vivienne's guilt

*They say you always
want what you can't have.*

HEATHER M. ORGERON

VIVIENNE'S GUILT

Cover Design:
Jersey Girl & Co.
www.jerseygirlandco.com

Cover Photos:
Adobe Stock
www.adobe.com

Editing:
Edee M. Fallon, Mad Spark Editing
www.madsparkediting.com

Interior design and formatting:
Jersey Girl & Co.
www.jerseygirlandco.com

BOOK DESCRIPTION

Vivienne
Guilt...
Like a cancer, it festers, slowly stealing your life bit by painful bit.
What do you do when you have betrayed the love of your life but he is no longer there to grant you forgiveness? How do you carry the weight of your gravest mistake knowing there is no way to atone for it?
I've made a terrible choice—one that can't be undone.
Hiding this secret is eating me alive.
But if it ever came out?
If it were ever discovered?
It would destroy everything.

Reid
They say you always want what you can't have.
From the moment I laid eyes on Vivienne Parker, I knew I was fighting a losing battle. I want to believe that I'm better than this—that I wouldn't cross that line—but deep down, I know if I were ever given a chance, there's no way in hell I'd refuse.
She's my uncle's wife, so why does it feel as if she is mine?

For ages 18+ due to adult language and sexual content.

one

Vivienne

"TILLIE, HONEY...LET'S GO!" I WHINE. Yes, whine. That is what spending every waking moment with a toddler has reduced me to. "Daddy will be here any minute!"

"No, no-no, no-no, NO! I'm not wearing this one!" my sweet angel screeches as she stomps her fat little foot on the bathroom tile. "I want the *pink* bow!" She turns her back to me and crosses her arms over her chest in a stance that lets me know she means business.

Dear Lord, here we go again with the freaking pink! If being the mother of a three-year-old girl has taught me anything, it is that they are serious about their pink, and you can't rationalize with three-year-old girls. *Ever.* About anything. From the moment Matilda Grace could walk and talk, she has been a little tyrant! I am sure Abbott and I don't help matters by catering to her every whim, but she is just too damn cute with her golden blonde hair, crystal blue eyes, and the deepest set of dimples you've ever seen. I know, we are going to regret it later, but we choose to enjoy her now.

"Baby girl, your dress is blue, just like your beautiful blue eyes," I tell her as I hold the pink bow against the silky blue fabric of her dress. "See, the pink bow won't match. Don't you want to look pretty for your date with Daddy?"

Tillie tilts her head to the side as she considers this for a moment before coming up with a solution of her own. "Ummm, I sink pink is fwitty, Mommy, right? You said pink is your favorite, too! Pink is my faaaavorite, Mommy! We can just pick something else to wear that's pink, and I get to wear the pink bow! That's a great idea, right?" she suggests, a little too pleased with herself.

Sure, it's a great idea. It's not like we went shopping for a "date dress" and matching shoes only yesterday. It isn't like it took her hours to pick a dress she liked. Now she wants to wear something else so she can match the dress to the bow, rather than matching the bow to the dress. I thought this stuff didn't start until they were teens. Mommy needs to get creative fast. Abbott really will be here any second to pick her up.

He's taking her to see Disney on Ice. She has no clue where they will be going, only that she has a birthday date with her daddy. She's bubbling over with excitement, and I could not be more in love with that man. Seriously, I thought I loved him before Matilda, but there is just something about watching a man dote on his baby girl that multiplies that love tenfold.

Wow! Our *baby* will be three tomorrow. Where has the time gone?

"It's a fantastic idea, sweetie, but I just remembered a surprise Mommy got for you. I think it will be perfect!" The word surprise, of course, captures her attention. She is all eyes as I rifle through the vanity drawer for a little crown that I bought for her to wear to a princess dress up party in a few weeks.

And there it is—that million-dollar smile. As I pull the hairpiece from the drawer, I know I have won this round.

"Oh. My. God! Mommy! Is that for me?" she asks, practically bouncing out of her skin. "I'm going to be like a reeeeeal princess!" Tillie squeals in excitement.

"You sure will, sweet girl. Now hop up here on the stool so I can get it in your hair before you're late."

"Can I wear some make-ups?"

"Makeup is for Mommies," I say as I slide the comb of the crown into the golden bun atop her head.

"Can I pleeeeeease just wear some lipsticks? Please? Please?

Pleeeeease?" she begs with a pout. Oh God. Not the pout. I can never refuse that pitiful look, and she knows it. Manipulative little shit.

We settle on lip gloss and light pink blush. Just as I finish strapping her sparkly, silver dress shoes, there is a knock at the door.

"I believe your date is here, baby girl! Go answer the door!" Tillie sprints across the living room to the door and opens it just as I power on the camera. The sheer joy that crosses my beautiful girl's face at the sight of her prince makes my heart skip a beat. Abbott looks like a dream in his suit and tie, perfectly styled blond locks, and the same striking blue eyes as Tillie. Her smile is radiant, and the look of adoration on Abbott's face makes my eyes well up.

My girl is living her own little fairytale.

God, I love that man.

Abbott crouches down to her level and pulls a dozen pink roses from behind his back with one hand and swoops her up into his arms with the other. "You look stunning, Bossyrella!" he says as he kisses her chubby little cheeks. "Are you ready for our date?"

"Yes, Prince Abbott. Do you like my fwitty dress? And look," she says as she points to the top of her head, "Mommy gotted me a real princess *crown!*"

"I love it!" he tells her as he leans over to give me a light kiss. "Great job, Momma," he whispers against my lips. His scent and the warmth of his breath leaves me momentarily flustered.

"You didn't do so bad yourself, Charming," I say, and I give him a lingering look that lets him know just how significantly he will be rewarded for his efforts. "You two better get going or you'll be late."

Abbott glances down at his watch. "Mommy's right. We better head out." He sets Tillie down and reaches for her hand. "You don't have too much fun with Cassie while we're gone...and make sure you're alone when we get back," he whispers suggestively into my ear. He brushes his nose along my nape, causing the baby hairs to stand on end as a shiver moves through my body.

I smother my sweet girl in kisses and instruct her to have a great time. As I practically shove both halves of my heart out of the door, a pang of guilt hits me because of how much I am looking forward to some girl time.

ABOUT THIRTY MINUTES LATER, CASSIE arrives armed with tequila and strawberry margarita fixings.

"Hey, hooker!" she says as she wraps me in her boney arms. "God, I've missed you!"

Cassie and I were roommates through all four years at Tulane University. We spent the first year together in the dorms before getting our own apartment. Both transplants from different states, we quickly became more than friends. Cassie and I are family. She is the only person I have beyond my mother, who still lives back home in Alabama, and Abbott. Abbott and I decided to settle down in Louisiana near the university because he's from Georgia and I'm from Alabama, so we didn't know how to choose. Also, I couldn't bring myself to leave Cassie. Cassie grew up in and out of different foster homes in Mississippi and has no one else. She has no family. Although we have been here nine years now, she has yet to find "the one" or even come close. Cassie is the sister I never had and Tillie's godmother. She spends every holiday with us, whether it is here in Magnolia Pines or back home at Mom's house. Cassie is always saying how lucky she is to have us, but I know without a doubt that we are the lucky ones.

I squeeze her tight and give her a peck on the cheek. "I know, right? Three. Whole. Days. How did you survive without the Parker casa chaos?" I tease.

"Speaking of chaos, I'm sorry I missed my little BFF. Was she excited? Show me pictures. I know you took some, paparazzi."

I pull out my iPhone and start scrolling through the pictures. "You should have seen her, Cass. She was so excited. Abbott got all dressed up for her and showed up with roses. If it wasn't so damn sweet, I might've been a little jealous."

"I need an Abbott. I swear he's the only good one left. Tillie's dating life is better than mine...and she's dating her daddy." She shakes her head. "I'm in such a rut, girl. My hand is tireddddd. I'm going through batteries like nobody's business," she divulges while waggling her eyebrows at me.

"You're right...it *isn't* my business. What happened to that one guy...Jared, Jacob, Jeremy...? What was his name again?" I can't keep up with this girl anymore.

"Jason? Yeah, uh, no. He was too into himself. I can't handle all that cockiness. If you're more into your own body than mine... you've gotta go. Doesn't he know this body is a temple just begging to be worshiped?" she teases while running her hands provocatively down her front, tracing her tiny breasts and hips.

I shake my head and laugh at her silliness. "Speaking of your body, you're looking really thin again, Cass. Are you eating? I swear you're withering away." Cassie has always been a stick of a girl. At 5'9", she dwarfs my 5'3" frame. She could best be described as a beanpole, but don't let that fool you. Cassie is absolutely stunning with her wavy red hair and green eyes. She could be a runway model. But I hate seeing her look sickly.

"I'm eating. It's just stress, and my thyroid's acting up again," she says with a shrug. *Sure it is.*

"You'd tell me if something was wrong, right? I don't want you making yourself sick again. I don't want to mother you or overreact. I'm just worried." Cassie has a bad habit of "forgetting to eat" whenever she's lonely. She swears she doesn't have a problem, but I lived with her long enough to notice that her stretches of not eating always occur during or immediately following a breakup. *Maybe she was more into this Jason guy than she's letting on.* I feel myself begin to sweat, and my throat constricts. I'm apprehensive, but I have to tread carefully, or Cassie will shut down on me. I will just have to keep a closer eye on her.

"I'm fine, love. I swear it. I'll even come over every night this week and hit up some of your good home cooking just to show you."

"I'll hold you to it. The boss'll be excited to have her favorite playmate over for dinner every night," I say as I wink at her. "Now, are you going to get this frumpy, old housewife drunk or are we going to sit here and stare at that bottle of Jose all night?"

"On it, sista!" Cassie grabs the blender from the pantry and sets up shop on the island counter.

I make myself comfortable on one of the bar stools and watch my best friend do her thing. Her tiny hips shake to the beat of some pop song blaring from her iPhone.

"So, how's Momma Anderson? Have you spoken with her lately?" Cassie asks while chopping the stems off a handful of strawberries before adding them to the blender.

"Ugh, no. You know how she is. She's constantly nagging me to visit her. No matter how often we go, it's never enough. I get tired of hearing it, honestly. She will never truly forgive me for settling down here instead of going back home. If she misses us so much, she should just move here. We have nothing there but an empty house filled with memories of my father. It's sickening. She keeps that place like a shrine to a man who *left* her for another woman. A woman ten years younger than him! It's not like he died, Cassie. He's out there somewhere with his new, younger wife and kids, and she's stuck in the same old place."

"Viv, I know she drives you crazy," she says, "but you're lucky to have a mother that loves you, worries about you, and *wants* you around. Don't ever forget that." Her face turns sad, and I'm having one of those all too frequent "foot in mouth" moments. "Some of us don't have that. You have no idea how much I would love to have a nagging, bitching mother."

"Oh God, I'm such a bitch. I know you're right. You know my nagging, bitching mother loves you like her own, right?" And she does. Most of the time I'm convinced she would take Cass over me as her daughter any day. "I know it's not the same thing, but you're family. You have a family. Don't ever doubt that."

"I know it. I do," she says as she wipes the tears just beginning to form in the corners of her eyes. "Gah, how did girls' night turn into a pity party?" Cassie sniffs. "Get your ass up out of that chair and shake that sexy booty, Momma!"

For the next two hours, my best friend and I drink margaritas and dance until we drop. Then, we cuddle up on the couch in front of the fifty-inch flat screen to catch a few DVR'd episodes of American Idol. It's nice to spend time with her like this. Just the two of us watching mundane TV. Just like old times.

Halfway through the second episode, I receive a text from Abbott. It's a picture of him and Tillie at the show that he must have had someone else take. I can't help the smile that spreads across my face at what a beautiful pair they are. She is his spitting image. Where I am unremarkable with my brown hair, brown eyes, and freckles, they are breathtakingly beautiful. I will never understand what Abbott saw in a plain Jane like me. Whatever it was, I hope he never loses sight of it.

"What are you making that shit-eating grin at over there? Is Abbott sexting you? He is, isn't he? Gross!" Then, she runs over to check it out because the girl does not know the meaning of the word boundaries. She snatches my phone out of my hand, and she too cracks a huge smile. "Wow, Momma. They are something, aren't they? Tillie is such a lucky girl to have a father that adores her the way Abbott does. Neither of us had that, ya know? I'm so happy our baby girl does."

Before I have a chance to respond, the phone dings again. And, being the nosey bitch that she is, Cass reads it. "It's lover boy again. He says I better be gone by the time they get back. They're leaving now. Damn. And all this time I thought we were cool," she jokes.

Thirty minutes later, as Cassie is packing up her things to head home, my phone rings. I don't recognize the number, and since it's after nine o'clock, I get a nervous feeling in my gut as I press the phone to my ear.

"Hello."

"Hi, is this the wife of Abbott Parker?"

"Yes, this is she. Who's this? Did something happen?" *Oh my God. Oh my God. Please let them be okay.*

"This is Officer Thomas. There's been an accident..."

two

Vivienne

"...MRS. PARKER, YOUR HUSBAND, AND I'm assuming your daughter, have been taken to Memorial. Do you have someone who can drive you to the hospital?" he asks. He sounds so calm, like this is just a routine phone call, while I feel like my insides are on the floor. Calm is good, right? Surely, it can't be too bad. If things were really bad, he would be more upset. He wouldn't sound like someone calling to sell me a magazine subscription.

"I...um. Yes. I do. Are they okay? Oh my God! My baby. Is she okay? Is Abbott all right? Can you tell me how serious it is?" I feel like I'm in a fog. Like this can't possibly be happening to me. No matter how badly I want to convince myself that it's not anything too serious, cops don't call for fender-benders. They don't ask you to have someone else drive you if everything is fine.

Cassie walks up to me and grabs the phone from my hand as I sink to the floor. I don't hear what she's saying. I just know that she's talking to the officer one moment and then helping me up and into her car the next. She talks to me in soothing tones the whole way to Memorial, but I don't hear a word she says. I must be in shock. I feel like I'm under water. My sight is blurry and sounds are jumbled. I don't know how I get from one place to the next, but my body must be cooperating because the next thing I know Cassie is rushing us through the emergency room doors. At that point, I come to enough to ask for my baby.

I run over to the registration desk and introduce myself. "I'm

Vivienne Parker. My husband, Abbott Parker and my...my daughter, Matilda Parker, were just brought in I guess thirty or forty minutes ago. I need to see them. Are they all right? Where's my baby?"

"Try to calm down and I'll see what I can find out for you, okay?" she says as she walks off through a set of double doors.

Cassie is rubbing my back and repeatedly telling me not to freak out until I know what's going on, but I can feel it. I know it's bad. I know that whatever news this woman brings back is going to rip my world to shreds. Because no one has it this good. No one gets to have it all and keep it. Eventually, something comes along to tip the scales. And the better you have it, it seems, the heavier the load.

Then suddenly I recognize a squeaky little voice and nothing has ever sounded better to my ears. I leave Cassie with instructions to come for me when the receptionist returns and follow the sweetest sounds I've ever heard. I arrive at a curtained off triage room and peek my head inside. There on the hospital bed is my heart, and I finally feel like I can breathe again. She's talking the ears off a male nurse, and neither has noticed my arrival.

"And then, Cinderelly comed out and her singed like this." Tillie gives her rendition of whatever song Cinderella sang and jumps right back into her story. "And Prince Abbott putted his fingers in his ears because him is a crazy Daddy! And then Cinderelly skaped around in circles." She demonstrates with her pointer and middle finger, pretending they are the legs and moves them around in circles. When she asks where her daddy is and if he can take her to him, I finally remember why I am here.

I rush through the curtain over to my sweet girl and swing her around in my arms. I cannot control the tears of relief that are flooding from my eyes. I kiss every inch of her little face and run my hands over her to assess for any damage.

"She's just fine, Miss. She may have a few bumps and bruises, but she appears to be just fine. Such a sweet girl you have here. I've enjoyed chatting with her about her date. Sounds like she had a great time," the nurse says.

"Mommy. Mommy, don't cry. Why are you crying, Mommy?" Tillie's eyes well up at the sight of my tears, and I try for all I am worth to suck it up and be brave for my sweet girl.

"Mommy is just *so* happy to see you, baby girl. So, so happy! I was very scared."

"I'm just fine Mommy, see? Don't cry. Big guhs don't cry, like the song. Like my Daddy says, right, Mommy?"

"Right, baby girl. That's right."

"Mommy, my Daddy was bleeding a lot. I didn't see him when I gotted here. I think they're getting him Band-Aids. Can we find my Daddy? I want to kiss him better."

I look over to the nurse to make sure that it is okay for me to leave with her and he assures me that she is good to go. He hands me some discharge papers and information on concussions that I should be on the lookout for and wishes us well.

I make my way back to registration with my heart literally in my hands. Cassie is pacing with a worried look on her face, which she does her best to cover when she sees us. "Hi, Bossyrella, I heard you had a hot date tonight. You look absolutely beautiful in that dress, my girl."

"Auntie Cass!" Tillie reaches over for Cassie, but I can't bring myself to let her go.

Cassie comes over and wraps her arms around us both and kisses Tillie's cheeks. "Hold on to Mommy for a little longer, Boss Lady. She had quite a scare. I'm not going anywhere."

"Okay, Auntie, I can do that. I'm a big guh, you know that? I'm gonna be free years old tomorrow!" She holds up four stubby little fingers to show Cassie. "Auntie, did you saw my daddy. Me and Mommy are going to find him and kiss his boo-boos. They taked him in another car. I don't know where he is."

"No, baby. I don't know where he is yet. We're waiting for someone to come tell us."

I walk around the waiting room for what feels like hours—but is probably no more than minutes—mindlessly reading the public service announcements and medical pamphlets on the walls. The sterile smell is making me nauseous, or maybe that's fear. I'm so terrified. What could possibly be taking so long? It's close to midnight, and surprisingly, the waiting room is empty. I'm grateful for that fact when a doctor comes out of those double doors and calls my name. I pass Tillie off to Cassie and walk over alone. The mother in me knows to protect her innocent ears from the news I am about to receive. It's that same part of me that manages to hold myself upright and not fall through that white speckled tile when Dr. Mullins' first words are, "I'm sorry."

three

Vivienne

"I'M SORRY" IS SUPPOSED TO make everything better—
not rip your fucking heart out. Those two little words are used
so freely—so carelessly. Seldom do we lend them much thought.
They are our free pass to forgiveness, which is most of the time
undeserved. "I'm sorry" took on a whole new meaning when they
fell from the lips of that emergency room doctor. "I'm sorry" just
tore my world apart. Those two little words hold more power than
I ever imagined.

I've heard those same two words countless times in the last two
days. Friends and family call to give their condolences, and always,
always they say "I'm so sorry" because we believe that those two
words somehow make things better. That they will help to alleviate
some of the pain or maybe it just helps us feel better to say it. But
"I'm sorry" no longer offers me comfort. Each time I hear those
words, I am taken back to that place. To the smell of ammonia and
medicine. To the single most devastating moment of my existence.

*"I'm sorry. We couldn't save him. The EMTs tried to revive him on the
way to the hospital, but they couldn't bring him back."*

They couldn't bring him back. My husband. The love of my life.
The father of my precious girl. Gone. His life dismissed with two.
Little. Words. Lost at the hands of a drunk driver—an eighteen-
year-old girl, who shouldn't have been drinking in the first place.
Her carelessness stole the life of the greatest man I have ever known.
I don't know how to even begin to process this—how to accept that

this nightmare is actually my reality.

I've spent the better part of the last two days hiding from my baby, and I feel like the world's worst mother. Who does that? Who hides from their own child? Their child who just lost her father. I feel selfish and vile. I feel unworthy, but I can't seem to pull myself together, and I can't let her see me fall apart.

I'm lying in our bed, my bed now, hugging his pillow and inhaling his scent. I need now more than ever to be wrapped in his strong arms. I need him to take this all away and make it better. Abbott always made everything better. I want to feel him—to taste him—and I know I will never again have that chance. I've replayed our last kiss over and over in my mind. It hardly seems fair that the last time our lips touched was a chaste, parting kiss. I want a do-over. I want to wrap myself around him and love him the way he deserved, to kiss him with everything in me. To leave him with a kiss that reflects how much he meant to me because, God, he meant everything to me.

The funny thing about being so young is that you think you have all of the time in the world to make important decisions, like where you will be buried. In the nine years that we've spent together, five of those married, Abbott and I never had this discussion. It never felt like a priority. We had the rest of our lives to worry about such things. Well, the rest of Abbott's life came far sooner than we ever could have imagined.

I need to pull myself together. I have arrangements to make and a daughter to care for. Taking a final sniff of Abbott's pillow, I make my way to the shower. I vow to find my inner strength and to be the rock that my daughter needs. If I can't be Abbott's wife any longer, I can at least be the mother he would want for our child. Tillie deserves more than this.

"MOMMY!" TILLIE RUNS ACROSS THE room and jumps into my arms. "Are you all better now? Auntie Cass said you were sick and to let you sleep. But I reeeeeally wanted to wake you up because someone bringed me some new toys!" She hops down and pulls me over to the kitchen table and waves her hand at all of the presents that our neighbors and friends have so graciously dropped off for her.

Yesterday was her birthday. Yesterday, on May 21st, my girl turned three years old, only hours after her father lost his life. I spent my daughter's birthday locked away in my room. I feel sick with guilt. I am so ashamed. I fight back tears and feign excitement for her benefit. "Oh, wow! You are a lucky girl. Look at all of this stuff!" *Lucky, hah!*

"People keep stopping by with gifts for Tillie and food. The fridge is loaded. Why don't you go grab something to eat, Viv?" Cassie begs. The irony that our roles have suddenly reversed is not lost on me.

Cassie has been here, loving my daughter, wiping her tears. She's fed her, sang her to sleep, and even celebrated her birthday. All while I wallowed in my own misery. No more. No longer will I put my own grief above my daughter and my best friend.

"I'm not really hungry."

"You need your strength," she says, looking at me sternly. "Tillie needs your strength," she adds in a whisper.

"Maybe I can eat a little something," I concede. "Are you hungry, baby girl?"

Tillie shakes her head at me. "No, tank you, Mommy. Auntie already feeded me. We ated some zahnia. It was soooo yummy!"

"Well, then, I must have some of this amazing lasagna." I walk over to the stainless fridge and pause to take in the photographs on the double doors. The first is of Abbott and me standing in front of our lake house. This was our dream home, and we brought it to life together. There's another of Abbott and Tillie when she caught her first fish only a month ago. She's beaming with that little perch dangling from her princess fishing pole. He was such a great father. I smile to myself and finally open up the fridge in search of this killer lasagna.

I prepare myself a plate, even though the last thing I feel like doing is putting food into my mouth. Then, I walk over to the breakfast table and scoot a few toys out of the way to sit opposite Tillie and Cass. They're putting together a ballerina puzzle. Matilda loves puzzles. Her face is all scrunched up in concentration. She brings me so much joy. I could just watch her for hours.

"Are you going to call your father?" Cassie asks hesitantly.

I scoff, "Is that a serious question?"

She shrugs.

"No. Honestly, I hadn't even thought of him 'til you asked. I doubt he even knows I'm married, and he wouldn't give a shit anyway, Cass. I haven't seen him since I was thirteen, and the last time I heard from him was a card on my eighteenth birthday with a check to pay for my college tuition. Even if he would care, which is highly doubtful, there's just too much that would need to be said between us and Abbott's funeral is not the time."

Cassie nods. "You're right. I don't know what I was thinking."

"Has his mother called again?" I ask Cassie, dismissing the subject of my father, as I take another mouthful of lasagna. I could be eating cardboard and wouldn't know the difference.

"Only a dozen times. That woman is a ruthless bitch."

"Cassie! She just lost her son, and she's..." I gesture my head toward Tillie and mouth *her grandmother.*

"Oh, I know very well who she is. Does she?" she asks as she too motions to Tillie with her head. "His *mother* hasn't seen him in years and thinks she has a right to dictate when the funeral is and where you bury him? You need to do what you feel is right. What Abbott would have wanted. And I can tell you that he would want to be here in the city where the two of you fell in love. Here with his daughter. Here where he was finally at peace and happy with his life. Why would you even entertain the idea of burying him back in Georgia where his grave would rot with neglect?"

"I know you're right."

"Damn straight I am! No one knew Abbott better than you, Viv. Even I knew him better than that shrew. I knew him enough to know that he would never want to be anywhere you're not, even in death."

"All right, then, I guess it's time that I contact the funeral home.

Do you think two more days is enough notice to allow time for any family members who want to come down?"

"Two days is *more* than enough time. Anyone who cares enough to be here will make it work. You can't keep thinking of everyone else, Viv. Be considerate, sure, but we need to not drag this out any longer. It's time to lay Abbott to rest and start figuring out how to go on without him." Cassie bends under the table to grab a few puzzle pieces that fell and asks Tillie if she wants to go outside and swim so that I can make some phone calls.

Matilda abandons her puzzle and runs off to her room to put on her swimsuit. I hear her little feet patter up the wood stairs and down the hall to her room.

While we await Tillie's return, Cassie pulls me into a tight hug. Through her own tears, she promises me that we will get through this. She's here for Tillie and me. She will help me raise my daughter, and I know she will. Cassie loves my little girl as her own. Together, I know we will be okay. We have to be.

Moments later, Tillie stands before us in her blue and white seersucker tankini with her initials embroidered on the front. It was Abbott's favorite. He loved her in anything blue because he loved the way it brought out her eyes. *His eyes.* She has his eyes. She has his face. I don't know how I will ever look at my girl and not see her father. It's comforting, yet it hurts at the same time.

"Mommy, will you come swimming with us?"

"That sounds like a lot of fun, baby girl. Let Mommy handle some boring business calls and then I'll be out there to join you and Auntie, 'kay?" She nods her head, and I slather on some sunscreen and tie up the back of her suit. "See you ladies in a few."

I MAKE MY WAY OUT back to my favorite area on the property: the pool. We really do have our own little slice of heaven out here. The goal was to feel like we were on vacation in our own backyard, and I am already feeling a little less tense. I watch Tillie climb up the rock steps to the slide, which doubles as a waterfall. She's such a big girl. Swims like a fish already. I jump in and surprise her when I catch her at the bottom of the slide.

"Mommy!" I will never tire of hearing the excitement in her sweet little voice every time she calls out my name. "Are you done wif your phone calls?"

"I am. How about we spend the rest of the afternoon out here? No more phone calls, huh? Does that sound like a plan?" I glance over at Cassie, who smiles in agreement and then rises from the pool, wraps herself in a towel, and collects our phones.

"I'm just going to put these naughty things away and grab us some lemonade. Be right back."

As I watch Cassie make her way back into the house, I feel Matilda's hand on my cheek, pulling my face back toward hers. "Mommy?"

"Yes, baby?"

"When is my daddy gonna get not dead anymore?"

My breath catches in my throat. *Holy shit.*

Shit! Shit! Shit! I am so not prepared for this. Be strong for Tillie. Be strong for Tillie—my new motto.

"Well, Daddy can't not be dead anymore, sweetie. When you die, you go to heaven with Jesus, and you don't ever come back." *He is never coming back...*

"But I don't want my daddy to be dead. I want him to come back home wif us." I don't know how I won't die from the pain of her broken heart. I could go my entire life without ever witnessing it again.

"Oh, baby girl, Mommy does, too. I want him with us, too. He can't come back, but we have our own angel. Daddy is up in heaven watching us now."

"Is heaven in the sky?" she asks as she looks up.

Is there a book on how to explain these things to a three-year-old? Surely I am not qualified. I do the best I can and wing it. "Yes, Tillie. Heaven is way-way up in the sky."

"Well...I don't want a angel in heaven. I want my daddy to come home. I want him to be in my house, not at heaven." She crosses her chubby little arms on her chest and releases some of the largest tears I've ever seen. My composure is lost. I hold my baby, and I cry with her. Because, Goddamn it, I want that, too.

So much for not letting her see me fall apart.

four

Vivienne

I STARE OUT BLANKLY FROM the altar of our church, and I am overwhelmed by the number of friends and family who've shown up to pay their respects. The shrew is here, front and center, and staring daggers at me. If looks could kill, let's just say that Cassie would be planning my funeral next and inheriting a child. Cass and Tillie are seated in chairs to my right. I wanted them up here with me. I need their strength if I am to have any chance of keeping it together. The three of us united. It's how it will be from now on.

I take one last look over at my girls and feel Cassie's cold fingers tighten around mine. Our eyes meet, and she gives me an encouraging smile as I rise from my seat, smoothing down the fabric of my black skirt. When I move to take a step forward, the room begins to spin. I close my eyes, pulling in deep breaths and blowing them out slowly. With measured, careful steps, I inch my way over to the podium and grip the wooden top with trembling hands. Tears well in my eyes, and my throat begins to collapse in on itself as my heart thrums loudly in my ears. *This is it,* I think to myself. *This is goodbye.*

Clearing my throat, I adjust the tiny microphone in front of me and introduce myself. "Hi," I begin, looking around the packed room. "Thank you all for being here today. For those of you who may not know who I am, my name is Vivienne Parker, and I was lucky enough to be married to that" —I motion to the casket on the left side of the room— "incredible man." Tears sneak out from the corners of my eyes and roll down my cheeks.

My eyes pause on the wedding photo that Cassie had framed. It sits high on a stand surrounded by floral arrangements of various sizes and colors. I stare at his beautiful, perfect face. Those dimples set so deep in his cheeks. Vibrant blue eyes filled with so much emotion. At the two of us, so young and in love and so anxious to begin our life together. A life that held so much promise...so many dreams.

"Abbott..." I cry, clutching my hands to my chest as silent tears stream down my face. "God, where do I even begin?" I whisper, shaking my head to myself, keeping my gaze lowered, unable to meet the tear-filled eyes that I know are staring at me. There aren't words to adequately describe the depth of my love for this man. Anything I say will fall short.

"They say that people come into your life for a reason, a season, or a lifetime. Abbott was my reason. Everything good in my life leads right back to him. The nine years that I was blessed enough to spend loving and being loved by this incredible man was a perpetual spring. Our season was cut short—ended far too soon. Ours is a love that without a doubt would have lasted a lifetime."

Taking a deep breath, I dab away my tears as I lift my head to address the crowd. "Who was Abbott Parker?" I ask, chewing on my lip and tasting the salt of my tears. Every set of eyes in the room seem to find mine at that moment. "I guess that depends on who you ask. He was so many things to so many different people...

"You see, Abbott wasn't just one thing. To me, Abbott Parker was everything. To his friends, Abbott was the life of the party. He was fun, and he was funny. Abbott was always trying to make those around him laugh, many times at his own expense." I laugh weakly. "Abbott was dependable and honorable and loyal. If you were lucky enough to cross paths with Abbott Parker, you found yourself a friend for life," I say, glancing up at the funeral party and watching as dozens of heads nod in agreement.

"To his business associates, Abbott was reliable. He was one of the most sought after architects in the area, and it was because Abbott took so much care and so much pride in everything that he touched. He would not rest until every project was absolutely perfect until every client was completely satisfied. He went above, he went beyond and made it look effortless because Abbott was not putting on a show. This is just who he was.

"To the autism community in and around the New Orleans area, my husband was a hero. He would hate that I just referred to him as such, but it's the truth." Looking back to my left, I whisper, "Sorry, babe," with a tear-filled smile. "When we were designing the lake house, it was his idea to include plans for a camp for children with Asperger's. That camp was his pride and joy. He looked forward to spending time with these children every summer, and I think I fell a little more in love with him for it." I pause, feeling my heart clench tightly in my chest. "This will be the first summer that I have to do this without him. It wasn't supposed to be this way," I cry, wiping tears away from my face. "As long as there is breath in this body, I will keep his work alive.

"He was smart, kind, and generous. Abbott was all of those things in spades. But, what I'm most proud of, was the incredible father that he was to our baby girl. Matilda Grace Parker was the light of his life. Abbott and I both grew up without our fathers. There was nothing more important to him than being there for our baby girl...than her knowing without a doubt how much she was loved and cherished. He was an active participant in every aspect of Tillie's life. We were a family. A *real* family. Abbott died...." A sob escapes, and I pause to collect myself. "I'm sorry. He died doing what he loved most: doting on his daughter.

"Abbott Jude Parker was the love of my life," I choke out. "He was my heart, my soul, my *everything*," I say, smiling wistfully through my tears. "He was my very best friend, and God, how I miss... him..." I bring my trembling fingers to my lips and feel the wetness of my tears. "I never imagined that I'd be standing here...a widow at twenty-six. That I would have to raise our baby girl without him," I say, my voice breaking. "I thought that I understood pain. I thought that I knew what it meant to feel sad...to feel alone...but I. Knew. Nothing," I sob. "Because what I didn't realize before was that you can only experience those emotions to the depth of which you've felt their counterparts. You can only feel loss as strongly as you've felt love, sadness as deep as your happiest moments, and you can't possibly know what it means to be truly alone until you've been so connected to someone else that you can no longer tell where they end and you begin, only to have them ripped away," I explain through a torrent of tears. "I have been loved to the depths of my soul. I've known love that most people only ever dream of, and now I know pain in equal measure. This is the consequence of all-consuming love." I wave my hands, gesturing to the mess that I've become. "And I hope that each of you is lucky enough to find a love with the power to completely destroy you because to experience that kind of love is worth any price." With my hand on my heart, I turn my face up to the heavens. "It was worth it. God, Abbott... loving you was more than worth it."

I look around the church and force myself to smile through tears at our guests. I open the floor to any friends or family that would like to share their memories of Abbott and take my seat next to Cassie and Tillie. After a few friends from school share their fondest moments with my husband, Cassie makes her way to the podium.

"Abbott was more than a friend. He was my *brother*. Abbott was my *family*, and family is not something I have a lot of. I don't have a mother or father...no aunts, uncles, or cousins. But what I have is worth so much more. I have a family who *chose* me. I may have been born to one who threw me out with the trash, but there is no way they could have ever come close to what I've found in Viv, Abbott, and Matilda.

"I know I'm not an easy person to love. I can be a royal pain in the...behind. I have issues a mile long. I'm selfish and high maintenance. But, Abbott never pushed me away. He accepted me and didn't make me feel like a third wheel.

"I don't know how to say goodbye to one of the only people who ever truly cared for me. Thank you for allowing me to be a part of your family. I promise to take good care of them. 'Til we meet again." Cassie kisses two fingers and raises them in the air, then she makes her way back to her seat, a sobbing mess. As I lean over to comfort her, I watch Tillie wander out to the center of the altar. "It's my turn now. Right, Mommy? You and Auntie gotted a turn. Can I talk now?" She looks so small standing up there in her pretty blue dress...her date dress. It was her idea to wear it, and she looks like a little angel. Abbott would approve.

I'm not sure what Tillie wants to say, and to be quite honest, I'm a bit scared. You just never know what will come out of that girl's mouth. But, Abbott was her father, and if she wants a turn to speak, then I am going to let her have it. "Go ahead, sweet girl. It's your turn." I nod in approval.

Tillie smiles over at me and then turns her back to the crowd. She looks right up at the crucifix and begins. "Jesus...Jesus, I'm mad at you cuz you taked my Daddy away. I'm not gonna be your friend anymore if you don't give him back. I don't want him to be a angel. I just want him to be my Daddy. Please let him go home. Amen." She puts her little hands on her hips and gives that statue the meanest eyes she can conjure.

Oh. My. God. I walk over and lift my baby into my arms. I whisper to her that I love her and that her daddy loves her so much. I apologize over and over, and I am not even sure why, but I keep saying it. "I'm sorry, baby girl. I am so, so sorry." There they are again. Those two little words. They feel so insignificant, but there is nothing else to say. I wish there were words to express how very sorry I am.

I peek out at the crowd, and even the manliest of men have tears streaming down their cheeks. Leave it to Tillie to make a bunch of grown men cry.

AFTER THE FUNERAL, WE ALL meet up at the lake house for a reception. We have a huge outdoor kitchen and covered pavilion with tables and chairs. Abbott's company catered a late lunch for the entire funeral party. There is so much food, and still nothing looks appetizing. I could not keep anything in if I tried.

Today was hard. One of the hardest days of my life, but I'm

relieved it's over with. The last four days have been brutal.

I walk over to my mother's table, where she is having quite an animated conversation with Tillie. Lord knows what that crazy girl is telling her Grammy. I hope she's not getting me into trouble. "Hey, Momma," I say as I lean over to hug her large frame. No matter how crazy she makes me, she still feels like home. Her smell is comforting. Her touch, soothing. "Thank you for being here. It means more to me than you know." It took Abbott's death to finally get my mother out to Magnolia Pines. She doesn't drive more than a few miles from her house, and flying is out of the question. But, she faced her fears for me and here she is. I hope it won't be the last time she makes an appearance.

"Oh, my sweet girl. As if I would be any place else," she says as she squeezes me tight. "You have a lovely home. The pictures don't do it justice. I'm so sorry it's taken me this long to visit. I'll try to get out here a few times a year. I promise."

She sounds genuine, but she always does. My mother is one who often says what she knows people need to hear. I don't think she intends to lie, but she seldom follows through. Time will tell. Either way, I'm just happy she's here.

"How long will you be staying?" I ask as I take a seat next to Matilda. I pull her into my lap and run my fingers through her waist long hair.

"Oh, I have to fly out tomorrow morning. We have a few girls out sick at the restaurant so I couldn't take more than a few days, but I'm going to plan another trip soon." *Sure you will.*

Before I have a chance to say anything, Abbott's mother walks over and gives a terse, "Hello, Vivienne." Then, she nods over to my mother. "Ms. Anderson."

I guess it's now or never. "Hello, Elizabeth. I hope you made the trip well." God, I can't stand this bitch. With all of the hell she's put me through in the last few days, it is physically draining to fake nice. It's my husband's funeral, and I will not turn it into a catfight. "This is my daughter, Tillie," I say as I look down at my pretty girl.

Cassie must have seen Ms. Parker approach me, and like the amazing friend that she is, I see her marching toward us. That girl always has my back.

"Why do you insist on such a ridiculous nickname? Call the girl by her given name for Christ's sake," she chastises. "Hello, *Matilda*, I'm your grandmother." *Bitch.*

Cassie arrives right as Tillie responds, "Ohhhh, grandmudder. Right, right, right...I know who you are." A look of recognition crosses her face as she continues. "You are the toofless bitch. Right, Auntie? I'm right, huh? I 'member that!" She holds up her pudgy little hand for a high five, and I don't know if I want to laugh or cry.

I'm lying. I do. I really want to laugh in her fucking face, but of course, I don't. Cass, however, is not so restrained. She immediately bursts out laughing and quickly turns her head to try to regain her composure. At least there's that.

"Tillie!" I admonish. "We don't use that word. Ever." That's about the best I can do to try to save this situation.

Ms. Parker is as red as a tomato and completely loses her shit. "Did that child just call me a...a...a...bitch?" she chokes out. "I always knew you were trash, Vivienne. My son deserved more. He deserved to marry a woman with class. A *real* woman would never allow her child to behave so...so...uncivilized!" The look she gives Tillie is one of pure disgust. I want to slap it right off of her plastic face.

Cassie is no longer laughing. In fact, she may be even more red in the face than Abbott's mother. My friend glances down at Tillie cowering in my lap and says, "Baby girl, it's ruthless not toothless," and then she lifts her eyes to meet Elizabeth's and continues in a voice just above a whisper, "but if you ever speak that way to Vivienne again...toothless just may work, too."

Shock.

Radio silence.

I pass Tillie to my mother and ask her to take her back to the house for some dessert. As soon as they are out of earshot, I turn to Elizabeth and finally give her a piece of my mind. "Ms. Parker, this is neither the time nor the place for your tirade. You don't know me, you didn't *really* know Abbott, and you most certainly will never have the pleasure of knowing our daughter. He wanted to cut off contact with you years ago. It is this 'trash'," I say, poking myself in the chest, "who convinced him to at least speak to you. I thought that *maybe* there was something worth saving, but Abbott was right all along. I don't know how such rotten people created that beautiful man. He must've had some amazing nannies because I know damn well that you had nothing to do with it. Abbott was proof that we are not merely a product of our raising and thank God for that! You may see your way out." I don't bother sticking around to witness her reaction. I've already had more of her than I can take. Without a parting word or a backward glance, I stalk off toward the lake to blow off some steam. *How dare she?*

I hear footsteps coming from behind as I approach the wharf and turn to see Abbott's brother, Dave, following a few yards behind. I hope he's not here to give me shit over his mother because I don't know how much more of this I can take. I seat myself at the end of the wharf with my feet dangling over the edge and wait.

I feel the wood give a little as he plops himself down next to me. "Hey, pretty girl. How ya holdin' up?" he asks, and I'm relieved to see that he appears genuinely concerned. Dave is an older version of Abbott: same hair, same eyes, same frame. He is exactly what I imagine Abbott would have looked like ten or so years from now. It almost hurts to look at him. The last time I saw Dave, Tillie was barely a year old. He and Abbott were really close before his mother started shit over the family business, and they've hardly spoken since. I can see the regret written all over his face.

"Ah, I've been better," I respond honestly. "I don't know if I can do this. I mean...I know I have to, but I'm scared. I'm so, so scared, and I just don't know how I could ever be truly happy without him." I use my sleeve to wipe my tears. *God, I am such a fucking mess.*

"I know there's nothing I can say to make this easier for you. I'm really sorry about Mother. I'm not sure what was said, but I know that you wouldn't have started anything today of all days. She just doesn't know when to quit," he offers, shaking his head. "I have so many regrets where Abbott is concerned. I wish I could go back and change things, but I can't. I'm sorry for that, too. More than you will ever know." Dave stares out into the water. "I want to help you. I know you have the camp starting up next month. Reid is graduating next week," he says with a smile.

I return his smile with one of my own. "He can't possibly be that old already. He is forever a ten-year-old little boy in my eyes." I haven't seen little Reid in years.

"It's been too long since we've gotten together. He's all grown up, Viv. Starting at Tulane this fall...following in his uncle's footsteps. He wanted to be here today, but he's in Europe on his senior trip and couldn't get back in time. I was thinking...maybe we could send Reid out here early to help you with the camp this summer. I know it'll be hard on you with Tillie and just losing Abbott. Reid can drive a boat. He's a great outdoorsman and kids love him."

"Oh, do you think he would want to? That would be amazing, Dave. I feel so overwhelmed right now. It would be a huge relief. I would love to get to know him again and for Tillie to spend some time with her only cousin. But only if he lets me pay him. No eighteen-year-old wants to spend their summer working for free." *Maybe something good will come out of this dreadful day after all.*

Dave's face lights up. I can tell he's truly excited about being able to do something for us. "Of course he'll want to. We're family, Viv. It's time we start acting like it. If you want to approach it as a summer job and pay him, I won't object. But you don't have to. He needs to get out here a little early for football conditioning, anyway. It'll give him a place to stay and the comfort of family. And it will give his old man peace of mind." He pats me on the back and then pushes himself up off the dock. "I'm glad we had this time to talk. I'll be in touch about Reid, but, unfortunately, I have to get going. My plane leaves in a few hours, and I need to get back to my hotel and pack my things...find Mother," he says with an exaggerated eye roll. "Don't be a stranger, Viv. We want to know that you and Tillie are okay." He helps me up and gives me a hug. It's warm and welcoming, and I can't help but wish it was his brother's arms instead. He takes a few steps toward the house and then turns and calls out, "You call if you or Tillie need anything, Viv. We want to help." And then he's gone.

five
Vivienne

I OPEN MY EYES AND strain to see the red numbers glowing on the alarm clock beside my bed: 2:32 A.M. *Well, if I can't sleep, might as well take advantage of the alone time.* I roll over and reach across the bed in an attempt to seduce my sleeping husband. When all I grasp are sheets and blankets, it all comes back. That piercing ache. My heart. My Abbott. *He's gone.*

I curl into a ball and clutch at my burning heart as I scream out in agony. It hurts. *Oh God, it hurts so badly.* I just want the pain to stop, and then again I don't. Because if I stop thinking of him, stop aching for him, then I will begin to forget. And, I can't ever forget.

His scent no longer lingers on my bed sheets. I can feel him slipping away, and it is too much, and still it's not enough.

Sweat beads on my skin and I can't breathe. *I can't breathe.* I'm suffocating in my grief. It's like burning lava coursing through my veins. A pain so excruciating, so unbearable, that for a moment I just want to die, too. I want to escape this agony and follow my heart to wherever he's gone. Because a life without him, this life I'm pretending to live, is almost too much to bear.

And that thought leads to guilt. How can I, even for mere seconds, want to leave my daughter all alone in this world? It's selfish, and it's wrong. *I'm a horrible mother.*

With trembling hands, I pull open the drawer to my nightstand and manage to open the prescription bottle and tap a Xanax into my palm. I take deep breaths and try not to pass out as I slowly ease into a sitting position. I open the bottle of water that I keep next to my bed, swallow the pill, and I wait. I wait for the medicine to calm my racing heart. To clear my clouded vision. To ease the dizzying nausea.

The panic attacks are worse now than ever. They usually come at night. At night, when I am alone. When I can drift off and for a blessed moment in time forget that my entire life has been upended. That I will never again feel his touch, taste his lips, or feel his hair slide through my fingertips. I will never again feel him moving over me—inside of me. And when that realization hits, it's like I'm standing inside of a burning building with no escape.

As the attack subsides, I glance back over to the clock: 3:03 A.M. *What will I do for the next three and a half hours?* I grab my phone from under my pillow and bring up the picture of Abbott and Tillie; the one he sent me right before the accident. I've spent countless hours staring at his radiant smile. That smile. That smile that will never again brighten my days.

I put the phone down and try to fall back asleep, but my mind won't shut off. Memories of Abbott flood my thoughts. I touch my fingers to my lips and smile as I remember our first kiss.

It was Halloween of 2001, my first year at Tulane, and my first frat party. My roommate, Cassie, and I decided to wear complementing costumes because that's what corny, college freshman BFFs do.

"How's my tail, Viv? Is it centered?" Cassie asks as she climbs out of the cab, stumbling over the curb.

"It's as centered as it's going to be. I'm not playing with your ass in front of all of these hot guys," I answer, shaking my head at how ridiculous she looks trying to see her own ass from over her shoulder. *"Find a bathroom and check it out in the mirror or something. It's hanging a little to the left."*

"That's what she said! Ba dum bum tsssss!" Cass jokes. *"Oh come on, Viv! I need you. You can't let me go in there looking a mess."*

Great. Now she's begging.

"No one will see. Just fix my ass. Fix it or I'll embarrass you. You know I will," she threatens.

And I know she will. Ugh. *"Hurry up. Get over here."* *I adjust the pin attaching the pointy black tail to her red spandex pants and then slap her on the ass for good measure.*

"*Vivienne? Is that you, angel? Where have you been all my life?*" *Oh God. Oh God. I know that voice. Of course he would be the one to walk up and catch me slapping another girl's ass.*

I'm so surprised that I choke on my own saliva. Way to be sexy. Why couldn't it have been anyone else?

"*Oh, shit, are you okay, Viv?*" *he asks as he rushes over to pat me on the back.*

I don't even attempt to disguise it as I openly check him out. Black fitted, v-neck tee, fuck me jeans, and damn he smells good. Like beer and cologne... "*I want to lick him.*"

Cassie lets out a loud guffaw, and I realize that I may have just said that out loud. Fuck Cassie for making me drink so much before the party.

"*You want to lick who, babe? Cuz if there's any chance that you meant me...lick away. And you don't have to stop there. I'm down for making all of your fantasies come true,*" *Abbott says as his hand stills on my waist.*

I look up and meet his gaze. I am frozen in place, hypnotized by those damn crystal blue eyes. I should be embarrassed. I would be if I could form a coherent thought.

"*Okay...so you two love birds have at that shit. I'm going to find me a drink and a man...in that order,*" *my best friend says before giving me a wink and walking away. She walks away!*

Abbott reaches up and adjusts my halo. If you haven't figured it out by now, Cassie is a sexy little devil, and I am her opposite: an innocent angel. Well, innocent is a stretch. There's not much innocent about this costume. I suddenly feel extremely underdressed.

"*Thanks, Abbott. I...ummm...*" *I cover my face with my hands and take a deep breath before I continue.* "*God, I'm so embarrassed. I didn't mean to say that. I'm sorry. Truly.*"

"*I really hope you don't mean that.*"

"*What? That I'm embarrassed?*"

"*No, not that. That you didn't mean it. Because I did.*"

"*Well, I mean, I didn't mean to say it, you know...out loud...*" *I stammer. Why am I so nervous? Abbott's my friend. We've been friends for months. Why do I suddenly feel like a stranger? Like I'm bumping into him for the first time? He must think I am an idiot.*

"So, you do want to lick me, then... That's good. Really good, Viv," Abbott slurs.

"Is it?" I ask in a whisper.

"Mmmhmm." He pulls me closer. My face is now even with his chest, his erection pressing against my stomach.

His erection. Holy crap, I gave Abbott Parker a hard on. At least I'm assuming it was me. Oh God, I am so drunk.

I look up to find him staring down at me. And as if my body has a mind of its own, I rise up on my toes and wrap my arms around his neck.

"Viv," Abbott whispers, and I can feel the warmth of his breath on my lips. "Yeah?"

Abbott places his free hand on my face and begins to slowly rub his thumb across my trembling lips. "Viv," he whispers once more, and there is so much yearning in the way that he says my name. I feel liquid heat pool in my belly as I slide my tongue out to taste his salty skin.

And that is all the permission Abbott needs to pull my face into his and press his lips to mine. He runs his tongue along the seam of my mouth, and I open for him. Our tongues meet in tentative strokes before finding their rhythm, and I am lost in his kiss. Nothing else exists but this moment. I slide my hands up the sides of his smooth face and into his short, blond hair, tugging gently. Abbott groans in response and moves his hands down to my ass and squeezes as he pulls me impossibly closer. Our kiss becomes more urgent. Lips melding. Tongues thrashing. Licking. Teasing. Tasting. And then he continues licking and sucking down my face to my neck. I rock into his erection and whimper, which seems to urge him on. He works his way back to my mouth and our tongues war with each other in primal need. My God, I never want this moment to end.

Through a haze, I register what sounds like hooting and hollering, and it takes a moment for me to realize that we are the cause. I break the kiss and whisper, "Abbott...Abbott, stop."

But he doesn't stop. He moves back to my neck, and I'll be damned if a part of me doesn't want him to just fuck me right here for all to see.

The cat calls get louder, and finally Abbott takes notice of the situation. He shakes his head in frustration and pulls at his lips with his fingers. "Fuck," he growls out.

My face is flushed...from the kissing or the embarrassment of being watched, who knows? I'm suddenly dizzy and nauseated, and I just want the ground to swallow me whole. "Abbott?"

"Yeah, babe?" he answers, still breathing heavily.

"I think I'm going to be sick." And then I gag. Because isn't that what all girls do after the best fucking kiss of their life?

"Oh, shit..." Abbott yells over to his friends. "Show's over, guys. Get the fuck out!"

The guys make their way back into the house, for which I am extremely grateful, when only seconds later I puke right there on the front lawn of the frat house.

I laugh aloud at the memory, and it's so good to feel something other than pure devastation when I think of my husband.

It's now just after 4:30 A.M., but I'm too afraid to even attempt sleep. I haven't felt this good since the accident, and I don't want to risk losing it. I stretch out my arms and legs then peel myself from my comfortable bed. I throw on workout clothes and running shoes and put in an hour on the treadmill.

AFTER A NICE HOT SHOWER, I sneak past Cassie sleeping on the couch, careful not to wake her, and into the kitchen to make my girls some breakfast.

Just as I finish scrambling a batch of eggs and frying a few strips of bacon, Matilda barges into the kitchen. "I smell bacon! Are you making me some bacon, Mom?" she asks and then lets out a big yawn.

"Yes, ma'am! Hungry?"

"Duh! I'm starvin' Marvin," she says with a giggle.

"Are you, Silly Tillie?" As I speak Abbott's usual line, a lump forms in my throat. I can't help but feel guilty when I say or do things that were "his." I know it's ridiculous. I know that it is not my fault that he isn't here to do it himself. But the guilt ensues nonetheless.

"Yep!" she says. "I am."

"I had a feeling you would be," I say with a wink. "Eat up, Bossyrella! We have a busy day today. Your cousin, Reid, is coming tomorrow. Wanna help Mommy clean up the pool house for him?"

Just then, Cassie comes trudging into the kitchen. "Damn, Momma, it's not even six yet. Why the hell are you up so early?" she asks, rubbing the sleep from her eyes. "Not that I'm complaining. Breakfast smells delicious!"

"I woke up a few hours ago and couldn't fall back asleep. My mind was on overdrive, so I got up and worked out for a bit and then decided to make breakfast," I answer as I pour each of us a glass of apple juice.

"That's great, Viv. You look really good. Are you doing okay?" she asks while chewing on a mouthful of bacon. "What am I saying? Of course you're not okay...but you know what I mean. Better today than yesterday?" she adds, looking hopeful.

"I feel really great, actually. I was remembering that Halloween party...at the frat house." I laugh. "Do you remember?"

"Oh my God, Viv. How could I forget? You puked on the freaking front lawn for Christ's sake." She laughs, shaking her head. "It was the first time you ever embarrassed me."

"And the last," I add with a smirk and a raise of my brow.

She laughs. "Definitely not the last."

"Mommy, why did you pupe in someone's grass? That's not nice, right, Auntie?" Tillie says with a disgusted look on her face. That girl is always listening. I really need to be more aware of what we talk about around her.

"Mommy was sick, baby girl. Mind your business and eat your breakfast," I tell her, pointing to her half-eaten plate.

"So, Reid gets here tomorrow. I thought maybe you should get back to work, Cassie. I love having you here. I mean...I don't know how I would have survived the last week without you, honestly, but I'm feeling a little better and will have someone to keep me company during the day. Your kids must be missing you like crazy. I hear you on the phone with them all day, and I'm just feeling really bad for keeping you from them."

Cassie is a social worker for the Department of Social Services. After being just another number on someone's roster for so many years, she wanted to make a difference. Cass loves her kids. I know that they must miss her. She says that they'll understand, but I can't help but feel guilty. *Guilt. It seems to be my new best friend.* For kids who have nothing, having someone who genuinely cares is *everything.* I hate knowing that I am the reason she hasn't been around.

"Are you kicking me out?" she asks with an exaggerated look of shock on her face. "After all I've done for you. You hear that, Tillie? Your mom is kicking me out."

"I sink you can stay. You can sleep wif me in my bed if you want to, Auntie," Matilda answers sweetly. "Mommy, why are you making Auntie Cass leave? Her's your best friend!"

"Aw, at least someone loves me," Cassie says to Tillie, giving her a kiss on the forehead. "I'm just kidding, though, baby girl. I can't stay forever. How about this weekend Auntie will come sleep over with you in your new big girl bed?"

"That's a great idea! And we can paint our nails, and do make-ups...and we can watch a movie...and eat popcorn!" Tillie's face lights up with excitement.

"It's a date!" Cass says to Tillie before turning her attention back to me. "So, you're sure you're okay with me leaving? I can take a few more days off if you need. But if you think you will be okay, then I probably should get back."

"I'm fine. I swear. It's already been a week. If I need you, I promise I'll call," I say between bites. I need her gone so that I can force myself to be a fully functioning human being. She can't continue to put her life on hold for me. And, I need to make things as normal as possible for my daughter. I can feel myself beginning to depend on her too much, and I can't afford to become that person.

"Okay, then. What's on the agenda for today? What needs to be done before Reid gets here?" Cassie asks.

"I was planning to clean out the pool house for him. Freshen it up. I want him to have his own space." I look at both Tillie and Cass and ask, "You two down for a day of scrubbin'?"

"Not me!" Tillie shouts. "I'm not cleaning. I'm just little. I'm just going to play toys...and watch tartoons, and not clean. I'm not doing that..." she says, shaking her little head vehemently.

ONCE WE FINISH WITH THE cleaning, the three of us spend the day splashing in the pool, and it feels like any other Sunday. I forget that I am now a widow. That my husband just died and that I should be mourning his death. I smile, and I mean it, but damned if I don't feel guilty about it afterward.

It's a crazy thing, guilt. I never realized what an all-consuming, crippling emotion it can be. Is this what my life will be like from now on? Guilt stealing what little happiness I manage to find along the way?

six

Reid

"BUT, REID..." KYLIE WHINES THROUGH the phone, "this was supposed to be our last summer together before school starts. I was looking forward to spending some time together. Do you realize how hard it will be to see each other when you're in Louisiana and I'm in Georgia?"

We've had this same conversation every night since my father told me that he'd promised my summer to Aunt Viv. I want to be pissed at him for volunteering me for shit without my consent, but even I am not that big of an asshole. I haven't seen the woman in years but she was still married to my uncle, and I'm just going to have to suck it up and get my ass out there.

Plus, he threatened to not pay for my schooling if I don't. So, yeah, there's also that.

"Babe, we've been over this. It's not like I can just fucking say no, okay? You think I want to spend my summer with my aunt and her kid? I'd much rather spend it in you..." I joke.

She doesn't laugh.

"With you, baby, with you. It was a joke. Chill out."

She sniffs. "God, I don't know how you can be so...so...whatever about this."

Kylie has been my girl, off and on, for almost three years. Our families are in business together, and we've always been friends. When high school and hormones came around, it just sort of made sense. We've taken a few breaks, and I've fucked a few other girls, but I'm pretty sure Kylie has only ever been with me.

I hate it when she cries...when any girl cries. I don't know how to handle that shit. I care about her, but right now she's really starting to get on my fucking nerves. I have a plane to catch...early. The last thing I feel like hearing is this shit again. It won't change anything.

"Listen, Kylie, maybe we should just start our break now."

Kylie and I discussed calling it quits during college. We'll still see each other when I come home, but I don't want to be tied down, and she doesn't want to lose me. It works for us both. I'm pretty sure we will one day end up married and do the whole kids thing. Nothing would please our families more, and I do love her. I think. But I'm not married yet. I want to enjoy my college years, and I want the same for her.

Her cries get louder, more forceful. *Make it stop.*

"Is that what you want, Reid? To break up?" she asks between sobs. "You going out there to hook up with some girl or something?"

"Jesus fucking Christ, Kylie! Yeah, I met a girl the last time I was out there eight fucking years ago!" I yell. "We talked about this," I say with a little more control.

"But...we were supposed to have the summer," she cries.

"Yeah, we were, but things changed. Look, I really need to get some sleep. I can't do this right now. Let's just end it now and I'll see you when I come home for Thanksgiving, okay?"

"Yeah, I mean...I guess I don't really have much of a choice, do I?" she asks with a twinge of hope in her voice.

"No, babe, not really. No regrets, remember?" I remind her. "I want you to enjoy these next few years. I don't want you sitting around crying over me. We'll still talk," I assure her. "I love you, baby. That's not going to change. We just need to experiment and experience life before settling down."

Kylie doesn't respond, just continues crying into the phone.

"Right, okay. Well, I'm going to get to bed. Call me tomorrow or something, okay?" I offer weakly. "Love you." And then I end the call.

AFTER GETTING OFF OF THE plane, I make my way over to the baggage area and see a poster with my name on it in colorful bubble letters held up by a woman, who I'm assuming is Aunt Viv. She's dressed in a simple pink tank top and jean shorts with flip flops. Her hair is in long waves down her back and those legs...long, lean, and toned that top off a perfectly round ass. *Fuck. When did Aunt Viv get so hot?*

"Looking for me?" I ask as I walk up to meet her and Tillie, who is bouncing around her feet.

Vivienne looks up from her daughter, and when our eyes meet, my heart starts thudding in my chest. She's fucking gorgeous. *What the fuck am I thinking? This isn't just some girl. This is my aunt. My dead uncle's wife.*

She looks at me strangely, and I'm wondering if she's feeling the same pull, or worse. Maybe she can read my mind. But, that's just stupid. She seems to catch hold of her thoughts when she pulls me into a tight hug. "Reid. It's so good to see you. Thank you so much for coming."

And sick fuck that I am, all I can think about is how great her tits feel pressed up against my chest. How right my arms feel wrapped around her tiny waist. *I need to get a fucking grip.*

"Mommy," Tillie calls to her mother, and it's exactly the bucket of ice cold water I need.

"Yeah, baby?" Viv answers.

"Why does Reid look like my daddy?"

seven

Vivienne

WHEN I LOOK UP TO see Reid's face—*Abbott's face*—I'm momentarily struck stupid. For a second, I forget how to breathe. It's all still so fresh, so raw. It's hard enough to see his face on Tillie day in and day out, but on another man...it's physically painful. When Tillie voices my thoughts aloud, it's like a punch to the gut.

Thank God Reid answers because I can't seem to find my voice.

"Because Reid's a lucky guy," he says, ruffling her hair. "And you are a lucky girl. We Parkers all look alike," he adds with a shrug. "Good genes."

"You have good pants?" she asks, confused. "I'm not wearing pants, silly. This is a dress, and it's pink. Do you like pink?" Tillie questions while batting her long lashes at him.

Just roll with it, I mouth to Reid, laughing silently.

He smiles and answers, "As a matter fact, I do like pink, Miss Tillie, and I love your dress." He compliments my daughter and my heart warms to him instantly.

"Okay," Tillie says. "Good. Cuz pink is our favorite, right, Mommy?"

"It sure is," I answer. Then, addressing them both, I say, "Come on, kiddos, let's get out of here!"

I do my best not to look at Reid on the way home from the airport. It's doing crazy things to my emotions and confusing the hell out of me. Each time I catch a glimpse of him in my peripheral, it's a shock to my heart. It's hard not to envision Abbott riding alongside me, where he has so many times before.

"So, Reid, how was your flight?" I ask while keeping my eyes straight ahead on the road.

"Well, I slept right through it," he laughs. "So, I'd say it was pretty good."

"Yeah, I'd say so. It was an early flight."

"It wouldn't have been so bad if I hadn't spent half the night on the phone with my girl. She isn't taking my leaving too well. You know how chicks are," he answers, sounding just like the eighteen-year-old that he is. His juvenile language reminds me that this is not Abbott, and these feelings are completely unwarranted.

"I'm sorry, Reid. Maybe you can have her come out for a few days in a couple of weeks once we get things situated. You'll have your own space in the pool house. It would be a nice vacation for her."

"Yeah? I might do that. Let's see how things go. You wouldn't mind?" he asks, looking a little skeptical. "Are you sure?"

"Of course. You're an adult. As long as it doesn't interfere with your work at the camp, then I don't see why not. I already feel bad that you'll be here working all summer. I mean, I appreciate it more than you know. But I was eighteen once. You should be having some fun, too."

"It's not a problem, Aunt Viv. I'm happy to help."

ONCE WE GET BACK TO the house, I carry my sleeping daughter to her room and grab the baby monitor from her dresser. Then, I lead Reid out back to the pool house so that we can get him settled in.

"Wow, Aunt Viv. This place is awesome. I'd never want to leave the backyard," he says as he scopes out the pool area.

"That was the idea, Reid." I smile at his excitement. "And this," I say as I wave my arm in front of the pool house, "is where you'll be staying."

"No way."

"Yes way. Let me show you around. Come on in." I wiggle the key into the lock, pop the door open, and usher him inside. "This is the game room, which will serve as your living room. There's a PlayStation and an X-Box in that console over there and a ton of games. The TV has satellite, and there's a channel guide in the drawer over there." I point to the end table beside the couch.

"Awesome," Reid says with genuine enthusiasm. "Do you play?" he asks, looking over at the pool table in the corner of the room.

"I love it. Abbott and I played often," I answer wistfully.

"Well, maybe you can show me sometime?" Reid asks, moving closer. "I've never played. Always wanted to learn."

"Sure, I'd like that." I force a smile and wonder if he can tell how nervous he makes me. My arms and legs are beginning to tingle, and I can feel the nausea setting in. I need to get this over with and get away from this boy for a bit. *Get your shit together, Viv.*

"Good," Reid says, coming closer still.

I smile and then quickly turn and show him his room, bathroom, and kitchenette area. "I'm sorry you don't have a full kitchen in here. But you have a fridge and a microwave, and you're welcome to have all meals with us up at the house and to come and go as you please. I wanted you to have your own space but don't feel like you have to stay in here if you're bored and want to hang out or talk, or if you need any food, drinks, anything at all. Make yourself at home, Reid."

"I will. Thank you. This is all really cool."

"You're welcome," I say, handing him a set of keys. "The keys are labeled. There's one for the pool house, the main house, and the storage building near the pavilion. You may need the last one for work," I add. "I'm going to run back to the house and check on Tillie. Come on over whenever you want. Dinner will be at 6:00. My best friend, Cassie, is coming over, and she's looking forward to meeting you," I say as I back my way out of the door.

"Sounds good, Aunt Viv. I'll probably lounge around for a bit and check in with my folks. I'll see you ladies at 6:00."

"Perfect," I answer then walk back to my house as fast as my legs will take me.

I climb the stairs to my bedroom and grab a pill from the bedside table and swallow it down with some water. My face is flushed, and my heart is racing.

What the hell is wrong with me? Why am I reacting this way to my nephew?

I didn't expect...shit...I don't know what I expected, but I didn't expect to feel...uncomfortable around him. I didn't expect him to look exactly like my dead husband. Surely, I am only feeling these things out of loneliness. Because I am missing Abbott so much.

I fall onto my bed and cry for what I've lost. I cry over my traitorous body and for the overwhelming guilt that I feel over it all.

CASSIE GETS TO THE HOUSE at a quarter to six, and Reid has yet to arrive. Tillie's watching a princess movie in the living room, and when I see my best friend, the tears flow like a river.

"Oh my God, Viv. What's wrong, babe?" she asks worriedly. "Is it Abbott?" She reaches out, rubbing my tears away with her thumbs.

I shake my head. "Yes...ugh. No? God, Cassie, I don't even know," I sob. "I'm feeling all these things, and they don't feel right." I dab my nose with a tissue. "I just...I'm a terrible person, Cassie."

"Bullshit!" Cass yells through clenched teeth. "That is fucking bullshit, Vivienne." She gets real close, pointing her finger in my face. "You are one of the best people I have ever known. You just lost the love of your life. You have a right to be a little messed up in the head right now. Cut yourself some slack, Momma."

"You don't understand, Cassie...I can't even look at him without seeing Abbott. It's scary how much he looks like him, and it's freaking me the fuck out! I had to stare out of the window the whole way home...Just the slightest glance and, God...it was like— like having him back for a split second and then losing him all over again."

"Listen, if he looks that much like Abbott, it's no wonder you're having a hard time. You're not a bad person, and you aren't doing anything wrong." She leans over, giving me a hug, and I hold on to my best friend like my life depends on it. Painful sobs wrack my body as I cling to comfort and try to remember how to breathe.

People often say that things are "as easy as breathing." I've come to hate that phrase. Those people must not know the pain of a broken heart. The way it sits on your chest and crushes your soul. The way it squeezes the air right from your lungs. Since losing Abbott, nothing in life is easy and each breath feels like a monumental task.

"Plus," Cassie adds, "you're on your period. All those extra hormones added to what you're going through. You have a free pass to be a complete basket case. No one would hold it against you."

"I know I won't," Reid says, coming in through the back door. *And I want to die. How long has he been standing there? What did he hear? Why do these fucking Parkers always walk up during my most embarrassing moments?*

Slowly, I lift my face from Cassie's shoulder and am met with the face of a very sincere Reid. I feel the heat in my cheeks as I apologize, "Reid. I'm so sorry. I didn't see you there." And then I cry some more because it seems that is all I do these days.

"Don't do that," he says, moving farther into the room. "Please don't be embarrassed. You've been through a lot, and trust me, I know what periods are," he laughs. "I have a mom and a girlfriend. In a few hours, we'll all laugh about this. So don't let it bug you," he adds. "Consider it forgotten."

"Holy fucking shit," Cassie whispers under her breath. "It's like looking at Abbott eight years ago. I mean, I know you said it... but seeing it is...just...wow!" she says in disbelief. "I mean, it's no wonder...you know...what you said. It makes sense, babe." I love her for trying to be discrete. Maybe he only caught the tail end of our conversation. *As if I could be that lucky.*

Reid sticks out his hand toward my friend. "Hi, you must be Cassie," he says with a grin, clearly liking what he sees. "I'm Reid. But, uh...I guess you already know that right?"

"Right, yeah...hi," Cass says, shaking his hand. "Go get cleaned up, Viv. I'll get the table set and my best girl ready to eat."

"What would I do without you?" I walk swiftly to my bathroom, desperate to get away. It's been a few hours since my last one, so I pop another Xanax and wait 'til I can feel the medicine start to work before heading back downstairs to have dinner with my family.

When I return to the kitchen, I see that Cassie has dished out all of our plates, and they are already sitting around the table, deep in conversation.

"Mommy...finally!" Tillie says. "We been waiting for you foreverrr. I'm starvin' Marvin."

"Are you, Silly Tillie?" I ask, playing along. "Well, then, let's eat."

Matilda is sitting between Cassie and Reid...and I am apparently seated on the other side of *him*.

"She asked Reid to switch places with you, Mommy. Tillie wanted to sit by her cousin tonight. I hope you don't mind?"

"No, it's fine. All good," I assure her, smiling sweetly. And I don't know which one of us I am trying to convince.

Over spaghetti and meatballs, we discuss how the camp runs and what will be expected of Reid. It's really a simple job. The campers come with their own supervision. We merely provide a fun place to visit and entertainment. Abbott and I were not willing to take on the responsibility of chaperoning as well. Reid's primary job will be to take groups out in the boat and to play with the kids. To make sure everyone is having a great time. He will help bait fishing lines and remove fish from hooks for squeamish children. We have karaoke on Friday evenings.

Camp Aspie was Abbott's pride and joy. His best friend growing up was a girl who suffered from Asperger's Syndrome. These children are socially awkward and have difficulty forming friendships. They were an unlikely pair, with Abbott being the social butterfly. But Gracie took a liking to Abbott and became borderline obsessed with him. Instead of being turned off by her attention, Abbott became her champion. He looked after her in school, and they became very close. They eventually grew apart after high school, and I've never actually met her. I could tell what a tremendous impact she had on his life. The way he was with these kids. It was just incredible.

"So the campers will arrive next week. They'll be here every day from eight to five and from eight to eight on Fridays for karaoke night. The camp runs every week until August 2nd."

"Sounds like a lot of fun. All I have to do is play with a bunch of kids. I can handle that," he says confidently.

"I love Camp Aspie," Cassie chimes in. "It's a really rewarding experience. I can't wait to meet this year's kiddos."

"It may take a little while for the kids to warm up to you...to all of us. I don't know what you know about Asperger's Syndrome, but the kids are a little...different. Mostly just shy. They need a little help making friends, but this camp is like therapy for them. You'll see so much growth from the time they get here until they leave. It's our hope that they make lifelong friendships," I explain, finally feeling a little excitement.

"So, do you have the same kids every year?" Reid asks.

"We have a few repeats this year. The camp is for children between thirteen and fifteen. So, we end up with a lot of newbies every year. We try to keep the kids close in age. It's easier for them to forge lasting friendships that way."

Reid nods his head in agreement while chewing on a mouthful of spaghetti. "Makes sense."

"Can I play wif Reid, too? I wanna go in the boat." Tillie was too young to really remember the camp last year. "My daddy always taked me in the boat, right, Mommy?"

"Right, sweet girl. Daddy loved taking you fishing," I assure her. "You'll be able to go out in the boat, too, but not with the big kids."

"I can take her tomorrow," Reid offers. "As long as it's okay with you, of course." I don't really have anything else to do for the next week. "I'd love to spend some time hanging out with you two."

How sweet is he? Reid really is a great kid. I need to get control of my emotions and just enjoy having him around. I'm going to use this time to get to know him again, and we are going to make this a great summer for my baby girl. I will give her a happy childhood, even if I have to fake my own happiness to make it happen.

"Thanks, Reid," I say, turning to look at him for the first time since sitting next to him tonight. "Really, it means so much. You spending time with her...with us. We could use a little fun, right, baby girl?"

"Right!" Tillie shouts with a mouthful.

"Don't mention it, Aunt Viv. It's what I'm here for. To spend some time with family and get to know my baby cousin. Isn't that right, Tillie?" he asks, nudging her with his shoulder.

"Yep, it is right! You can be my prince since Daddy got dead!" Tillie announces excitedly.

My jaw drops.

"I think that's a great idea...You can call him Prince Reid," Cassie suggests. "Daddy will always be your Prince Abbott, baby girl." Then she looks at me as if asking permission. "But, a girl can never have too many princes. Right, Momma?"

Reid looks my way apologetically as I give a strained response. "Yeah...Right. Can't have too many," I say, trying not to cry. "I'm sorry guys..." I push up from the table, feeling the all too familiar burn behind my eyes. "I'm starting to feel a little sick again." I look over to Cassie with pleading eyes. "Would you mind getting Matilda down for me just one more night?"

"Of course, Momma, you know I don't mind. Anything, remember? You can ask me for anything. We're in this together."

I give Cassie a hug and then step around Reid to hug and kiss Matilda good night. My sweet girl. My whole world. She is all I have left, and once again I am pushing her off on Cassie. But, as I feel the burn of the tears threatening to fall, I know that I am not strong enough for this right now. I have to get out before I completely break down in front of her. I can't scare her like that. She's seen enough of my tears. I turn back to Reid, wishing him a good night, and then carry myself on wobbly legs back to my sanctuary.

I throw myself back onto the bed with tears streaming down my cheeks and reach for my phone. Without thinking, I open to the contacts and my finger hovers above his name. He's always been my first response...my go-to. And, when I realize what I've done, it's like losing him all over again. How can a heart already so broken continue to break? I stare at his name, crying so hard that I can barely make out the letters, and then I press my trembling finger to the screen. Abbott's phone is dead, so it goes immediately to voicemail. I listen to his greeting over and over again. *"You've reached Abbott Parker, and I'm unavailable at the moment, but if you leave your name and number, I'll be sure to call you back. P.S. If this is my gorgeous wife... Vivie, I love you."* I love you too. God, I love you so much. I'm like an addict getting her fix. His voice is music to my starving ears. It sends chills down my spine and a knife right through my heart. One day, I will be able to listen to it and smile.

But, not today. I'm not there yet.

eight

Vivienne

"COME ON IN, VIVIENNE, AND have a seat," Dr. Benson beckons from behind his cluttered desk. He's an older man in his fifties or sixties with a full head of salt and pepper hair. He's fit, very attractive for his age, and has the kindest eyes. "I'm very sorry to hear about Abbott," he adds sincerely as I seat myself across from him in a worn armchair and inhale deeply to calm my frazzled nerves. His office smells of paper and dust—like an old library.

I began seeing Dr. Benson a few weeks after Tillie was born. That's when the panic attacks first started. I wasn't sure what was happening to me. I thought that I was dying. Random spots on my body started to go numb. I was dizzy and having heart palpitations. Abbott ended up bringing me to the emergency room when I almost dropped Tillie one night. After a battery of tests was run to rule out any neurological or heart problems, I was diagnosed with postpartum. And still, after a clean bill of health, I was sure that those doctors hadn't a clue what they were talking about. Women with postpartum hate their babies, right? I was convinced that they just couldn't figure out what was wrong because I saw the moon and stars in my baby girl's eyes. There was no way that she was the cause. But, at the hospital's recommendation, I came to see Dr. Benson, and he confirmed that postpartum is not always depression and that what I had was anxiety. He put me on a daily pill for a few months, and after I was feeling better, he prescribed Xanax to take as needed.

I look up to meet his glistening brown eyes with tear-soaked eyes of my own. "Thank you...I still can't believe that he's gone," I say, already fighting back tears. "That he isn't just on a business trip and coming back home to me."

"I can only imagine how hard this all is for you. I would ask how you're doing, but I don't really think that's necessary," he says, folding his slightly wrinkled hands together on the top of his desk. "Why don't you start? Tell me what you're feeling."

Dr. Benson patiently waits while I gather my composure. I really like that about him. I know it is his job, but he is so calm—never pushy. "I don't really know where to start," I say, and those damned tears fall anyway. "I feel like I'm losing my mind," I choke out.

He passes me a handful of Kleenex, and I dab at my eyes and nose. "I'm trying so hard to be normal for Tillie. She can't lose me, too. But, I'm so scared...I'm scared that I won't be able to stop that from happening." I curl up into the chair and hug my knees to my chest.

With a look of concern, he asks, "What do you mean by lose you, Vivienne?"

I can see where he is going with this.

"Not, ummm, not physically, of course," I say, looking up at him through wet lashes. "Don't worry about that. I could never ever do that to her. I just mean mentally. I can't focus, and I'm so sad. I can't stop crying. I've been so distant with her, and I know that she needs me, but I don't feel like I'm able to be what she needs right now, and I hate it! I hate the person that I'm becoming, but I don't know how to stop it...I feel like I'm failing her," I cry. "I'm failing my baby."

"Vivienne, you are *not* failing," he says, meeting my eyes. "Listen to me. You're an amazing mother to that little girl, and you were an amazing wife to Abbott. You will get through this. Maybe not today or tomorrow, but eventually you will find happiness again. You'll find it in your daughter and your loved ones, and your days will get easier. I'm not saying you will ever stop loving Abbott or missing him, or even that you'll move on romantically; although, that's okay, too. Each person is different and whatever path you choose will be the right one for you. But, you'll learn to live again. I've been doing this for such a long time. Believe me when I tell you that you will get through this."

The passion in which he delivers his words makes me almost believe them. I want to believe so badly that I will come out of this okay. That someday I won't be merely surviving but *living* again, but right now my future feels so bleak. If it weren't for Tillie, I would have no reason to get out of bed in the morning. That is my truth.

"Do you have anyone helping you?" he asks, interrupting my thoughts. "Someone to help occupy your time and distract you from your grief?"

"Cassie was...until I sent her home yesterday. I was depending on her too much. I need to do this on my own. I want Tillie's life to be as normal as possible and watching her godmother take care of her mother is not normal," I say nervously, now questioning my own decision.

"You can't put a time limit on grief. We all have to grieve in our own way and at our own pace. I'm afraid that you're trying to rush yourself, Vivienne. Abbott hasn't even been gone two weeks. Please allow your loved ones to be there for you. I'm really concerned about you being in that big house all alone."

"Oh, I'm not. I'm not alone, and I don't mean Tillie," I add. "Abbott's nephew, Reid, came to help with the camp over the summer, so he's staying with us."

I don't tell him that Reid is technically next door in the pool house, and that is about as close as I can handle right now, or that I really don't know him at all. I don't tell him how crazy I have felt since laying eyes on him at the airport yesterday or that the panic attacks have more than doubled. I don't tell him that the emptiness I've been feeling since Abbott's death is slowly being replaced by guilt.

"Great. That's good. I'm glad you have him there with you." I can hear the relief in his voice.

"Reid is great. He's out fishing with Matilda right now, actually."

I have a feeling they'll be really close by summer's end," I say with a forced smile.

The doctor looks at me questioningly. "Am I sensing some animosity? Has something happened that I should know about?" he asks, wrinkling his forehead.

I have no poker face.

"No. Not really. But...well...he looks just like Abbott. It's sort of messing with my head a little. It's just...It hurts seeing him. I know it's not his fault. Reid really is great. It's my issue. Not his," I ramble. "And Tillie...God, I don't know how to say this without sounding like a child," I say, placing my head in my hands.

Dr. Benson shakes his head at me. "There is *nothing* you can say that would make you sound like a child. You're entitled to your feelings, however juvenile you may think that they are."

I nod. "I'm afraid that Tillie is trying to replace Abbott with Reid..." The tears are now falling freely. It hurts more than I imagined to speak that thought aloud. "Abbott *just* died." I grab for more tissues and wipe at my wet face.

Nodding, Dr. Benson replies, "That's perfectly normal, my dear. Tillie is so young. She can't possibly understand. She just wants her life to go back to normal. Children that young don't fully grasp the permanence of death. They don't grieve the way adults do. She's not trying to replace Abbott. She's trying to fill that gap...but no one will ever take the place of her father."

"So, I should just encourage this?" I ask incredulously.

"No. I wouldn't say encourage as much as allow it. Allow Tillie to grieve and to deal with her pain in whatever way works for her. If hanging out with Reid is bringing her happiness, then you shouldn't try to take that from her. And if it's the thought of her forgetting about Abbott that's the problem, then you should talk with her about him. Spend a little time each night remembering her father. And if you cry, that's okay, too. It's not the end of the world for Tillie to see you cry. It's a normal part of grieving. A normal part of life," Dr. Benson explains.

"Okay. All right, I can do that." I've avoided even saying Abbott's name around Tillie unless she brings him up for fear of upsetting her or myself. I realize now that by doing so, I'm helping her forget. I have to find ways to keep her father alive.

"You mentioned the panic attacks. How are you handling those? Do you still have medication?"

"No, I was using the pills, but I'm out." *Liar.* The truth is, I do still have half of a bottle, but I have been taking them more frequently and don't want to run out. The thought of doing this without them is terrifying.

"All right. What about the dose? Is the .25 mg tablet still working for you?"

"Yes. It is. Well, it was," I answer, and I feel bad for lying. But, the anxiety of running out of medication overrules any guilt that I feel at this moment.

Dr. Benson hums while flipping through my chart. "I want to put you back on the Zoloft for a while. I think you need something for every day. It's been three months since the last time that you refilled the Xanax. I'm going to keep you on that as well. It'll help you to shut off your mind and get to sleep at night. But I want you to remember how addicting these medications can become. They are really just a Band-aid to reduce your symptoms and allow you to function more normally until you've dealt with your grief. That will come with time. You can use the medication to counteract those attacks."

I nod. "That sounds good."

"I'm going to keep you on the .25 mg Xanax, and you can take it at night to sleep or during the day if you get a really bad attack. I don't want you taking them more than you absolutely need to. No more than three times a day, and you need to wait at least six to eight hours between pills. If it's not working, then I want you to come back and see me, okay?"

"Of course."

"I know that you've taken it before, but remember to be careful driving. Benzodiazepines can cause extreme fatigue," he warns. "Do not consume any alcohol while on the medication. Alcohol greatly increases the side effects because they are both downers. The side effects can be so severe that they have even been used as a date rape drug. Coupled with high amounts of alcohol, they can cause memory loss and in some cases even death."

"I remember the side effects, Doctor. I'm not really a big drinker, anyway. That won't be a problem for me. I just want to be able to get through the day, you know?"

"All right. Well, I wish you the best, Vivienne. With time, it will get easier. You hang in there and enjoy that sweet girl of yours," he says as he writes out the prescription on his little pad. "I'd like to see you back here in two or three months to touch base. Of course, you can come sooner if you feel like you need it."

"Thank you so much, Doctor," I respond, taking the prescription from his hand. "And thank you for seeing me on such short notice."

I PULL UP TO THE house, admiring the scenery. We have a long winding drive lined with oak trees that form a canopy overhead. The front and side yards have a few large oaks as well. The largest is to the left of the house and my personal favorite. Abbott recently hung a tire swing for Tillie from one of its thick, mossy branches.

I chuckle to myself at the memory of him trying to get the cable up and over that branch. He'd tied a small brick to one end, and it took forever for him to get enough oomph to make it. I remember heckling him about his throwing arm, and when he finally got it over he did his stupid little victory dance. Anyone who knows Abbott has witnessed it. It was just this silly little cross between the Carlton and the running man. It used to embarrass the hell out of me, but now... now I would give anything to see him do that godawful dance just one more time.

My mind drifts to the first time I ever saw Abbott's moves...It was only a few weeks after the Halloween frat party. Abbott and I were sort of an unofficial couple. We did everything together. I'd even started attending his football games on Friday nights. They'd just won against their biggest rival, and Abbott made the game-winning touchdown.

"Come on, Cass. I want to get to the house before the guys make it back,"

I urge.

"I'm coming, Vivienne. I need to be 'fuck me' hot. The place will be swarming with all sorts of football player yumminess!" she says, waggling her eyebrows. "What's the deal with you and Abbott, anyway? Are the two of you together...officially, yet?" she asks while applying another layer of mascara to her lashes.

"He hasn't asked me to be his girlfriend or anything. Do guys still do that? I don't know what we are. I just know whatever's going on...it's really good, Cass. It's so much more than anything I've ever had with a guy."

"Well...let's go. What are you waiting for? We need to get to this party before one of those skanky cheerleader bitches gets her claws into your man!"

I shake my head at my best friend and grab my purse and keys as we head out of the door.

IT TAKES A FEW TRIPS *around the block before we find an empty spot to park. Cassie and I have to do some serious walking to get to the house. We somehow arrive just before the guys all show up, and thankfully only have to hang out with the frat bitches for a few minutes.*

When the players walk in, their fight song is blaring through the speakers and everyone cheers and rushes to greet them.

Everyone but me. I just hang back and observe.

The smell of beer permeates my senses as the cheerleaders pass out overflowing Solo cups to the team. I look on as they hang all over the guys. Sluts.

Finally, I spot Abbott in the center of a crowd of people chanting his name and push my way through the gaggle of girls to find my man. At least, I think he's my man. I hope he is...

What is he doing?

Oh my God...he is quite possibly the worst dancer I have ever seen. He's got the attention of the whole room, and where I would, no doubt, die from embarrassment, he just eats it up. He's shaking his hips and doing some running man thing with his legs. I can't even...

And then he spots me and crooks his finger toward me.

I shake my head, laughing.

He continues motioning for me to join him and then mouths the word "please" while poking his bottom lip out. I can't leave him hanging, so against my better judgment, I make my way through the crowd.

Oh God. Am I really going to embarrass myself in front of all of these people?

I'm a pretty good dancer, actually, but Abbott is hopeless. He's terrible and adorable, and damn does he smell like heaven. "Hey," I say as I approach him, and the sight of his still damp hair and those dimples is doing crazy things to my girlie parts.

Abbott flashes me a sexy smile and then pulls my body against his. He kisses my temple and works his way down to my ear and whispers, "Hey," as he continues down my neck to my collar bone.

The next song comes on—"Back That Ass Up"—and the house goes wild. Booties are popping everywhere, and I'm relieved that we are not the sole focus of every pair of eyes in the room any longer.

Abbott and I are barely moving. I grind my ass into his crotch as he continues making out with my neck and whispers, "Babe?"

I turn my face to meet his and answer, "Yeah?"

"They clowned when you passed, yeah," he sings, eying the group of girls in the corner.

I bust out laughing and look over to the flock of girls gawking at us and give them the stink eye.

"Let's give 'em something to stare at," he says. Then he places his hands on my hips and begins to really move against me. And the boy can move. He slides one of his hands up under the hem of my shirt to caress my flat stomach, and I lift my arm over my head and around his neck, pulling his face against my own. Being this close to him has me tingling in all the right places.

I look back at him and ask, "What the hell was that...thing," I say, waving my free hand in the air, "you were doing when you walked in? I can't even call that dancing. I was scared."

Abbott cracks up. "That, babe, is called a victory dance. It's supposed to be silly. You thought I was serious?" He laughs even harder.

"Well, I was a little embarrassed for you, truthfully, and really embarrassed for me, too. I'm glad you can actually dance."

"Are you, now?" Abbott asks as he pulls my waist into his, pressing his bulge into my ass. "Speaking of slangin' wood," he whispers as he reaches the hand that's still under my shirt up to grab my breast.

"What wood?" I tease. And boy am I ever joking. He is huge and hard and my body is on fire.

"Whoa, Vivie's got jokes!" Abbott laughs.

I turn in his arms to face him. "Who says I'm joking?" I ask, running my hands up his chest, around his neck, and into his short blond hair.

"That sounds like a challenge?" he questions, raising his right brow.

Yes, please! We've been doing this dance for weeks, and I'm so ready to be with him. Every time things get a little heavy, Abbott backs off. I don't want to be a slut and rape the boy, but I am not far from begging.

I reach down and palm him in my right hand, eliciting a hiss from his lips.

"Fuck me," Abbott growls, releasing a long breath.

"I'm trying..." I say, biting my bottom lip. God, could I be any more desperate?

"Not here, Viv. Not yet," he says, brushing my hair out of my eyes with the back of his hand. "Not at the frat house. Not when we've been drinking. I want our first time to mean something. You mean more to me than this, Viv."

"Do I?" I ask seriously. "What is this Abbott?" I motion between the two of us. "I think you like me and I really, really like you. I want you so bad, and you just keep pushing me away. You've probably slept with half of the girls in this room, so I know you have no aversion to sex. Is it me?" I ask with tears in my eyes.

I am so pathetic.

"Come here, baby," he says as he grabs the sides of my face in his hands and pulls until our noses are practically touching. "Yes, it's you," he says, massaging my scalp with his fingers. "But, not the way you're thinking so stop it." He looks right into my eyes. "I have never wanted anyone the way that I want you and it scares me and excites me all at once. I don't want to fuck this up," he says, wiping my tears away. "Don't let me mess this up, Viv."

BANGING ON MY CAR WINDOW snaps me back to reality. I look out to see Reid and Tillie with huge smiles on their faces, and my heart is feeling lighter than it has in days. I smile back, turning off the engine and unbuckling my seatbelt. I open the door to my silver Maxima and Tillie rushes into my arms.

"Mommy! We hadded so much fun and we catched seven fishes," she says, holding out three fingers.

"Did you now?" I ask giving her a tight squeeze and looking over at Reid.

He ruffles Tillie's hair. "Yes, ma'am," he says. "Seven catfish. We were just about to clean them out back on the wharf if you want to help."

"Sure," I answer. "Just let me run inside and change out of these jeans."

Reid nods. "So...was your appointment good? Everything go okay?"

"It was great. It went great," I say, smiling back at him from the front porch steps. "I'll be out in just a sec."

I run up the stairs to my room and change into a yellow, knee-length sun dress, and a pair of metallic gold flip flops. After running my hands through my hair, I swallow one of the pills on my nightstand and head out to the lake.

I FEEL THE WOOD OF the wharf creak beneath my feet and smell the fishy lake odor that I've become so accustomed to. Ahead, I see Reid and Tillie laughing and teasing each other, and I know in my heart that having Reid here will be good for the both of us.

I'm getting over the initial shock that I felt when he first got here. With the help of the medication and talking to Cass and Dr. Benson, I'm able to see things more clearly.

"*Ewww!*" I hear Tillie yell. "Mommy, hurry! You have *got* to see this. Prince Reid just cutted the fishies head *off!*" she shouts, excited and a bit disgustedly.

Reid is holding the fish head out toward her, and she's squealing like a happy little girl. It's a beautiful sound.

"Hey, crazies," I say, handing Reid a large metal bowl for the fish and a pair of skinning-pliers. "I hope you don't mind if I just watch. Abbott always cleaned the fish. I'm a bit of a girl," I say, crinkling my nose in disgust.

Reid shakes his head. "I don't mind, Aunt Viv." He takes the pliers and gets to work on the decapitated fish.

I watch the muscles in his forearm contract as he pulls the skin back. It's such a disgusting task, yet here I am fascinated by the way his muscles flex with his movements.

I realize I'm staring and turn to watch Tillie playing with the container of worms. She definitely gets that from her daddy. I still can't bring myself to touch the nasty little things.

"Hey, Reid?" I call out while staring absently out at the water.

"Yeah?"

"Would you mind not calling me *Aunt* Viv?" I cringe. "It just makes me feel old. Vivienne is fine or just Viv...Please?"

"Yeah, sure," Reid answers, "No problem, Viv," he adds with a wink. Damn those Parker eyes. This boy is gorgeous, and he knows it. He is going to be lethal to the heart of every female he encounters. Poor girls won't know what hit 'em.

nine

Reid

I SEE VIVIENNE WATCHING ME from the corner of my eye and damned if it doesn't make my pulse quicken. I'm not sure what it is about her that has my dick stand up and take notice, but notice he does...and it's fucking distracting as hell.

Vivienne is everything I normally steer clear of in a girl. She's damaged and fragile. She cries all of the time, and I do *not* do tears. But I want to take away the pain. I want to make her feel whole and beautiful and wanted. Somehow, I sense that she needs that from me.

Maybe it's the fact that her tears are not superficial. They aren't a means to get something from me like every other female in my life. Vivienne is truly hurting, and I have this uncontrollable urge to make her smile, and not that half-assed, fake smile that she gives for everyone else's benefit. I want to make her light up. *In more ways than one.*

I know it's wrong to want her, but I can't fucking help it. I would never betray Uncle Abbott that way, but showing her a little attention and lending her a shoulder to cry on is harmless, right?

I try to concentrate on skinning the last couple of fish, but my eyes keep wandering over to Vivienne in that short yellow dress. She's standing a few feet away, watching Tillie pull worms out of the bucket, and that should totally be a turn-off...seeing her with her daughter. But everything about her calls out to me, even the way she dotes on her kid.

Hell, Vivienne Parker just fucking turns me on. Period.

I drop the last of the fish into the bowl with a splat. "Hey, ladies...all done here," I call out, rinsing my hands in the lake water and then drying them off on my shorts.

"Oh, awesome!" Viv shakes herself out of her daze and rewards me with a huge smile. "Why don't we go inside and I'll make you two some sandwiches for lunch?" she offers, reaching out for the bowl. Her hand barely brushes against mine and the sensation is enough to set my soul on fire. "I'll put these in the fridge and fry them up for dinner."

She's radiant this morning. It's the only word I can find to describe her. This is a whole other level of attraction, and if I don't watch myself, I could be in deep shit. I thought she was beautiful before—beautifully broken—but a smiling Vivienne, a happy Vivienne, is a sight to behold.

I catch myself staring at the freckles that dot her cheeks and give her a tense smile. "Sure, Viv. That sounds great. I'm just going to go grab a shower, and I'll meet you and Tillie up at the house," I say, already walking backwards away from Vivienne.

I PLACE ONE HAND ON the shower wall and the other around my painfully hard cock. One touch from this woman and I need release. I stroke up and down, picturing that perfect ass. Those impossibly long legs. I allow myself to pretend that she's here in front of me. I hike up that yellow dress, pull her panties to the side, and ram into her over and over. I squeeze my shaft as I pump harder and faster, imagining that it's her tight pussy welcoming my every thrust. I feel the tightening in my groin as I cum...hard...with my *aunt's* face on my mind.

Sick bastard.

ten

Vivienne

THE SCREEN DOOR SLAMS SHUT just as I'm returning to the kitchen from putting Matilda in her room for a nap. "Hey, Reid," I call out, "in here."

I watch as Reid saunters into the room wearing gray cargo shorts and a light blue tee; the color against his eyes is striking. He has a presence about him that is welcoming and comforting. Maybe it's just his likeness to Abbott, but now that I am over the shock and on my medication...it just feels *good* to be around him.

"Hey, Aunt—ugh, hey, Vivienne," he chuckles. "That's gonna take a little getting used to. Sorry," he says with a guilty shrug.

"Don't worry about it." I wave him off, grabbing our plates from the counter. "Let's have lunch out on the porch. It's such a gorgeous day. Would you mind getting us each a Coke from the fridge?" I ask as I push the door open with my hip.

Reid grabs our drinks and follows me out to the table on the screened in porch. It's a warm day, but there's a nice breeze coming off the water, and the ceiling fans offer some added circulation.

We enjoy a comfortable silence as we eat our lunch, the only sounds coming from the whirring of the fans and the birds in the trees. I love that Reid can appreciate the beauty of our surroundings. I watch his profile and fixate on the movement of his jaw as he stares out at the water. There's something magical about being able to offer someone peace with your presence alone. I've only ever gotten that from Abbott and Cassie. It's nice to have another kindred spirit.

"So, when do you start football practice?" I ask once I've finished my lunch. "I need to make sure I work around your schedule with the camp."

"Officially, practices won't start until the end of July," Reid says as he checks the calendar on his phone. "July 26th is when we have our first. We pretty much practice every day after that. Sometimes in the morning and others in the afternoon," he says, placing his phone back down on the table.

"That's the last week of camp. I can hire one of the neighbor kids to take the day shifts that week if you can still handle the Friday evenings."

Our neighbor, Mrs. Sue, has a few high school aged boys that are always on the water. We've paid them to cut our lawn in the past. I'll have to contact her anyway to set that up regularly now... since Abbott is no longer here to do it.

Abbott's gone...

And that's all it takes to kill the pleasant mood I've found myself in since returning home this morning. My hands begin to shake, and my heart suddenly feels too big for my chest.

Reid notices the change right away, and I hate that just like that I've ruined our good time. I hate being so weak...so dependent. "Are you okay, Viv?" Reid asks as he gets up from his seat and walks over to kneel in front of me. "Did I say something to upset you?" he asks, placing his hand on my knee to stop it from shaking. I can see the wheels turning. Reid is frantically searching his head for a reason for my sudden change in mood.

I shake my head and squeeze my eyes shut tight, willing the dam not to break. Slow deep breaths do little to calm my racing heart, and when Reid wraps me in his arms, the floodgates open. He holds me tight against his body, and it feels so good to be held... to be wrapped in a man's strong arms...*arms that do not belong to Abbott.*

My good friend guilt makes her appearance, and I am burning inside. My knees buckle, and I cry out for my husband. "Abbott...oh God...I need him. I *need* him, Reid. I can't do this," I cry, clenching the fabric of Reid's shirt, pulling him closer...further incinerating my own heart while my conscience is screaming that I should be pushing him away. *This is wrong.*

"Shh," he whispers, running a hand through my hair. "It's okay, Vivienne. It's okay...cry. Let it out."

And I do. I soak his shirt and cling to the strength that he's offering. I'm not sure how long we stand there like that...Reid supporting my boneless form as I spill my pain all over him...my heart and body at war with each other. Eventually, he carries me up to my room and sets me down on the bed.

Reid crouches down in front of me and takes both of my hands into his own, and I need this right now. I need the warmth and the kindness that his touch offers me. It's an indescribable feeling when your body seeks comfort in the very place that's filling your heart with gut-wrenching guilt. At this moment, my body wins, and I know that my heart will not go down easily.

"Do you need anything, Viv? Some water maybe?" he offers, grabbing the box of Kleenex from my nightstand and pulling a few from the box. He mops up my tears and then tosses them into the wicker trash bin.

I grab a few more tissues and blow my nose. "My, umm... my pills are in the drawer," I say, pointing. I hardly recognize my own voice. It's rough and gravelly from the workout I've just put it through.

Reid gets my medication from the drawer and hands me the bottle along with my water. I swallow a pill and pass both bottles back to Reid, who is still crouched before me. I'm embarrassed to have lost it like that in front of him. I'm sure that this is not what he thought he was signing up for.

"Thank you," I whisper.

Reid pushes my tear-soaked hair behind my ears as he rises. "You're welcome. Why don't you get some rest, Viv? I'll go watch TV in the living room and wait up for Tillie."

Liquid gratitude sneaks down my cheeks. "I'm so sorry, Reid," I say, feeling the heat in my face.

"You just lost your husband. I'd be worried if you weren't a mess," he says simply as he opens my bedroom door. "Get some sleep. You look exhausted. Don't worry about Tillie." Reid switches off my light and shuts the door behind him, leaving me to my thoughts.

After just a few minutes, I feel the ache in my chest subside as my heartbeat returns to a normal pace. The guilt is only a fraction of the weight it was just moments ago. It's still there...always there, but I'm back to a place of rational thought. The pain numbs to a dull ache, and I'm tired. So very tired.

WHEN I OPEN MY EYES, the first thing I notice is that it is dark outside. *Shit.* What time is it? It wasn't even one in the afternoon when I came up to bed. I throw off the covers and sit up to see that it is almost seven o'clock. I've been asleep for six hours!

I go into my bathroom to pass a brush through my bed-tangled hair and brush my teeth. Then, I walk back out to my bedroom and take one of my pills. I can't afford a repeat of this morning.

When I open the door to my room, I'm greeted with the smell of fried food. I hear rock music blaring from the kitchen and the sweet, sweet sound of my little girl's giggle.

On tip toes, I creep down the stairs and through the house to the kitchen entryway. There's a pan filled with fried fish and another with fries sitting on the island. Reid has Tillie kneeling on a stool beside him at the sink and they are...washing dishes? Well, Reid's washing dishes. Matilda is dipping her hands in the water and waving them in front of Reid's face to spray him with the droplets. The floor is full of soapy water, and he is dripping wet.

My heart swells.

I can't believe he did all of this. I don't know how to ever thank him for everything he's done for me today.

I clear my throat loudly to get their attention and two-megawatt smiles trimmed in identical sets of dimples turn my way.

"Hey, sleeping booty," Tillie says as she jumps off of the stool and rushes at me, slipping and sliding on the wet floor the whole way.

Reid dries off as best he can with a dish towel. "Ah, don't worry about it. Dimples and I had a great time, didn't we?"

Dimples? He gave her a nickname? *Huh...I like it.*

"It was *so* fun, Mommy. We played Barbies and Play-Doh...And Reid letted me play water guns in the *house!*"

Reid's mouth falls open in mock surprise. "Hey, now...don't go telling all our secrets. You trying to get me in trouble?" he asks, playfully swatting at her with his towel.

Tillie giggles. "Oops, I mean we didn't did that, Mommy. I was just joking," she says, attempting a wink at Reid but looking more like she is having a seizure.

"Oh, you two are trouble!" I laugh. "Dinner smells great, Reid. Thank you so much for cooking for us...and cleaning...and entertaining my daughter while I slept...and, well...for earlier, too," I say, blushing.

"Pffft. It was nothing," Reid says, waving me off. "Really. But if you want to do something to thank me...maybe you could give me my first pool lesson after Dimples goes to bed. You should be good to go for a few good hours now, right?" he teases, lifting an inquisitive brow.

"I'd love to," I answer as I grab the mop and bucket from the closet and begin mopping up the water from the floor. "We have another pool table in the game room upstairs. Let's play here since Tillie will be sleeping."

AFTER I'VE GIVEN MATILDA A bath and brushed her teeth, I tuck her into her bed and climb in beside her. I'm taking what Dr. Benson said to heart and starting a new bedtime routine.

"How about instead of reading a story tonight we share some of our favorite Daddy stories?"

She looks at me with the hugest of smiles. "I like that idea, Mommy. How do we tell Daddy stories?" she asks.

"Well, you just talk about some of your favorite things you did with Daddy or your favorite things about Daddy."

"Can you go first?"

I smile and brush my fingers through her hair. "Sure can... hmm...One of my favorite days with Daddy was the day we got married..." She is obsessed with weddings and loves to hear all about ours.

Tillie's face lights up as she interrupts, "On the beach, right? You gotted married by the ocean!"

I smile at her and answer, "Yes, sweet girl, on the beach. The sand was white, and the water was crystal blue. And Daddy...Daddy looked like Prince Charming."

"But he was Prince Abbott, right?"

"Right! Prince Abbott made Mommy feel like a princess, always. It was one of the most special days because it meant we would get to love each other forever."

Little did I know how short our forever would be.

For some, love doesn't come easy, but for us...it was effortless. Even if I had known how it would end, I'd still choose Abbott every time. Those precious years that we did have are worth more to me than a lifetime of mediocrity with anyone else.

I just wish we'd had more time...but no amount of time would ever be enough.

"And when you get married, you get to live in the same house together, right, Mommy?"

"That's right, Tillie. Now it's your turn. What was one of your favorite days with Daddy?"

She considers it for a moment. "Well, my date was my bestest day ever! It was *so* fun. Daddy taked me to eat at Miss Donald's and then we goed to the ice skaping ring and I gotted to see all of the princesses." Then she gets a sullen look and says, "But then my daddy gotted dead. So that was not my favorite anymore."

I pull her close and hug her tight as I place light kisses on her forehead. "I'm glad you and Daddy had a great date, sweet girl. You made him so happy. He sent me a picture before y'all left to come home. Do you want to see?"

I feel her nod her little head and pull my phone out of my pocket. I've missed a few texts from Cassie that I will need to respond to later. I bring up the picture and show it to her.

"We look so fwitty, Mommy," she says, running her little finger over his face. "I miss my Daddy." Her little body starts to shake, and her whimpers cut me deeply.

"I miss him, too, baby. So much. It's okay to miss him. It's okay to talk about him, okay?"

She lets out a huge yawn and nuzzles her head further into my shoulder. "Okay, Mommy," she says between cries.

I snuggle with Tillie until her body goes limp and she's breathing heavy. Once I'm sure that she's asleep, I slip my arm out from under her head and slowly slide myself from the bed, careful not to wake her.

After shutting the door very slowly, I damn near have a heart attack when I turn around and bump right into Cassie. "What the hell?" I whisper-yell. "Cassie, you scared the shit out of me!" I shove past her, down the stairs, and into the living room.

She follows, hot on my heels, and chastises, "Well, so did you. I've been texting you all day, and you've been ignoring me. What's up with that, Vivienne? I came over to make sure that you were all right."

I spin around to face her. "I just noticed all of your messages while putting her down and was going to call you when I got out of her room. I'm sorry that I made you worry. I sort of freaked out earlier, and Reid watched Tillie so I could take a nap. I ended up sleeping all afternoon."

Her expression cools and is replaced with a sympathetic smile. "I'm sorry you had a rough day, Momma. Do you need me to come back? I can stay here with you."

"No," I respond a little too quickly. "I mean, it's okay. Reid was here. He was really helpful and great with Tillie."

I can tell I've hurt her. "Oh, umm, okay. Well, I'm glad you have *Reid* to help you," she responds dejectedly.

"Come on, Cass. You know it's not like that. I just don't want to keep you from your life, and I'm trying really hard to do this on my own. I'm very thankful that Reid was here, but I don't plan on needing him. It's just nice knowing someone is here in case. I don't want to disrupt your life, too."

"It's fine, girl. I get it. And for the record...you and Tillie *are* my life. You don't disrupt anything. I love you, Vivienne, and I *want* to be here for you. You need to do this in your own way, and I respect that. Just know that I'm always a phone call away. You don't have to do anything alone."

I walk over to Cassie and give her a big hug. "I don't know what I would do without you, Cassie," I say, taking a step back. "You and Tillie...you're all I have left. I'm sorry if I'm hurting your feelings. I don't know the right way to do this. I'm just winging it and hoping that I am doing the right things."

She shakes her head. "No, I'm sorry. I shouldn't be making you feel guilty." She pulls a gift bag from behind her back and holds it out to me. "Forgive me?" she asks with a pout.

"Of course, there's nothing to forgive," I answer. "What's this?" I ask, reaching out for the bag.

Cassie nibbles on her lip. "Don't be mad, okay? I got you something."

Oh God...

"What? Why? It's not my birthday, and I've been a moody bitch lately."

A grin lights her face. "That's precisely why I got you this... *amazing* gift." She reaches out to stay my hand and adds, "Just keep an open mind...I know how prudish you can be."

I glare at her. "What did you do? And I'm *not* a prude." I reach into the bag and pull out..."A dildo?" I shriek. "Seriously, Cassie?"

"A vibrator," she says proudly.

"There's a difference?"

Cassie rolls her eyes. "Duh." She grabs it from my hands and removes the packaging. After inserting two AA batteries, she turns it on before passing it back to me. "A vibrator...vibrates. A dildo...is just a rubber dick. It doesn't *do* anything."

I can't even..."Why the hell would I need this, Cassie? That's the farthest thing from my mind."

"Because, *Vivienne*, you're a woman. A woman who had a very active sex life and just lost her husband. You're going to have *needs*, and I know you aren't going to go off and sleep with anyone else. You'll be thanking me soon. Trust me," she says, winking at me. "I can't have you taking out all that sexual frustration on my goddaughter. Just looking out for my favorite girls."

How is *this* my best friend? She's so crude and inappropriate.

"I'm not going to use this," I say, trying to hand it back to her. She pushes it away. "Oh, you will. I wasn't sure on the size. I figured Abbott must have been well endowed to keep your prude ass craving his dick. This one is nine inches with a thick girth. But, if it's not right, we can make a trip to the sex store. There are different sizes and..."

I raise my hand, palm out, cutting her off. "I'm not a whore, Cassie!"

"Hey! I resemble that remark. And besides, you have to fuck *real* dick...attached to actual men to be a whore. Plastic and fingers don't count."

A cough draws both of our attention to the doorway. "Uh, I thought that we were going to get in that game of pool tonight? I... uh, let myself in. Bad time?" Reid asks, trying to stifle a laugh.

Perfect fucking timing, as usual. I'm sitting on the sofa with a vibrating penis in my hand, and I'm sure he just got an earful of that titillating conversation.

I throw the vibrator at Cassie. "Turn it off!" I say, glaring at her.

She's laughing so hard that she can't catch her breath, and I must be the only one who fails to see the hilarity in this situation because Reid is in hysterics against the wall.

"Goddamn it, Cassie. Turn the fucking thing off!" I'm furious, mortified, and on the verge of tears.

That slut gets up and starts chasing me around the living room with the buzzing vibrator, and I'm screaming like a little girl being chased by a cockroach. Reid has plopped himself on the couch to watch our shenanigans with a shit-eating grin plastered on his face.

I feel Cassie poke me in the butt with it, and I fall to the floor in hysterics.

"Stooooop!" I yell, slapping at Cassie, who is now on top of me, attacking me with the vibrator.

Cassie always has been the fun friend. She never fails to cheer me up or force me out of my comfort zone. We're opposite in so many ways, from our looks to our sense of humor. She's overtly sexual, and I guess I am a bit of a prude, although I will never admit that to her. Somehow, we just fit.

"Hey. No fair. Can I try the sword?"

I turn my head and see Tillie staring at Cass and me wrestling on the floor. We must have woken her up with all of our noise. "Umm, hey, baby," I say with a forced smile.

Cassie switches off the vibrator and tosses it to Reid on the couch like she's playing hot potato.

Just shoot me.

"Here, Reid, go put your toy away before someone gets hurt," Cassie says with a smirk.

Reid shoves the vibrator into the gift bag and places it on the top shelf of the entertainment center. Our eyes meet and his are filled with mirth.

"Hey, Dimples," he says to my daughter, his eyes never leaving mine.

"Why can't I play, too?" Tillie whines.

I push Cassie off me and sit up, brushing my hands off on my shorts. "Well, because it is past your bedtime, young lady," I say, panting. "I'm sorry we woke you up. We won't play any more games without you."

Standing, Cassie reaches out for Tillie, wiggling her fingers. "Come here, sweet thang."

Tillie leaps into her arms. "Auntieee!"

Cassie begins walking in the direction of the stairs. "I'm going to read the princess a story and get her back to bed," she says guiltily.

I watch them round the corner and snort out a laugh.

"So, ummm, that wasn't awkward at all," Reid says, reaching his arms out to help me up from the floor.

"You ready to run back home yet?" I ask as we make our way to the kitchen.

"What? Are you kidding? Why would I? Mom's house is so boring. Believe it or not, I've never encountered hot women wrestling with sex toys in her living room," he teases. "I love it here."

"Spoken like a true man," I say, rolling my eyes at him.

"Oh, I'm all man," Reid says, puffing up his chest. *Yes, you are.*

"Right...Okay, well, I guess rain check on the pool lesson. I didn't know Cassie was coming over. She just showed up with her incredible *gift*," I say with an exaggerated eye roll.

"Yeah, no problem...That was, ummm...very thoughtful. I didn't realize women gifted those to each other," he says with a grin.

"Hah! Yeah, she's thoughtful, all right. I'm pretty sure *most women* don't buy each other sex toys. But, as I am sure you've realized by now, Cassie is not most women."

He jams his hands in the front pockets of his jeans and rocks back and forth on his heels. "Yeah, she's something..."

What does he mean by that? Does Reid have a crush on her, and seriously...why do I even care?

"Yeah, so...if we could never mention tonight...ever again, that would be great," I say, nervously biting the inside of my cheek.

"Don't sweat it. I haven't laughed so hard in forever. It was nice to see you having a good time," he says, grinning to himself. "You have a beautiful smile, Vivienne, and a laugh that begs to be heard."

Tucking a lock of hair behind my ear, I look up to meet his eyes. "Thank you, Reid." That sinking feeling in the pit of my stomach returns. "It's harder than I ever imagined...living without him." I shake my head. "I don't just mean physically being without him; that's just as devastating as I ever thought it would be. But, trying to *live*, to smile, to be happy, to find joy...it all feels wrong. I smile, and I think what the hell is wrong with me? Abbott's dead. I laugh, and I feel like a horrible person because I should be miserable. He's gone. And, in those brief moments, I forget. I forget that he is dead, and I feel so guilty, Reid. It hasn't even been a month. I shouldn't be happy. Not even for the briefest of moments."

Reid closes the short distance between us. "Vivienne, don't. Uncle Abbott wouldn't want you to be miserable. I can't say that I understand the pain that you feel, because really, how could I? But, you can't feel guilty for being alive. None of this is your fault.

No one expects you to be a walking corpse, and that's exactly what you're describing. To live your life with no emotion, no happiness, no laughter—that's not living." Using his shirt, he wipes away tears from my face that I didn't even realize were falling. "It wouldn't be good for Dimples, either. That little girl needs you to be whole. She needs to see you smile and laugh and *live*."

I nod. He's right. Rationally, I can see that. But my feelings. My grief. This pain...It's far from rational. "Do you want to sit out on the porch? I need some air." I'm starting to feel as if the walls are caving in on me.

"Whatever you need, Viv," Reid says as he follows me out to the front porch swing.

We each sit on an end and the swing sinks with our combined weight. The chains rattle as we shift around to get comfortable. Turning to face Reid, I pull my legs up, resting my chin on my knees. I close my eyes and listen to the calming sounds of nature: the breeze rustling the leaves, crickets chirping, the movement of the water.

After a few minutes, I'm starting to doze off when Reid finally breaks the silence. "So...Viv, what do you do?"

"What do you mean?"

"Sorry, I mean do you work or stay home with Tillie? Obviously, you would need some time off. I'm just wondering if you have a job that you need to get back to." How shitty is it that my own nephew has no idea what I do for a living? I wish Abbott would have been able to be closer to his family.

"No. I was a teacher. I taught kindergarten for a few years until Tillie came. Abbott and I decided that I would stay home at least until all of our kids were in school..." I trail off. *And the hits just keep on coming.*

"You all right?" Reid asks. "You got kind of quiet there."

"Yeah...I just...I just realized that there won't be any more babies...Tillie won't have any brothers or sisters."

He reaches out and rubs my knee with a look of apology. "I'm sorry, Vivienne."

I place my hand on top of his. "It's okay. Just another dream I'll have to get over, right?" I say, giving his hand a squeeze in return. "At least I have Tillie."

A smile spreads across his face at the mention of her name. "She's really something, Viv...coolest kid ever!"

Just then, Cassie comes barreling through the door with a bottle of wine, two glasses, and a Bud Light. "Out like a light! Let's get this party started," she says, handing the beer to Reid. "You look like a beer drinker."

Reid responds with a nod of approval. "Thanks."

eleven

Reid

I GRAB THE BEER FROM Cassie's hand. I'm so fucking relieved that she showed up to distract Vivienne from her thoughts. Viv's moods make my head spin. One minute we're laughing and having a great time and then right before my eyes, she crumbles.

Cassie's arrival seems to have worked. Vivienne rises up from the swing and follows her friend over to the patio table where they are all whispers and giggles while pouring their wine.

"To best friends," Cassie says, holding out her glass to Vivienne. "I love you to the moon and back."

Vivienne raises her glass as well. "To sisters," she says to Cassie as they clink their glasses together. "And to new friends," she adds, looking in my direction.

I reach out and tap the neck of my bottle to the tops of their glasses. "To *beautiful* ladies," I say, giving them each a flirty grin.

"Can we keep him?" Cassie begs.

Vivienne laughs. She laughs, and I see so much in that carefree giggle: a glimpse of the woman who's still in there somewhere, hidden beneath the pain. I want to bring that girl out to play. I want to see her uninhibited and free. I want...I want things that I definitely should *not* want from her.

It's only been a few days, and I was hoping that this infatuation would begin to wane, but if anything, it only gets stronger with every moment I spend in her presence. I find myself jealous of Uncle Abbott for finding her first...for being free to date her and love her...and fuck her. If she were anyone else, I'd be all over that. But she's not anyone else. She's my aunt—my *dead* uncle's wife and completely off limits.

We sit out on the porch for about an hour, drinking and talking. I mostly listen. Those two women rarely stop to breathe. They have a bond unlike any friends I've ever known. The girls reminisce about their college years, and Abbott's name is a constant. I try not to let the mention of my uncle sour my mood. It's absurd this jealousy. I'm generally a good guy, and I know this is beyond wrong. The feeling is so foreign, and I don't know what to do with it. I barely knew my uncle, and maybe that's why it's so hard for me to think of Viv as his. I'm confused as fuck because really, I barely know Vivienne. It shouldn't be this hard to put her in the "friend zone." I keep telling myself that I wouldn't touch her—that I'm not *that* guy. But deep down, I know that I wouldn't be able to stop myself if she gave me even the slightest hint that she'd be into it.

"All right, guys, it's been real, but unlike *some* people," Cassie says, looking back and forth at Vivienne and me, "I have to be up early for work tomorrow." Cassie pokes out her bottom lip as she pushes up from her chair. "I'm having issues with one of my placements...Sierra...again," she says to Viv. "I don't know what I'm going to do with that girl..." she trails off. "Anyway, I probably won't be back 'til this weekend. I'm going to spend the next few afternoons with her and see if I can figure out what's going on. But call me if you need anything...and answer my damn calls!"

Vivienne nods slowly as if it takes a concentrated effort to hold her head upright. "I will, I promissssse," she slurs.

Is she drunk? Surely she couldn't have drunk that much in the little time we've been out here.

"Reid, would you mind walking me to my car?" Cassie asks.

"Yeah, sure." I start to rise as Viv returns to her spot on the swing, and my movement throws her balance off. I reach out and grab her by the arms before she falls flat on her ass.

"Shit!" she shrieks as I lift her up to my chest. "Oh my God! You did that on purpose!" she yells, swatting at me. "Why'd you move the sw-the swing?"

Fuck, she's cute tipsy.

Cassie erupts into a fit of laughter. "Oh my...that was *great!* You should've let her bust her ass." Her eyes glisten with tears as she hugs her stomach, trying to contain herself.

"Fuckkk youuu, bitchhh," Viv slurs. "He moved the swinggg," she says, poking me hard in the chest as she looks up at me with murderous eyes.

"You aren't usually this much of a lightweight, Vivienne. Did you start before I got here?" Cassie taunts.

"Shut your sasshole!" she spits out, leveling her gaze on Cassie, who is still clearly amused. "I t-toldd you I'm fineee. It's not myyyy f-fault he moved the swwwwing." Her body begins to tremble, and I can tell she's really getting upset. *Does she honestly believe I would try to make her fall?*

"All right, ladies, that's enough," I say, trying to prevent Viv from going over the edge. *When did I become the voice of reason?* I hold the swing steady with one hand and lower Viv back into her spot. "You sit here until I get back. I don't think you need any more of this," I say, grabbing the wine glass that she somehow still has clutched in her tiny fingers.

"What do you knowww? Hmmm? Y-you don't knowww w-what I neeeed."

"Oh, but I do..." Cassie teases. "It's on the top shelf of your entertainment center," she whispers loudly and then scurries away from Vivienne before she has a chance to attack. She yells back over her shoulder, "You're welcome!"

Shaking my head, I push Viv back down in her seat. "Stay...let her go."

"What's she talkinggg abouttt? On my enter-entertainment centerrr?"

Maybe she did start drinking earlier because she is fucking lit. I'm not about to explain that one. "Just, please stay right here. I'm going to walk your scaredy-cat friend to her car, okay?"

I feel her begin to relax when I whisper, "Be right back," into her hair.

What the hell is going on?

I jog to catch up with Cassie, who is almost to her car by now. I could've just let her go by herself...I'm pretty sure she only asked me to follow her for a chance to get me alone. That probably sounds cocky, but I'm really good at reading chicks, and Cassie *isn't* very good at hiding her signals.

"Cassie, wait up," I call out.

She stops in her tracks and spins on her heels, rewarding me with a seductive smile. "Didn't think you were coming," she says, flirting with her eyes. They are beautiful eyes...green with yellow flecks that shimmer in the moonlight. Cassie is a huntress...a little vixen.

Shit! Why can't I be interested in the one who is clearly interested in me? Why do I have to fall for complicated? Complicated? No, not just complicated...fucking impossible.

I avert my gaze, staring out at the lake. "I wasn't, but I wanted to see if you have any idea what's up with Vivienne. I've never seen her drink, and I didn't think you girls drank that much tonight."

A frown mars her beautiful face. I've made it clear that I'm not interested. My concern for her friend, however, softens the blow. Cassie doesn't strike me as the type that gets shut down often.

She shrugs. "Viv doesn't drink much. She probably had a few before we arrived and the wine was too much. She's a funny drunk...really sensitive," she laughs. "Just stay with her 'til she goes to bed, okay? Call me if you need anything, but she should be fine. She'll pass out soon."

"Okay...I'll do that. Thanks, Cassie."

She opens her car door and curls into the front seat. "No problem, Reid. Thanks for being here and looking out for her, even if she thinks she doesn't need it. She shouldn't be alone right now."

"That's what family does, right?"

She gives me a tense smile as she turns the key in the ignition. "I wouldn't know." Then she drives off, leaving me staring after her.

WHEN I ARRIVE BACK AT the porch, I find Vivienne curled

into a little ball, fast asleep. *God, she is so beautiful.* I lean against the brick and stare at the milky white skin of her exposed shoulder and the way her long lashes fan those freckled cheeks. She's such an enigma. What is it that has me so drawn to her?

I need to get laid. Maybe I should take her up on having Kylie come and spend a few days...or weeks. I could use a distraction. This obsession with my aunt is disgusting...and not going away.

She stirs and lets out a soft moan, and my cock grows rigid in my jeans. *Seriously?*

I walk over and tap Viv on the shoulder. "Viv...? Vivienne...?"

She peeks at me with one eye, shuts it, and rolls back over, grumbling.

Laughing to myself, I reach out and shake her this time. She opens her eyes and a smile that could light the night sky spreads across her face. I've never been looked at with such adoration. It feels good. *Real good.* I don't know how I'm supposed to get past this when she keeps making me feel like maybe...maybe she feels something for me, too.

"Hey, you," she says groggily, reaching her hand out to me.

"Hey...ready to go up to bed?" I ask, clasping her hand in mine and pulling her up to her feet.

"Mmmm," she moans her approval. "That sounds like heaven. Let's go." Vivienne tugs my hand in the direction of the door, and I follow. I would allow this woman to lead me straight into the fires of hell if it meant that I could put my hands on her.

When we reach her bedroom, she starts stripping out of her clothes right in front of me. "Holy shit," I breathe out. *What's she doing? Not that I mind, but what. Is. She. Doing?* I try not to look, but, well...I'm a guy and completely infatuated with this woman...so I don't try too hard.

When she's down to just her black lace bra and panties, she pulls back the blankets and crawls into bed. *Thank God.*

Vivienne yawns and pats the space beside her. "I know I...I know I drankkk too muchhh tonight, but can you just ho-hold me?"

A better man would say no—would tell her good night and walk out of this room without looking back. But when you're eighteen and the cause of your raging hard on invites you, half-naked, into her bed to cuddle...you fucking cuddle.

Sorry, Uncle Abbott.

I convince myself that it is okay so long as I remain on top of the blankets. She needs me. This is what I'm here for, right? What kind of man would I be if I didn't comfort this woman?

I round the bed and climb in on the opposite side, careful to remain on top of the bedding. I'm nervous. I'm never fucking nervous around women, but I don't know if this is okay.

No...I know this is definitely *not* okay.

I don't know what she'll think when she's sober, and I don't want to give her any reason to believe that I am trying to take advantage of her delicate state. I scoot up next to Viv and lay on my side, facing her back...but not touching. I couldn't hide the bulge in my pants if I tried.

I'll let her decide how this is going to go.

Vivienne reaches over her shoulder and grips my hand. Shimmying her body back, she pulls my arm around her waist and snuggles into my chest. Viv begins to grind her sweet ass right into my cock, and I know she has to feel it. *Fuck!* I can't take much more. Placing my hand on her hip to still her movements, I whisper, "Just sleep, Viv." My voice is strained, my heart beating out of my chest.

What am I doing here?

Vivienne stiffens at my words. "Oh, sorry. Yeah, o-okay... goodnight."

Removing my hand from her grasp, I reach up and begin to rub her hair. "Goodnight, Viv. Sweet dreams."

twelve

Vivienne

THE SUNLIGHT PEERING THROUGH THE window beckons me to open my eyes, but I can't. I just can't. I felt him last night...felt his breath on my neck as I slept wrapped in his warm embrace. It was heaven, but now, as morning creeps in, so is reality, and I can't bear it. I want to sleep, to dream, where it doesn't take every ounce of my strength just to *be*.

I close my eyes tight and will the dream to come back.

Abbott, come back to me. I need you. Please don't go...

He left me and along with him went the very essence of my being. I don't know who I am without the glue that has held me together for so long. I'm losing myself a little more every day. It's not getting easier. This grief is like an open wound, growing more tender and poisoned with infection by the day.

My shoulders begin to shake as I try to hold my tears at bay. Try as I might, I can't get the dream back. I'm cold and alone, and this is who I am now...who I will be for the rest of my life.

Is it this hard for everyone? How? How do people go on with their lives?

I stare at my salvation through water-filled eyes...a prescription bottle that I don't want to depend on...but can't function without. Tears bead up in the corners of my eyes and roll down my cheeks. I taste the salt of my pain as it slides down my lips to my chin and neck. I lay motionless and let silent tears soak my pillow.

My mind, body, and heart wage a silent war as I drown in my sorrow. I am coming to hate those pills because I want to be a real person without them. I don't want to break down in tears every day, fifty times a day, when something...anything...everything reminds me of Abbott. He's so deeply ingrained in every part of my life, of my being, that it's impossible not to be constantly reminded of what I've lost.

Gripping my pillow, I bury my face inside and scream out in pain. "Arghh!" My entire body convulses with the force of my heaving sobs. "Why, God? Why *him*? Why *my* husband?" *It's not fair.*

Finally, when I've exhausted myself and am left gasping for breath, I give in to the pills taunting me from two feet away.

My body is spent.

I lie awake in bed and crave my husband. I crave his mind, his body, his touch...those expert hands that knew just how and where to touch me. I ache in places only he could ever reach. I miss the feel of his lips on my neck...The way my back arched off the bed and my toes curled when he made love to me. Abbott knew my body better than I did. Each time we connected, I could feel it in my heart...my soul...to my marrow.

Abbott was the first man to ever make love to me. What we had was sacred, and I know that I could never allow another to taint that. I don't even know what it feels like to just have sex, but I know that without that emotional connection—that spark—that I would only be disappointed.

And the guilt...the guilt would be unbearable.

I *hate* this.

I know that I'm lucky to have found my soul mate. I'm lucky to have been worshiped and adored. Many people go their whole lives searching for that to no avail.

I cherish what we had. I do. But, to be without it for the rest of my life...to know exactly what I am missing. God, it hurts.

All I have left are memories...and how long will it take for those to fade, too?

I CHECK THE ADDRESS I'VE written down against the one on the

mailbox one last time before turning into the drive. Abbott asked me to meet him here tonight. I'm anxious...excited. We've been dating for two months, and I've never experienced sexual frustration of this magnitude. This is all I've wanted... all I've thought about. I've gone to bed every night imagining it. Now that the moment is here, I feel edgy. My heart beats to the rhythm of a hummingbird's wings—like it could take off and fly right out of my chest.

The driveway seems to go on forever. It's pitch dark out, and as I venture deeper and deeper down the wooded path, my anxiety starts to get to me. There are no lights, and I'm just on the verge of freaking out when I finally spot the little log cabin on the lake, and Abbott's white Mustang parked to the side of the house. I breathe out a sigh of relief as I pull my old Honda Civic up next to his car.

Laying my forehead on the steering wheel, I sit for a few minutes and try to compose myself—to prepare myself. What the hell is wrong with me? My palms are sweating, and I can't believe that I'm this worked up over sex. Hell, I don't even know for sure that we are having sex.

Oh God...We'd better be having sex.

"Aghhh!" I scream and nearly have a heart attack when I turn and see Abbott peering in at me through the window. I press the button to let it down. "Abbott! You scared the shit out of me! You cannot sneak up on me in the forest like this."

He chuckles. "I'm sorry, baby. I saw you just sitting here. You aren't thinking of turning around and leaving me out here all alone, are you?"

"Abbott..." I cry, pleading with him to be on the same page for once...to need me the way that I need him.

Abbott reaches in, unlocks the door, and pulls it open. "Viv?" he questions. "What's wrong, baby?" he asks as he pulls me out of the car.

"I'm scared," I answer honestly.

Abbott's face falls. "Of what? Are you really that scared of the woods? We can leave. I just...I thought it would be a nice romantic weekend. Some alone time, away from the guys at the house. But it doesn't have to be here. We can go to a hotel, or we can just go back home."

Shaking my head, I press my pointer finger to his perfect full lips. "No...I mean, yes, I...I was, but, I'm not anymore."

"Then what is it, Viv? What are you scared of?"

"You..."

"*Me?*" *he asks, clearly stunned.*

"*Abbott, I've built this night up in my head. I've allowed myself to believe that this is finally going to happen. I've only just realized that I could be wrong—that maybe I am completely off-base. I can't...I just can't handle any more rejection from you. I want you Abbott—more than I have ever wanted anything else. I know you think that you're being noble, and I appreciate that, but please tell me that we're on the same page. Tell me that tonight is the night... that you brought me here to finally have sex with me,*" *I plead.*

"*I didn't bring you here to have sex with you...*" *he says, and my mouth falls open.* "*I brought you here, Vivienne, to tell you that I love you,*" *he says, backing me up to the car.* "*To show you how much I love you.*" *He places a hand on either side of my face and leans in. I can feel the warmth of his breath when he says,* "*I am so—*" *kiss* "*—crazy—*" *kiss* "*—in love—*" *kiss* "*—with you.*"

Throwing my arms around his neck, I jump up and wrap my legs around Abbott's waist. "*I love you too, Abbott. So much it hurts.*"

"*I'm sorry, baby. I don't ever want to hurt you. I want to make you feel good. Let me make love to you, Vivienne,*" *he says as he presses my back into the door, kissing my neck.* "*Be with me, baby...not just tonight. Be mine. I want you to belong to me, Viv. Only me.*"

I swallow past the lump that has taken up residence in my throat and croak out, "*Only you...*" *I run both of my hands up the back of his neck, into his hair, and tug his head back. His hungry eyes meet mine. Those crystal blue orbs devour me whole.* "*Inside...now...*" *I say with urgency because I doubt he's held out on me this long for our first time to be a quickie up against my car.*

"*Right. Yeah, good idea,*" *he says as I untangle my legs and slide down his body. When I'm once again standing on my own two feet, he takes a moment to check me out.* "*Sorry, that got a little intense. You look beautiful, babe,*" *he says, scraping his bottom lip through his teeth.* "*Fucking gorgeous...*"

I feel myself blush. "*Thank you.*"

Abbott sends me a sexy smirk before lacing our fingers and tugging me toward the house. "*Let's get inside.*"

I stumble over my own feet as Abbott eagerly leads me into the house. He looks at me expectantly—like a little boy, he's waiting to gauge my reaction. When I step through the door, I'm blown away. The floor is blanketed with rose petals. There's a fire crackling in the fireplace and a pallet of blankets and pillows scattered before it. Straight ahead is a table with a white cloth and candles. Dinner smells delicious. The table faces a wall of windows overlooking the lake. The scene before me is breathtaking, like something out of a movie. My feet are planted on the ground. I'm stunned. No one has ever made me feel so special. I'm suddenly a lot less annoyed with the fact that Abbott has made me wait so long. This...this feeling makes it all worth it.

"Viv? Viv? Yoo-hoo," *Abbott calls, snapping his fingers in front of my face.* "What are you thinking?"

"It's...wow..." *I stammer.* "This is incredible, Abbott. It's beautiful and so romantic. How did I get so lucky?" *I ask, pinching myself for effect. Abbott grins.*

That smile...

"Are you ready to eat?" *he asks.* "I've got steaks marinating, ready to throw on the grill out back whenever you get hungry. I made mashed potatoes and corn as sides. I hope that's okay."

"It's perfect, Abbott. Everything. All of this. It's like a dream. I will never, ever forget the way you've made me feel tonight." *I turn and clutch the fabric of his dress shirt. Rising up on my toes, I whisper,* "But if you don't make love to me right now...I cannot be held responsible for my actions."

I don't even know where this false confidence is coming from.

"Hmmm, option B doesn't sound half bad," *he says with a shrug.* "Lucky for you, I've been looking forward to A for a long time now."

"Have you?" *I ask, trying to play coy.*

Abbott grips the back of my neck with his hand. "Oh yeah," *he growls just before capturing my mouth in a ravenous kiss. He leads me over to the bed of blankets in front of the fire and slowly lowers me to the ground, his mouth never parting from mine. Abbott's kiss becomes reverent. He's worshiping my mouth with his tongue, leaving no spot untouched.*

When breathing becomes a necessity, he pulls his lips from mine and just looks at me...I mean really looks at me. It's as if he can see straight down to my soul, and I would give anything to spend the rest of my life in this moment...the moment that emerges between heartbeats. That instant just before his lips meet mine and the rest of the world ceases to exist.

"Viv," *he whispers, nudging my nose with his own.* "You're shaking. Is this okay?"

I have a sudden urge to cry. I've pushed for this for so long and now that this moment is here, I'm scared. I'm overwhelmed with love and fear and...awe. I'm in awe that this beautiful man actually loves me back. I've never felt so many conflicting emotions all at once.

I'm also nervous and feeling guilty. He doesn't know, and how could he? I've been after him like a whore at a truck stop and haven't said a word. Now, I'm scared that if I do, he will stop, and I don't want him to stop.

I lift my head and press my lips to his. "It's more than okay," I whisper, undoing the buttons of his shirt.

He rises up onto his knees and shrugs the offensive material off, tossing his shirt across the room.

I'm not sure what to do now. Do I begin taking my clothes off, too? Wait for him to do it? Why didn't I ask Cassie about proper sex etiquette? She should have told me...How could she send me here so ill prepared?

I'm going to kill her.

"Should I, ummm...do you want me to take my clothes off now?" I ask uneasily, and I want to take the words back the moment they leave my mouth.

Could I possibly be less sexy?

Abbott chuckles. "Do you want to take your clothes off now?"

Great. He's laughing at me. I'm not ready for this.

What the hell am I saying? I'm probably the last eighteen-year-old virgin alive. I'm so ready for this.

I wonder if I should tell him. He's going to figure it out soon, anyway.

He sits back on his heels...shirt off...belt undone...breathing heavy...

So. Fucking. Hot.

My skin begins to warm as he stares at me through hooded eyes, and I can both feel and hear my heartbeats echoing in my ears. My every sense is heightened.

Abbott reaches down and begins massaging my feet and works his way up the backs of my legs, his gaze never leaving mine. His broad chest towers over me. "Relax, Viv," he breathes out, his brilliant eyes filled with so much emotion.

Sweet Jesus. I could come just from the feel of his hands on my body.

He moves them up higher, lifting my dress as he goes. "Let me help you out with your little problem," he says, trailing his fingertips up my sides and finally pulling my dress up and over my head.

I'm lying before him practically naked in my pink lace bra and panties, and surprisingly, I've never felt more confident than I do at this moment. The way he's looking at me eases any reservations that I may have felt. My nerves quickly morph from fear to desire.

"You are so beautiful, Vivienne," he groans.

Every inch of my body tingles with need. "Abbott," I whimper as I grind my body against his. Heat radiates from his bare chest, melding with my own, and I'm dizzy with want.

I taste salty sweat as I lick and nibble on his neck. Reaching between us, I unbutton his pants and push them down past his hips.

After wiggling the rest of the way out of his pants, Abbott lies on his side facing me. He runs the backs of his hands down my cheeks and neck...to my breasts.

My nipples pebble beneath his touch and I arch into him, begging him to ease the ache that's building in my core.

Fisting one hand into his blond hair, I mold my lips to his. Our bodies are pressed so tightly together that I can feel his cock hardening against my belly, and I'm overwhelmed with a need...a desperate aching need unlike anything I've ever felt.

I run my fingers beneath the band of his boxer briefs and release him.

Holy shit.

He's huge and rock hard. As nervous as I was earlier, I am so turned on that fear has taken a back seat to desire. I need him inside of me. I can feel myself growing wetter as Abbott rubs me through my lace panties. The friction created by the material has me ready to jump out of my skin.

I moan and writhe against him. "Abbott." I gasp. "Oh God. Now...please, I need you."

"Almost, baby," he whispers, sliding my panties down my legs ever so slowly. It's exquisite torture. I'm a bundle of nerves, and his touch is electrifying. I squirm beneath him as he trails kisses up my belly. Abbott cups my breasts and squeezes as he makes his way back to my mouth.

He slips a hand behind my back, unhooking my bra, and then slides the straps down my arms, and for the first time ever, I am completely bare to him. Resting on his elbows, Abbott gazes into my eyes and whispers, "I love you, Viv. I've never made love to a woman before. I knew it...I knew you would be worth the wait. Thank you." Kiss. "Thank you for being my first...and I hope—" kiss "—my last."

His first...His last.

Tears spring to my eyes. "You are a dream, Abbott. I love you so much...so much. I can't imagine sharing this with anyone else."

There...that was sort of a confession, right?

"Shit," he hisses. "I threw my pants over to the couch, babe. I need to get up and get a condom."

"I'm on the pill, and I'm clean. I trust you," I say, tightening my grip. I don't want him to leave me, even for only a few seconds.

"I've never had sex without a condom before. Are you sure?"

Nodding my head, I answer, "I'm sure."

Abbott's lips meet mine at the same time that he enters me and my body tenses. He stills in response. I feel so full and stretched.

It's too big. Oh my God, I'm too small.

It's not the excruciating pain that I'd imagined, but it burns. I let out a moan and squeeze my legs tight around his torso, trying to allow time for my body to adjust to his size.

"Ohh," he moans. "Viv...you are so tight, baby."

He has no idea.

Abbott begins to move, and I cry out, digging my nails into his shoulders.

"Oh shit, Viv? Baby, are you all right? Am I hurting you?"

I feel a lone tear escape and roll down my cheek as I bite my lip, trying not to cry.

"I'm sorry, Abbott. I should have told you," I cry.

Confusion and worry are clearly written on his face. "Told me what, babe? I don't understand."

"I've, ummm...I've never done this before...had sex, I mean."

"Oh, no. Oh, Viv...why didn't you say anything? I'd just assumed..."

"I know. I know I should have told you, but I was scared that you'd want to wait even longer, and I wanted it to be you, Abbott...It's really not that bad."

"Just what every man wants to hear. 'It's not that bad,'" he jokes, but the look of concern he's giving me is a clear contradiction to his words.

I shake my head and let out a nervous laugh. "That's not what I meant, and you know it. I just thought it would be really painful. It stings, and I think that maybe I'm just not big enough. Does it hurt? Are you hurting? You can get out if you need to."

Abbott chuckles. "No...no, it doesn't hurt. You feel amazing, baby. I just hate that I'm hurting you. Do you want to stop?"

I shake my head. "No, I don't want to stop. Can you just...just kiss me?"

And he does. Careful not to move his hips, Abbott slants his mouth over mine and kisses me with a passion that shakes me to my core, annihilating any and all rational thought. It's a kiss of desperation, of pure and unadulterated need. It's earth shattering—soul shaking. It is a kiss by which to measure all others.

We are so consumed in each other that I barely register when he starts to slowly rock in and out. The pain now forgotten, I can't seem to get enough.

Abbott laves at my breast as he pumps in and out, rubbing my clit and sending sparks of pure bliss throughout my body.

I can feel my climax growing closer with every thrust. "Abbott," I moan. "Oh...oh God...don't stop."

He picks up the pace and takes me over the edge. Every muscle in my body tenses as we explode together. My fists clench and toes curl. For an instant, it feels as if the entire world stops on its axis. I can't breathe...can't think—only feel. This feeling is indescribable. It's like I'm falling off a cliff but there's no fear...it's freeing and exhilarating. I'm floating...flying...soaring. I feel a rush of euphoria followed by an overwhelming feeling of love in my gut.

Brushing the hair out of my eyes, Abbott asks, "Viv, are you okay, baby?"

I nod my head and bite my lip. I can't seem to form a coherent thought. "Yes, God...that was...wow..."

A huge grin lights his face. "That good, huh?"

"Mmmmhmm," I moan. "Better."

He puffs up his chest with pride. "I'm glad...I didn't hurt you, did I?"

He is so freaking cute, worrying over me.

"Not too much. Really, I just sort of forgot all about the pain. It was incredible, Abbott. You're amazing."

He kisses the tip of my nose as he starts to withdraw.

I groan and try to hold him in. "Don't," I whine.

Abbott laughs. "Baby, I need to clean us up and make sure you're okay," he says as he kisses my pout.

I watch him walk off through the bedroom to the bathroom, and his absence is overwhelming. I feel like I could burst into tears. What the hell? He is coming right back, Vivienne, chill!

"I wish you would have told me," Abbott says as he walks toward me. "I could've prepared better...taken things slower for you."

I shake my head as I take the warm, wet towel from his hands. "That's precisely why I didn't want to tell you. Abbott, you couldn't have planned this any better if you'd known. It just would have been more awkward for me, and if you'd taken it any slower, I might have joined the nunnery for fear that something was wrong with me," I joke.

"There is absolutely nothing wrong with you, Viv." He rakes his eyes over my body. "I've never seen a more beautiful sight. It would be such a shame to waste it on a life of nunhood," he says as he lies down behind me and pulls me into his chest.

I scoff, "Seriously, dude? You've seen half the female student body naked. And 'nunhood'...is that even a word? I don't think that's a word, Webster."

I feel his chest vibrate with silent laughter. "I haven't been with as many girls as you think."

"No? You care to share a number?"

Abbott coughs. "Uh, no, not really. I didn't exactly keep track. Those girls meant nothing, Viv. They were just fun."

I turn over in his arms and meet his eyes with my own. "Is that what I am, Abbott? Am I just fun?"

"You," Abbott says, meeting my gaze, "are forever. Mark my words, Vivienne Anderson; I'm going to marry you someday."

"Awful sure of yourself, aren't you, cocky?" I tease while sending up a silent prayer to the heavens that he is speaking the truth. Could I actually be lucky enough to spend the rest of my life with this Adonis?

He shuts me up with a kiss that leaves me breathless. "You can't tell me you didn't feel that, Viv. This," he says, grasping my chin and rubbing the pad of his thumb over my bottom lip, "this doesn't come along every day. We have something special. This is what forever feels like. It has to be."

"Forever, huh? I like the sound of that," I say, smiling against his lips.

I SMILE AGAINST TREMBLING FINGERTIPS as warm tears pool in my eyes. *Forever.* Forever seems like an infinite amount of time...until it's ripped away...gone in an instant. My boy kept his word, though. He gave me forever, and what a beautiful forever it was.

After drying my tears with the backs of my hands, I take my pill and then pad down the hall to check on Matilda.

When I reach her room, I stand in the doorway for a moment, just watching the slow rise and fall of her chest as she sleeps so peacefully. In the silence, I can hear the soft purr of her little snores, and I watch as the morning sunlight bounces off her bed-tangled hair. My heart fills to bursting every time I look at our baby. We *made* this perfect little angel. She's a living, breathing representation of our love. I've never seen anything more beautiful and a love more perfect has never existed...of this I'm certain.

Our girl.

Careful not to wake her, I climb in and curl my body around hers. Burying my nose in strawberry-scented hair, I fall asleep holding what's left of forever in my arms.

I miss you, Abbott.

thirteen

Vivienne

AS I FRENCH BRAID MY long hair, I can't help but take notice of the washed out reflection staring back at me. *Ugh.* I look as exhausted as I feel. I try to disguise puffy, tear-swollen eyes with a little makeup, but I'm not sure why I even bother. We're going tubing with Cassie and Sierra, and makeup won't last five minutes in the water.

The past few days have been spent swimming in the pool and fishing on the lake with Reid and Tillie. It's been nice, if not a little weird. Reid seems a bit off, and I can't help but wonder what I may have said or done to cause his change in mood. I can't remember a thing past the dildo episode. *God,* how I wish I could erase that embarrassment from my memory. Maybe it made him more uncomfortable than he let on. Ugh, I don't know. I could just be imagining the whole thing. I guess I should be happy that I've been so preoccupied with what I may have done to push Reid away that I haven't had time to have any major breakdowns.

Cassie thinks that I'm worrying over nothing. She swears that I was no more than drunk and silly, and unless she's hiding something, I can't see why that would make him pull away. I could just be oversensitive. He hasn't said or done anything all that obvious. It's more the little things he *isn't* doing that have my mind wandering.

He still shows up for all of his meals and is polite and extremely attentive to Tillie. That girl is smitten with Prince Reid. But, he leaves after dinner and hasn't asked about his pool lesson again. He spends a lot of time on his phone, more than he did when he first got here for sure, and when Tillie goes to take her nap; he excuses himself back to the pool house.

I just feel like he's avoiding spending any time alone with me specifically, and to be honest, I miss the attention. It sounds stupid, but he made me feel beautiful and desired...all of the things that Abbott always made me feel. Even though I know it was only his southern charm, I miss it. I miss him and the friendship we were building. I miss feeling like a real woman again for those brief moments.

Whatever, I don't have time to dwell on it anymore today.

I take one last glance in the mirror before heading downstairs to join the rest of the gang.

REID'S LAUGHTER BOOMS DOWN THE hall as I make my way to the kitchen. It takes me back for a moment. I miss Abbott's laugh. I miss the way it filled my heart so completely just to see him smile. Our house was always filled with happy sounds. The silence that threatens now is deafening.

I walk into the room and am so grateful for the people in it. Without Cassie and Reid breathing some life into this place, it would be one dreary day after another. And I can't forget Tillie. That sweet girl saves me every single day. She gives me a reason to wake up each morning and a billion reasons to keep smiling.

"Hey, guys," I call out. "Y'all just about ready to go?"

Reid turns to answer, and I notice him check me out in my light pink bikini and lace cover-up. It's not the first time he's seen me in a bathing suit, but it's definitely the first time I've noticed that hunger in his eyes.

I answer his look by raising my brows. Reid scrubs at his face with his hands and looks down in embarrassment. "Hey," he mumbles to the floor before turning to grab the ice chest and keys. "Yeah...I'm ready," he calls over his shoulder as he pushes out of the door, letting it slam shut behind him.

Why is he being so weird?

"I'm ready, too, Mommy," Tillie answers, never one to be outdone.

"Come here so I can get some sunscreen on those white arms of yours, Princess."

"Hey, hooch!" Cassie shouts as she crosses the room. She tilts her head back toward the door. "I see he's still acting special..." She throws a thumb over her shoulder. "What'd you do?"

Laughing, I answer, "You probably shouldn't be calling me that in front of the kids...And, yeah...see what I mean?" I ask, shaking my head. "I knew I wasn't imagining things."

"Pffft. Whatevs!" she says, hugging me from behind. "I've missed your sexy ass this week," she whispers into my ear before tracing her tongue lightly along the edge.

Choking, I swat her away. "Yeah? Thanks for whispering. You're hopeless! I can't believe *you* work with *children* for a living."

She gasps loudly, placing a hand on her chest. "I'm a wonderful role model. The picture of a lady. The epitome of what these girls should strive to be," she says, grinning back and forth between the girls. "You two start taking notes if you haven't already."

"Slow down, woman. Let's not get carried away," I tease, knowing full and well that I would love nothing more than for Tillie to be just like her godmother.

"Girl, Tillie is used to me. She knows not to repeat the things Auntie says, doncha, baby girl?" she asks, ruffling her hair.

Tillie smirks. "I'm gonna be just like Auntie when I'm all growed up."

Narrowing her eyes into slits, Cassie glares at my baby. "You little traitor!" she shouts, taking a step forward, and pretending that she's going to chase Tillie. Tillie takes off screaming, and Cassie waves Sierra over. "Sierra, do you remember my friend, Vivienne?"

"Yeah, I do. Hi, Mrs. Vivienne," she answers a little hesitantly.

My answering smile is an attempt to set her at ease. "Hey, Sierra. I'm so glad you're coming with us today."

She chews on the inside of her lip...a nervous habit. "Me too. Thanks for inviting me. I hate it at the Clawsons' house."

How does Cassie do this and not have a house full of kids? This girl is breaking my heart after only five minutes. If I hadn't just lost Abbott, I'd be tempted to keep her myself. I swallow hard, trying not to show the emotion I feel. "I'm sorry to hear that, Sierra. I hope things get better for you really soon, sweetie."

Pushing a lock of raven hair behind her ear, she nods. "Thank you. You too...I hope things are better for you soon, too." I know that she is referring to Abbott, and I can tell how hard it was for her to get those words out. I can't imagine how such a sweet and shy girl could be the same child that Cassie has described mouthing off and running away from the Clawsons.

As they do anytime someone offers their condolences, my eyes well up. I offer a strained "Thank you" and start gathering my things. "Let's go, girls, before Prince Reid leaves us behind," I say, clearing my throat to disguise the hurt.

fourteen

Reid

FUCK! I HAD TO GET out of that house. The sight of Vivienne in that little bikini had me ready to nut in my shorts. I can't get the woman out of my head. Holding her the other night and not being able to really *touch* her was brutal. I want her...and I can't want her. I can't have her. I can't do anything about the feelings I am developing for her, and it's fucking with my head.

She's fucking with my head. Why would she invite me into bed with her? I get that she's lonely and needs someone to comfort her, but that felt...it felt *wrong*. When I ran into her the following morning, she acted as if nothing had happened at all...and maybe to her nothing had. But for me...for me it was excruciating. She has no idea how close I was to doing very dirty things to her in that black lingerie. I'm not this guy...but, fuck...I'm no saint either. I can only take so much temptation.

I reach the wharf and begin loading our things into the boat. When I'm almost through tying the tube to the back, I glance up and see the girls making their way over. When Tillie spots me, she comes running.

"Heya, Dimples. You ready to go have some fun?" I ask as I finish up the knot. It's crazy how quickly I've become attached to this kid.

She climbs onto my back, hugging my neck. "Uh huh," she says, cupping her hand over my ear and whispering, "Auntie Cass told Momma that you are acting weird, Prince Reid. Don't tell her I telled you that, okay?"

Shit. So they have noticed..."Never. Your secrets are safe with me," I say, crossing my hand over my heart.

"Okay, cuz...I don't want to get in trouble," Tillie says, her eyes getting big.

Just then, Vivienne, Cassie, and Sierra arrive with their arms filled with enough shit for a weekend long camping trip. *Women.* Where the hell do they think we are going? I can't help but shake my head and laugh.

"Hey, Reid, you rushed outta there real quick...Somethin' wrong?" Cassie asks as they approach the boat. Her face looks innocent enough, but I know that she's trying to stir shit up.

"Nope, just ready to get this show on the road," I say as I begin loading their things into the cubbies beneath the boat seats.

"Hmmm...okay. I was just askin' because it seemed...*Ow!*" she shouts when Vivienne not so discretely kicks her in the shin.

Vivienne shoots her a death glare that only a mother could properly deliver. Cassie storms off and takes a seat on the other end of the boat, grumbling a string of curses the whole way.

When Viv turns to follow, I reach out and grab her hand. That little touch alone sends my heart racing. It's further confirmation that I need to do something about this insane attraction. I can't trust myself around her.

Vivienne looks at me, clearly waiting for me to speak. *Why did I just do that?* "Hey..." I say like an idiot. "You okay?"

Her brow furrows in confusion. "Yeah, Reid. Why wouldn't I be?"

I shrug my shoulders in answer. "You just seemed upset with Cassie. I don't want you two at odds because of me. She just enjoys getting a rise out of me..." I say with a little smirk...because I just can't help myself. "I'm a big boy, Viv," I add, widening my eyes. "I can handle it."

Why am I still playing with this woman?

She rolls her eyes, but I see the slightest hint of a smile before she replies, "Yeah, well, she shouldn't be messing with you like that. She needs to learn that sometimes she needs to keep her big mouth shut. You're my nephew and my guest. She shouldn't be taunting you."

If I wasn't certain before where Viv's feelings lie, her mentioning my nephew status is a dead giveaway. "It's all good," I say curtly. "Hey, umm, you said it would be all right for me to invite my girlfriend over. Does that offer still stand?"

Vivienne swallows hard. "Of course, Reid. You're an adult," she says before turning and walking off to meet her friend.

fifteen
Vivienne

THE WIND CUTTING MY BREATH and whipping my hair is just what I need to make me feel alive. I can see Tillie and Cass cheering me on from the back of the boat as I attempt to rise up from my knees to stand. I wobble, and just when I think I'm going to fall, I manage to steady the board and...and I nail it!

Gliding across the water, I feel free and happy. I can almost picture Abbott's beautiful face smiling down at me. He's practiced with me for years, and I've never been able to do it.

That was for you, baby...

Closing my eyes and turning my face up to the sky, an incredible sense of peace washes over me. I feel him near. I can just picture him here shouting his praise, and I imagine the way it would feel when he would lift me into his arms and spin me around, celebrating my victory. He was always my biggest cheerleader and my greatest teacher.

I TAKE OVER DRIVING THE boat and allow Reid a chance to show off. Much like Abbott, he's a natural. Tillie and Sierra are hypnotized by his spins and tricks.

For a moment, it's like having him back. My guy...my handsome, sexy, sandy-haired boy playing on the water...the warmth of the sun beating down on my damp skin...the smells of sunscreen and beer. The motor rumbling and our baby girl's high pitched squeals. It's almost as if he never left at all and a part of me wants to pretend just for today that my heart hasn't been shattered into a million tiny pieces.

Reid, Cassie, and I take turns riding with the girls on the tube. It's a wonderful day and the most fun I've had since the accident. Seeing the smiles on Tillie and Sierra's faces is fulfilling in a way that I can't even describe. These girls have both lost so much. They are such an inspiration to me. If these children can overcome loss and come out happy and smiling...maybe there's hope for me, too.

When the sun begins to set, we head back to the house, and I am overcome with a feeling of dread. I don't want to leave. I don't want to go back to my house that no longer feels like home. It's a mausoleum of memories—a million reminders of what I've lost.

My heart rate begins to speed up, and the anxiety is creeping in. Our home used to be my safe haven. I hate that the place we built out of love now makes me so uneasy.

CASSIE HAD TO LEAVE RIGHT away when we returned home from tubing to take Sierra back, and we haven't seen Reid since unloading the boat at the wharf. So, it's just my girl and me tonight.

Tillie and I are curled up on her bed watching a movie. This right here is my home now. She keeps me grounded and gives me purpose. Tillie holds all of my broken pieces together.

"Mommy?"

"Yeah, baby?" I say, pressing a kiss to her forehead. "What's up?"

She rolls onto her back, staring up at me. "One day when I am bigguh, you'll be a grandmaw?"

Smiling, I answer, "I certainly hope so."

Her little eyes fill with tears. "But, when you get old, you die..." she cries. "I don't want you to be dead, too, Mommy."

Oh, no.

"Baby, that's such a long time from now. Let's try not to worry about that, okay? Mommy plans on being here a very long time." The words feel like shit coming out of my mouth because how can I promise her that? How can I tell her I will be here when I have no more control over that than I did over Abbott's death? But how can I not do something to ease her little mind?

I want to throw something—break something. I am so fucking angry at life. Why? Why has my baby girl had to lose her innocence? Why must her pretty little head be filled with fears of death and loss?

Why did it have to be him?

sixteen

Vivienne

JUST AS I'M FINISHING UP the breakfast dishes, there's a knock at the front door. I dry my hands on my apron as I cross the living room to answer it. Peering through the sheer curtain, I see a beautiful, young girl with long blonde hair and caramel colored skin. Her eyes are emerald green, and she's dressed like a model straight out of a magazine. She's stunning, and my first thought is that she must be lost.

I fumble with the messy bun on top of my head as I pull the door open. There's an awkward moment where she just stands there appraising me. Immediately, I feel inferior. She makes me feel homely in my worn jean shorts and threadbare tee. "Ummm...hi, can I help you with something?" I ask.

The girl flashes me a smile, holding out her perfectly manicured hand. "Hi. My name's Kylie...I'm here to see Reid?"

"Reid?" I ask with surprise. *Who does he know around here?*

"Oh no! Do I have the wrong house? I told him to come and pick me up, but he said he would send a cab for me." The poor girl's face turns bright red with embarrassment.

"No, no. He's here. You have the right place," I assure her, ushering her in. "I just didn't realize he knew anyone around here, is all."

Another dazzling smile. "Oh, I'm not from here. I came all the way from Georgia. I'm his girlfriend, Kylie."

Aha! Now I remember Reid asking about her. Damn, he didn't

mess around, did he? "Now that you mention it...he did say that you might be coming to spend a few days. Come on in, Kylie."

We walk inside to the living room where I introduce her to Matilda, who of course immediately adores her. Tillie has never met a stranger. She's so much like Abbott that way.

"Kylie, if you want to help Tillie with that princess puzzle, I'll go and see if I can find Reid for you," I offer.

I WALK OVER TO THE pool house and knock a few times. When there is no answer, I assume that he is asleep and use the key to let myself in. Shutting the door quietly, I walk into the open bedroom to wake him.

Reid is lying on top of the blankets. At first, I think that he's asleep, but then I hear his heavy breathing and deep throaty moans. *Oh my God*...I can feel my pulse in my throat as I stand there in the doorway, rooted in place. I can't seem to move or to find my voice. Warmth spreads throughout my body, and my heart begins to thrum loudly in my chest.

Say something, Vivienne...

But, I don't. Like a creeper, I stand there until he's finished, and when he sits up in bed and notices me staring, I want to run away, but I've lost all bodily control.

"Shiiit!" Reid groans as he pulls the blanket over his waist in a hurry. "Vivienne?"

"Reid...I ummm." *Oh God...I'm going to be sick.* "I'm sorry. I thought you were asleep, and I-I let myself in." Panic wells in my chest.

Reid runs his bottom lip through his teeth really slowly. Staring at his mouth, I swallow hard. "You wanna turn around so I can get dressed?" he asks.

I nod my head, but I'm frozen in place.

Reid furrows his brow. "Are you okay, Vivienne?" he asks when I continue to stand there with my mouth hanging open. I'm so dizzy, and his words sound like they're coming from so far away. It's like I'm watching this scene play out from a distance and have no control over the outcome.

I shake my head, and that's when the tears start. My legs give out, and I slide down the frame of the door into a heap on the floor. After what seems like only seconds, Reid is on his knees in front of me in a pair of basketball shorts. "What is it, Viv?"

"I'm sorry, Reid. Oh God," I cry, my entire body visibly shaking. "I couldn't move. My body...it just...it wouldn't cooperate. I should've said something," I say, trying to avoid looking at his face.

Reid chuckles. "Really, Vivienne? I'm the one caught with my pants down, and you're embarrassed? I think it's my turn, don't you?" he teases.

I raise my face to meet his, sick with guilt. Seeing him this close after just watching him...like *that*...I take a deep breath to try and calm down, but, *oh God*...he *smells* like sex. My pulse quickens as I stare at the light sheen of sweat on his bare chest.

"I didn't see anything," I say weakly.

Reid rolls his eyes. "Yeah, you did, and it's okay, Viv."

"No," I say, shaking my head in disbelief. "No, Reid...I'm sorry. What's wrong with me?"

"Vivienne, stop it," he says in a tone boding no argument. "You were shocked and froze up. You didn't do anything wrong. I'm not upset."

I want to be able to excuse myself as easily, but I know what was going on in my head. I know the way my body responded to his. Worst of all, I know that Abbott knows.

It's crazy how ever since Abbott's death people want to excuse all of my actions. Reid should be outraged, not coddling me.

He analyzes my face. "Stop it. Just stop whatever you're thinking," he chastises, placing his finger against my lips. "You came here to tell me something. What was it?"

I try to clear my head and to remember why it was that I came over here to begin with. And then I remember the pretty young girl in my living room, and a ridiculous sense of jealousy creeps in.

I tamp those feelings down, answering, "Yes. Kylie's here...well, at the house with Tillie. I was coming to get you."

A strange look crosses his face. Regret? Dread? It's definitely not the excitement one would expect. "Awesome," he says, forcing a smile.

What is up with that?

REID GOES INTO THE BATHROOM to get dressed, and I use the time to collect myself.

We walk back over to the house together and find that Cassie has arrived during my absence. She, Kylie, and Tillie are intently working on another puzzle. Reid clears his throat to get their attention.

When Kylie notices Reid, her face completely lights up. She rushes into his arms, wrapping her whole body around him, kissing his neck. It takes all I have not to burst into tears again because I would give anything to be able to feel Abbott's body against mine... *anything.*

Reid loosely embraces her. "Hey, babe," he says, kissing her forehead and setting her back onto her feet. "How was your trip?"

She scrunches up her face. "Long...but it's okay cuz I'm here now. Did you miss me, baby?" she asks, fluttering her fake lashes.

"Of course," he answers simply giving her a weak smile.

Why'd he even invite her over? He seems to barely be able to tolerate her.

Cassie notices right away that I am a bit off and walks over to stand near me. "You okay?" she whispers into my ear.

"Mmmhmm," I nod, even though I'm anything but.

Kylie is rubbing herself on Reid like an animal in heat, and I am trying not to let it show on my face how much it bothers me. *It shouldn't bother me.*

"Hey, I'm going to go get Kylie settled in," he says, grabbing her hand. "We'll be back over for lunch."

"Yeah sure. That sounds good. Lunch will be ready around noon."

LUNCH IS A HOT MESS. I keep catching Reid staring at me, and every time he looks at me, I blush. The longer that I am forced to be in his presence, the guiltier I feel. I feel guilty for watching him like that, but the way that my body reacted makes me sick with it. It makes no sense. I know that I am not attracted to him sexually. Abbott just died, and I am still crazy in love with him. But, my body...my body is a traitorous bitch.

By the time that they leave, and I get Tillie down for her nap, I'm in desperate need of my best friend. I walk down the stairs and find her waiting for me on the couch. The moment my eyes meet hers, my already weak foundation crumbles.

"Oh, Viv," she says, "come here, babe." Cassie lifts the blanket for me to curl up next to her and holds me in her arms while she cries with me. "Shh," she whispers through her tears. "Tell me... what happened today Vivienne?"

I sniffle and my breath shutters, trying to calm myself enough to speak. "I don't know who I am anymore, Cassie. I'm so lost," I choke out.

Cassie rubs her hand up and down my back in slow, soothing strokes. "But what happened, Vivienne? Something must have happened...I saw the way you and Reid were dancing around each other tonight. I hate to even ask it but did something happen between the two of you?"

My gut reaction is to be upset that she would even suggest it, but then I realize that she isn't that far off-base. *What kind of person am I?*

Sobbing, I recount to her exactly what happened at the pool house earlier, and she does the very last thing I would ever expect...

She laughs.

"You know I love you, right?" Cassie asks between bouts of laughter. "God, you're so cute."

I don't even know how to react. I stare at her stupefied.

"Babe, you walked in on the man beating his meat...That's fucking hilarious," she says, swatting tears of laughter away.

"You are such a bitch sometimes, Cassie. It's not just that I walked in...I stayed there like some perv, and I *watched* him, Cassie. My God, it turned me on," I whisper.

She rolls her eyes. "Viv, what do you think happens when people watch porn, hmm? When you watch someone, *anyone* getting off, it's going to have that effect on you. It's not cheating, and it's not something you can control. If I flicked my bean right here in front of you, I guarantee your little nub would get a chub and you don't have a crush on me do you?" she asks, lifting her eyebrows.

"Excuse me, a what?" I burst out laughing. "Did you seriously just say nub chub? Where do you even come up with this shit?"

Cassie shrugs. "It's a gift. What can I say?"

How does she always manage to make my disasters seem so insignificant? This is why I need her in my life. She talks me out of my own head.

"Well..." I say, smiling through tears. "You are kinda hot."

"Kind of? Have you seen me lately?" she teases.

I let out a little laugh and lean in for a hug. "Thank you, Cassie."

seventeen

Vivienne

I LIE AWAKE IN BED, staring at shadows dancing across the wall. In just a few hours, the campers will arrive, and it will be the first time that I have to do this without him. My heart just doesn't feel in it. I don't know how to do this alone. I'm scared. I'm sad, and I hurt.

I can't. Oh God, I can't do this. I should have canceled the camp. What was I thinking? Panic rises in my throat as the shadows draw nearer. I feel as though they are smothering the breath right from my lungs. I lie on my back, facing the ceiling, and clutch the sheets for dear life. The room is spinning, and I can't catch my breath.

"SO, YOU'VE REALLY NEVER LOVED anyone else?" I ask Abbott for the millionth time. We're lying in bed, only hours after our wedding, and I know that I need to let this go, but it bothers me that he has been with so many women, and I have only ever been with him. Not that I want to be with anyone else. I just can't help thinking that he must think of them—compare me to them—and I have nothing to compare him to.

Abbott, ever patient and used to my insecurities by now, feathers kisses down my collarbone before answering. "You are the only woman I have ever been in love with."

"*Mmm...what about puppy love?*"

"*Nope. No puppy love. I did have this friend growing up, and I loved her...a whole lot. I just wasn't in love with her. Not in the way that I am with you,*" he answers as his face takes on a faraway look.

"*Well, who's this friend and why haven't I met her?*"

"*Grace. Her name is Grace Adler. She moved next door to me when we were twelve and that summer we got really close. When school started, she had a really rough time. She was shy and already I felt like she was mine to take care of, and so I did. We were best friends all through junior high and high school, right up until graduation.*"

"*Do you know where she is now? I'd love to meet her.*"

Shaking his head, he answers, "*Nah, babe, I'm afraid that's not possible. She doesn't want anything to do with me anymore, and I have to respect that.*"

"*Who dumps their best friend after graduation? That's pretty shitty, babe.*"

"*No. It wasn't her. It was completely my fault. I got caught up in the moment, and I kissed her...I broke her heart. I couldn't take it back, and I lost my best friend. Gracie was special to me. She just couldn't handle it, Viv, and she chose to stay away. I knew she was in love with me. I could see the longing in her eyes every time she saw me with another girl. I fucked up, and I can't fix it...I tried. I went to her house for weeks, and her mother wouldn't let me see her. She begged me to just leave her alone...said that seeing me only made it worse for her. That if I loved her at all, I would just let her go. It's one of the hardest things I've ever done.*"

Wow. My heart aches for him. "*I'm so sorry Abbott,*" I say, smoothing his hair back. "*I can't believe one kiss was worth throwing away years of friendship, though...I just can't understand why she would overreact like that.*"

"*Grace has Asperger's. It's a form of autism. I didn't know about it until we'd been friends for a few years. She was just a normal girl with me, but with everyone else, she was so mousy. Grace was shy and tripped over her words. She had trouble making friends. She obsessed over the things that she cared about, and I was one of those things. I knew how much she cared for me, and I should've taken better care with her. She was my best friend, and I disrespected her. I, of all people, knew better.*"

I can't help but feel a little jealous at how much she meant to him.

"*Don't be so hard on yourself, Abbott. I don't know her, but I'm sure she knows how much you regret what happened and how sorry you are. You made that very clear. You can't blame yourself for her reaction. You tried, and that's all you can do. It sucks that things ended the way they did…but she would be crazy to think anything but amazing things about you. You're a great guy,"* I say, sprinkling kisses over his face. *"And you are really——" kiss "——really——" kiss "——sexy,"* I say, running my hands up his smooth chest.

Abbott smirks. *"Keep it coming. I'm great, and I'm sexy, and…"*

"And, you have a really…big…ego!"

"So, is that what we're calling him now? Ego?" he questions as he grinds his hardening cock into my leg.

Again?

"You better put your ego away before I can't move, Casanova."

"Married only a few hours and already it starts!"

Shaking my head, I answer, *"I'll take care of your ego later, don't you worry. Just give Virginia time to recover."*

The bed shakes with the force of his laughter. *"Virginia? That's really unoriginal, babe. I'm disappointed by your lack of effort. Naming privates is a very big deal,"* he says, looking down at his impressive ego. *"Pun intended."*

I scoff, *"Privates? What are we in, kindergarten?"*

"Touché," he says, flicking my nose. *"Naming your pussy…"* Abbott whispers, drawing out the word as he runs his finger along my slit, *"is a big deal. It should be something sexy. Virginia…"* he says, shaking his head, *"is not sexy, baby."*

"My bad." I arch my breasts into his chest as my heart beats rapidly at his touch and breathily respond, *"My apologies, the fine china needs time to recuperate from the pounding your ego put her through over the past eight hours."*

He purses his lips, scrunching up his face. *"Meh, that's a little better. We'll keep working on it."*

BANGING ON MY BEDROOM DOOR pulls me back to reality. I must have dozed off again after taking my medicine.

"Rise and shine, lover!" *Ugh, her voice is like nails on a chalkboard.*

"Go away!" I shout, pulling the covers back over my head.

She raps on the door once again. "Come on, Momma. They're going to be here soon."

I groan. "Cass..."

"Yeah, babe?"

"I can't," I cry. "I can't do it."

"I got it, babe. Just come when you're ready."

I shut my eyes and drift in and out of sleep.

"SO," ABBOTT SAYS, MASSAGING MY scalp with his fingertips. "I was thinking..."

I widen my eye. "Uh-oh, that's rarely a good thing."

He gives my hair a gentle pull. "Shush. I really have an idea."

"I'm sorry, baby. What's up?"

"Well," he says, rubbing the back of his neck, "I was thinking that when we get home from our honeymoon and start building the lake house...that we could add in plans for a summer camp for kids with Asperger's? Kids like Gracie."

The loss of his friendship with Grace obviously still bothers him a lot. Abbott is so hard on himself sometimes. Maybe this will finally give him some closure.

"I think that's a great idea, Abbott," I say with genuine excitement.

The look he gives me in return is one of sheer relief. "You do?"

"I do," I agree, smiling at his cuteness.

"Good. I just got the feeling that you didn't like her much when we were talking earlier."

"I don't like that she hurt you, and I don't think you're the only one to blame for the loss of your friendship, but that doesn't mean that I don't see how much she meant to you and how much you need some closure. I understand that she had issues, and you know how much I love children. Helping kids could never be a bad thing, and if it helps you in the process, then all the better."

"You're the best wife ever," Abbott declares, pulling me in for a hug. He buries his scruffy face into the nape of my neck, eliciting a chill as his warm breath on my sensitive skin awakens a fervor in me.

I roll my head back, giving him better access as my heartbeat becomes erratic. "Abbott..."

"Yeah, babe?" he whispers into my ear.

"She's ready," I moan breathily.

"Who?" he teases.

"Ummm..." God, this feels so good. *"Uh, ohhh...I can't think right now, Abbott,"* I whimper.

"Come on," he urges, sucking on my earlobe, *"give me something, Vivie."*

"Pink taco," I blurt out. *Pink taco?*

He snorts...Snorts!

"Pink taco?" he questions, his voice filled with laughter.

"You're killing my buzz," I warn, glaring at him.

Abbott chuckles, raising his palms out in surrender. *"Pink taco...okay...we can work with that. Sounds delicious. Mind if I have a taste?"*

I don't mind. I don't mind one bit.

I JOLT UP IN BED. *What the hell am I doing?* This camp was so important to Abbott. Now is not the time to wallow.

After the world's fastest shower, I throw on a sundress and apply a little makeup to cover the dark circles that have become a permanent fixture on my face then head downstairs to greet this year's campers.

"GOOD MORNING, PRINCESS MOMMY," TILLIE calls from the breakfast table.

I walk over and plant a kiss on her chubby little cheek. "Good morning, Princess Tillie. How are those eggs Auntie made for you?"

"Delicious," she answers, spraying little fragments of scrambled eggs onto the table.

The screen door squeaks open, and Reid walks in dressed in a pair of khaki cargo shorts and his camp polo. "Reid Parker, reporting for duty!" he announces with a salute. *Someone's in a good mood this morning.*

"Good morning, Reid." I smile. "Where's Kylie?"

He scoffs, "Are you kidding? That princess won't be out of bed for hours." Reid rolls his eyes. "Beauty rest and all that..."

"Oh my God!" Tillie screams. "I knewed it! I knewed her was a real Princess!"

The room erupts with laughter.

"Oh, Dimples. She likes to think so, baby girl. She likes to think so," he says, shaking his head with a huge grin plastered on his face.

"Don't we all?" Cassie adds with a smile.

"All right, so...the vans will be here in about an hour, and the maid service should be just about finished with the pavilion and outdoor bathrooms. I think we're all set once that's done." I'm giddy with excitement. Even when he can't be here physically to keep me going, Abbott shows up in a memory and saves me.

THE THREE OF US ARE out on the front porch watching Tillie run around in the yard when the vans pull up. There's a twelve passenger van with six boys and two male counselors and another with six girls and two female counselors.

The kids file out as we walk over to introduce ourselves.

The two male counselors are Jordan and Tyler, and the girls are Sarah and Lila. They all seem nice enough. Three of the campers were here last year, and I can't believe how much they have grown in such a short time. Jace, Zavier, and Julie are fifteen and our repeat campers. Eric, Emma, Molly, and Charlotte are fourteen. The thirteen-year-olds are Michael, Cruz, Matthew, Rose, and Jessica.

"Where's Mr. Abbott?" Zavier asks. The smile on my face disappears. I can't say it. I can't make the words leave my lips. I don't know how to say that my husband is dead without completely losing it, and I *will not* break down in front of these children.

Reid overhears and like a white knight swoops in to save the day. "Viv, why don't you go get the kids' snacks together and Cassie and I can take them on a tour of the grounds?" he offers.

I nod and clear the lump from my throat. "Sounds good. I'll see you all soon." I can hear Reid speaking to the group as I walk away with Tillie's tiny hand clasped in my own. I can't make out what he's saying, and I'm extremely glad for that. I should've been prepared for this...the question was inevitable.

"I want to go with Reid and Auntie, Mommy," Tillie whines as I practically drag her back to the house.

"I know, sweet girl. Mommy needs your help, though, and they'll be right back. You can go next time, okay?"

She pokes out her lip in a pout but finally starts following me on her own.

ABOUT A HALF HOUR LATER, Reid and Cassie are back with all of our new guests. They crowd into the kitchen and begin filling their plates with finger food. We spend a few hours getting to know one another, and no one mentions Abbott again.

I see a few of the kids pairing off already, and I know that Abbott would be proud.

After a while, I notice that Cassie is nowhere to be found and sneak off to look for her. I find her alone in the downstairs guest bedroom in what looks to be a pretty heavy conversation. I can hear her begging the Clawsons for just a little more time. She's on the verge of tears and doesn't seem to be winning her argument. "Please, Mr. Clawson. She really is a great kid, and Korie will be lost without her big sister." She listens for a moment. "Just give me enough time to find someone to take them both...I can't send her to a group home...What if I keep her with me all day, and she promises to behave...Just one more chance." She listens, and I see her features begin to relax. "Thank you so much, Mr. Clawson...I'll make sure that she's on her best behavior."

As she hangs up the call, Cassie rests her head against the wall and cries. I've never seen her look so defeated.

"Cassie?" I whisper, wrapping my arms around her waist and resting my chin on her shoulder. "Are you okay?"

Suddenly, her body goes limp in my arms. Her legs give out, and her head falls to the side.

"Cassie!" I shout while dragging her over to the bed. Before I can even lay her down, she comes out of it.

She quickly wipes her tears away and turns to me with a weak smile. "Hey."

"What the hell just happened? Cassie, you fainted in my arms."

"Did I?" she asks, looking a little dazed. "Hmm. My thyroid must be off again. I'm okay. Don't worry about me, Viv."

She is clearly not okay. I take a good look at my best friend and notice how worn out she looks. How scrawny she is. I feel like shit because I have totally dropped the ball with her. I've allowed Cassie to take care of my daughter and me, and I've forgotten to take care of her. I'm her person. I look out for her. We look out for each other, and she has had no one these past few weeks. "I'm so sorry, Cassie. I haven't been here for you."

She gives me a look that says that she thinks I am completely insane. "Really? I don't need you to be there for me right now, Viv. It's my turn to help you. My problems are nothing compared to yours."

"Cass, don't do that. Don't shut me out because you think I can't handle it. You don't get to decide that your problems aren't worth sharing."

She shakes her head. "Seriously, Vivienne, do you hear yourself? You're asking me to dump my shit on the shoulders of my best friend who just lost her husband. I'm not that selfish."

I want to choke her.

"It's not selfish to confide in me. Yes, I'm sad and I'm depressed, and I probably will be for a very long time. Maybe even forever," I say with tears building in my eyes. "But I'm not dead, Cassie. It doesn't mean I don't care. It doesn't mean I want to lose my best friend, too...I've already lost so much, Cass. Please don't leave me, too," I cry.

"Never, Viv. I'm not going anywhere, and I'm sorry for not confiding in you," she says, taking my hand into hers. "I'm just running out of options with Sierra, but I'll figure something out. Don't worry about it," she says, using her sleeve to dry her face.

"Why don't you bring her here instead of making her hang out with you at work? If she wants to, of course...I could use a babysitter for Tillie during the day. They seemed to hit it off well when we went tubing," I offer.

"Okay. Maybe I will," she says, starting to rise from the bed.

"Oh, no," I say, grabbing her by the arm and pulling her back down. "No way. What was up with you fainting? And don't lie to me and tell me that bullshit about your thyroid. You don't have problems with your thyroid."

"I don't know. I guess it's all the stress with Sierra and losing Abbott. It's just a lot. That's never happened to me before, I promise," she says. After studying her face, I decide that I believe her.

"Cassie, I think that you need to see someone. You aren't eating right. I probably should have made you go to a therapist a long time ago for this. You have a problem. I'm not saying you aren't stressed, but you're skin and bones."

The panic in her face takes me by surprise. "No. Viv, I can't. If my job found out...CPS is really strict about those things. I can't risk losing my job. I will eat. I swear," she begs with tears in her eyes.

I don't know what to do. I know that she needs help. I also know that losing her job would kill her, and no one would care for her kids the way she does. "I don't know, Cass..."

"I swear I'll come over and let you watch me eat every day, Viv. I know that I haven't been eating right, but I swear it's not because I'm trying to lose weight. I just get so stressed out that I don't feel hungry," she explains.

"Fine," I answer with a resigned sigh. "But I'm watching you, and you can't keep shutting me out."

Cassie leans in and gives me a hug. "Thank you, bestie," she whispers into my ear. "I love you."

I return her hug, feeling the bones in her back, and it makes me cringe with guilt. "I love you, too, babe. Let's go get some food in you before you pass out again."

AFTER FILLING OUR BELLIES, CASSIE takes off to pick up Sierra before she can get into any more trouble, and I walk down to the lake to join everyone else. Reid left a note on the fridge saying that he had taken Tillie and where to find them so that I wouldn't worry.

Everyone seems to be having a great time. After fishing, we pull out the life jackets and let the kids take turns in the paddle boats. When Cassie returns with Sierra, she too straps on a jacket and joins right in with the other kids.

Cassie and I lay out in the grass, watching the children play, and I notice the way her whole face lights up as she watches Sierra and how much more relaxed she seems now that she's here. She will make a great mom someday.

"She's not a bad kid," Cassie says, breaking the silence.

"No," I agree, "she's not. Did you talk to her about helping me out with Tillie for the summer? I'd love to have her, and it will give you time with your other cases."

Cassie nods. "I spoke to her on the way over here. She's really excited." Cassie turns to me and smiles. "Thank you for giving her a chance, Viv."

"No thanks needed. We're family, and that's what family is supposed to do. We take care of each other, Cass. Your people are my people."

Finally, five o'clock rolls around and I've never been so happy to see those white vans depart. I'm both physically and emotionally drained. We survived our first day of Camp Aspie without Abbott, and while it wasn't quite the same without him, I do think the kids really enjoyed it.

Reid comes over and asks to borrow the car so that he can take Kylie out to eat, and I'm relieved that I won't have to entertain them tonight.

Cassie and Sierra stay for dinner and a movie. Once they leave, Tillie and I grab a quick shower, brush our teeth, and climb into her frilly pink bed. I fall asleep amid mountains of stuffed animals and toys with my own little doll cradled tightly in my arms. Even with my arm completely numb under the weight of Tillie's head and various little girl things poking me in the back, it's the best night's sleep I've had in a while.

eighteen

Vivienne

WE'VE JUST FINISHED WITH ANOTHER successful day of camp, and I feel so much relief as I wave goodbye to the children and watch those white vans roll down the driveway. I don't ever remember being this exhausted by the camp. It was something that Abbott and I enjoyed so much that the days all flew by in a blur. Now, they seem to drag on endlessly.

We stand there waving until they're out of sight, and then Cassie, Sierra, Tillie, and I meet Reid and Kylie at the pool to cool off.

Reid and Kylie...

I can't stop watching the two of them together. I'm obsessed with the way his hand is caressing her inner thigh when he thinks no one is watching...her body's reaction. The slight flush in her cheeks and the promise in her eyes.

I'm overcome with jealousy because I want to feel that way, too...to feel my body come alive beneath my husband's touch. I want his hands on my thighs, in my hair, on my breasts...whisper soft kisses and his warm breath on my skin.

I know that I should turn away, but I hesitate for a moment too long, and I'm caught. Reid's eyes find mine over her shoulder and my heart begins to race. Blood pulses behind my ears. Blue eyes that are as familiar as the back of my hand. The same blue eyes that I fell in love with so long ago. My heart clenches tightly in my chest as I struggle to look away.

With all of the restraint that I can muster, I rip my gaze from his and turn over in my lounger, diverting my attention to the other end of the pool. Reaching into my bag, I retrieve a pair of sunglasses to hide the frustration now seeping from my eyes. Knots form in my gut as I watch my baby girl and my best friend splashing around seemingly without a care in the world, and I'm even jealous of them. I can't remember what it feels like to not carry the weight of the world in my chest.

I don't know why everything has to hurt so much. I'm suffocating in this new life—a life I didn't choose...and a life I'm not sure that I want.

Tillie's laughter fills the air, and instead of bringing me feelings of joy and happiness, I'm consumed with guilt and so much shame. She should be enough. She *is* enough.

Why can't she be enough?

WHEN CASSIE LEAVES TO TAKE Sierra home, Tillie and I go inside to change into dry clothes and figure out what to do for dinner. I'm emotionally drained and not sure how much longer I can put on a happy facade for everyone around me. The last thing I want is to let them know how much I am hurting. I don't need to burden them with my feelings, and I don't want them hovering over me any more than they already do.

Sometimes, I wish that I could just be left alone in my grief... to lie in this bed and never get out. I want to cry and scream and to break every fucking thing that I can get my hands on without having to answer for it, without having to worry about how crazy that would make me and how much it would scare my baby. But, life doesn't stop. It goes on, and I have no choice but to flounder around trying to keep up. I'm harboring all of these pent up feelings with no place to release them, so I bottle them up, and I go through each day feeling like at any moment the pressure will become too much, and my body will implode.

As I am leaving my room, I catch the prescription bottle on my nightstand from the corner of my eye. It's only been four hours, and I know that it is too soon...but the desire to feel a little relief is too strong to pass it by. With a guilty conscience and a racing pulse, I swallow another pill before going downstairs to meet Tillie.

I FIND HER DRESSED IN a Cinderella gown, complete with matching heels, dancing around in the kitchen. *God, to be so young and resilient.* Most of the time she seems completely unaffected. Tillie's plastic slippers clomp on the tile as she spins, her golden hair floating behind her like a cape flapping in the wind.

"May I have this dance?" I offer, holding out my hand to my pretty princess.

Tillie flutters across the room and takes my hand. "My honor," she says, bowing, and I feel my heart swell with so much love for this incredible little person that I am lucky enough to call my own.

We hum and twirl around the kitchen, her chunky little hands clasped in my own. In this moment, I feel a sense of hope. Hope that maybe...just maybe, eventually everything will be all right.

"Princess Mommy, I decided what I want for supper," she says when she's finally exhausted herself. *Who knew ballroom dancing could be so draining?*

I collapse on a bar stool to catch my breath. "What would you like to eat, Bossyrella?"

"How about...*pizza?*" she suggests, bouncing in her heels.

How can I say no to her? "Pizza it is!"

"Can Prince Reid and Princess Kylie come, too? I weared my princess dress, so I can be a real princess, too," she explains, fluffing the front of her dress.

*Princess Kylie...*I inwardly cringe. "Of course, baby."

I call Reid's cell, and it goes right to voicemail. It must be dead.

"Tillie, Reid's phone is dead," I call out to the playroom. "I'm going to walk over and invite them to dinner, okay?"

"Okay, Mommy!" she yells back.

"Stay in your playroom until I get back. I'll just be a few

minutes," I tell her, now standing in the doorway.

She looks up from her princesses and flashes me those heart-melting dimples. "I will, Mommy. I promise."

Leaning down, I plant a kiss on the top of her head and then walk over to the pool house.

The door is ajar, so I push it the rest of the way open and step inside.

Reid and Kylie are there on the couch. His broad muscular shoulders hunched over her as he nibbles on the exposed skin of her breast. She moans...loudly. They are both naked from the waist up and so consumed in each other that they don't even pause when I gasp in surprise.

For a moment, I just stand there, unable to digest the scene before me. The sounds of their heavy breathing and whispered words of affection make my head swim. How many times have Abbott and I made love on that same couch? What I wouldn't give to be in their place...in *our* place, together again right now. *This is so unfair.*

My chest heaves with silent sobs and tears pool in my eyes. My knees buckle, and I fall back against the wall with a thud. That's when Reid finally turns his head in my direction and finds me standing there staring.

He covers Kylie's body with his own, shielding her from my view, and offers me a crooked smile. "We've got to stop meeting this way," he jests, breathing heavily.

He's joking...This is funny to him? I. Am. Dying. My heart is ripping open inside of my chest, and he has the nerve to *laugh?*

That's the moment when it all becomes too much. The moment when it's either going to have to come out, or it's going to kill me. Fueled by all of the pain and jealousy, the hurt, the anger, and embarrassment, all of the emotions that I've allowed to build up over the past few weeks, I push off the wall, and I explode.

"Have you ever heard of shutting and locking a fucking door?" I scream. The room falls completely silent. "Did you even consider for one moment that you're in someone else's home? That my daughter—my *baby* could have just walked in here?" I yell, kicking over the little table next to the door and watching its contents scatter across the floor.

That felt so good.

Reid rises from the couch, creeping toward me slowly as if he's approaching a wild animal...and he might as well be. I have lost my fucking mind.

"It's okay, Viv," he coos, reaching his hand out to me like I am a child.

"No!" I yell, slamming my fist into the wall. "No, this is *not* okay!" I shout, inches from his face. "Nothing...none of this is okay. Stop saying everything's okay when nothing will ever be okay again!"

His face is panicked when he answers, "I know. I-I'm sorry, Vivienne. I wasn't thinking."

I glance over to Kylie, who is balled up and crying on the couch, and then back at Reid's bewildered face. "You need to have more respect for other people," I say weakly, tears streaming down my face.

"I'm really sorry," he apologizes again.

"Do you have any idea how hard it has been to watch the two of you?" I ask through clenched teeth. "To see you touch her and, my God, you were about to have sex with her on my couch," I grit out between sobs.

He places a hand on my shoulder and I recoil. "Don't...touch... me..." I fume, reaching for the door knob. "And lock the damn door," I add, slamming it shut behind me.

WHEN I WALK BACK INTO the house, I am forced to grab ahold of the counter to avoid collapsing onto the floor. I brace my head in my hands as my entire body begins to quake with violent sobs, the force of which leaves me gasping for breath.

"Mom.... Mommy...*Mom!*" Tillie calls, pulling on my shirt.

"*What?*" I finally snap. Can't she see that now is not the time?

"I said...where's Princess Kylie?" she repeats, placing her little hands on her hips and tilting her head to the side.

I can't handle this right now. I just need a fucking moment to myself. "Tillie," I say very slowly, "will you *please* just leave me alone for a few minutes?" It takes a concentrated effort to remain calm. My pulse is racing, and my hands are shaking uncontrollably.

"Ughhh, I just wanted to play wif Princess Kylie. You told me you were getting her for me," she sasses.

"Goddamn it!" I yell, slamming my fist down onto the counter. "Just give me a goddamned minute, will you?"

Tillie's face crumbles as she runs off crying. I want to go after her, but I need to calm down first. I've never yelled at her like that. *What has gotten into me?*

nineteen

Reid

WHAT IN THE HELL JUST *happened? I think to myself as the door rattles on its hinges. Vivienne has completely lost her mind. I mean, yeah, I guess I should have shut and locked the door, but she more than overreacted. If I'd realized that having Kylie over would have this kind of effect on her, I never would have invited her.*

"Reid?" *Kylie calls from behind me.*

"Yeah?" I answer, still staring out of the window, trying to decide if I should go after Vivienne to make sure that she's okay.

"What was that all about?" she asks, resting her hand on my shoulder. My body tenses. I don't want her touching me, and I don't know why. It's not like what just happened was anymore her fault than mine, but suddenly her touch repulses me. "Is something going on between you and Vivienne?" She sniffs.

"No," I snap...*Yes? Maybe?* "Did you seriously just ask me if I have something going on with my aunt, Kylie?" I ask, shrugging her hand off my arm.

"Why else would it bother her so much to see us together? She's acting like a jealous girlfriend," Kylie whines.

"She is not acting like a jealous girlfriend. Jesus, Kylie! She's acting like a pissed off mother and a depressed woman whose husband just died," I say condescendingly.

Kylie starts to say something, but I cut her off when I see Tillie running toward the lake and Vivienne nowhere in sight. "I have to go, Kylie. Wait here," I say curtly as I step into my shoes and fling the door open.

"What? Where are you going, Reid?"

I don't waste time on an answer. I have this sinking feeling that something bad is about to happen as I take off running after her.

"TILLIE!" I SHOUT AS I get closer to the lake. I know that I saw her running this way, and I can't find her anywhere. "Matildaaaaa," I call as I scan the lake.

Finally, I spot her approaching the wharf, and I thank God because it's almost dark out and I was beginning to really panic. She's still a good distance away, but now that I can see her, I slow my pace.

What happens next is the single most terrifying experience of my life.

Cupping my hands around my mouth, I call out to Tillie once more. When she turns to answer, I watch her slip on the wet wood, falling backward into the lake. *Nooo!* I run after her, pumping my legs as fast as I possibly can. It's as if I'm moving in slow motion... running against a current. My heart hammers against my ribcage and seconds feel like hours. I can't get to her fast enough.

How long does it take to drown?

My lead feet pound the wood of the wharf, and I scan the lake, afraid of what I will find. The sun has begun to set, making it difficult to see. Bile rises in my throat as I stand there, unsure of what I will do if I don't spot her out there. How would I find her? And I *will* find her. The alternative is unthinkable.

Hold on, baby girl...I'm coming. Just hold on.

Time is a tricky thing...speeding up when you want to savor every second and damn near stopping altogether when you are in a moment of sheer desperation.

After what feels like an enormous amount of time—*too much time*—I spot her flailing soundlessly in the water a few yards from where I first saw her fall in. With no time to think or feel anything, I dive in after her, fully clothed. My shoes are slowing me down, so

I kick out of them and pray that I reach her in time. My pulse is pounding in my throat when I finally reach out and lift her head above water. She chokes and gasps for air as I pull her to the shore. "Are you okay?" I ask, and I have a sudden urge to cry with relief, but I steel myself. There will be time to break down later. Right now, I need to focus on Tillie and making sure that she is all right.

Tillie coughs and coughs, spitting up so much water. She's unable to speak and that moment of relief passes. Now that I've got her, I don't know what to do. I pat her on the back and lift her arms above her head because that's what my mom always did when I choked as a kid. I don't know if it helps, but it makes me feel better to do something.

I have no phone with me to call for help, and I'm not trained in CPR. I mean...she's crying, so she's breathing...but the gurgling sounds coming from her throat, and the way she's gasping for breath is worrying me. My stomach knots as I lift her trembling body against my chest and rest her head on my shoulder. "It's okay, Dimples. We're going to go find Mommy, okay?"

She continues hacking but nods her little head. When we're a few yards from the house, I hear Vivienne frantically calling Tillie's name in the distance.

"She's here, Vivienne. She's with me," I yell out to her.

Vivienne is shaking with fear, and when she takes in our wet clothes and hears Tillie coughing and crying, she bursts into tears. "Oh, baby..." Vivienne reaches out, taking her from my arms. "What happened?" she cries while shushing Tillie.

"I saw her running toward the lake through the window. She was by herself, so I followed her, and I must've scared her when I called out her name." I take a breath, placing my hand on my burning chest...I don't think my heart has ever beaten so fast. "She was running on the wharf, and I saw when she slipped and fell in, but I was still a few yards away. I got there as fast as I could, Viv," I explain, talking a mile a minute. "She seems okay, though, right?" I ask, hopefully, needing some reassurance as I wipe my sweaty palms onto my wet shorts. *Lotta good that did.*

"Oh, my girl. I'm so sorry, baby. I'm so sorry that I yelled at you," she chants over and over while hugging Tillie tightly to her chest.

"Vivienne," I say forcefully, trying to keep her attention. "Do you think that we should take her to the hospital or maybe call an ambulance?"

"Mommy..." Tillie croaks, her voice shredded from all of the heaving. She sounds so weak, and it worries me to see this normally vibrant child so frail.

"She seems okay, but I think we should get her checked out to be sure. Would you mind calling the ambulance?" she asks, sniffling. "If we can avoid going to the hospital..."

The last time she was at the hospital was the night of the accident, and I can understand her hesitation.

"Sure. Yeah," I answer. "Do you have your phone? Mine's back in the pool house."

Viv reaches into her back pocket and hands me her phone. I call for the paramedics while we walk back to the house.

WHEN THE AMBULANCE ARRIVES, THE three of us are sitting in the living room on the floor. They take Tillie from her mother's arms, and I fill them in on the situation while Vivienne paces a hole into the floor.

Life is so fragile. Knowing that had I been even seconds later that this baby may no longer be here has really shaken me up. It's beginning to hit me just how badly this could have ended.

After they examined Tillie and gave her the all clear, I suggest that Vivienne go and give her a warm bath and get her into some dry clothes while I go back to the pool house and get cleaned up.

"Please, don't leave yet," she begs, clutching my arm. "I don't want to be alone."

After the day we have had, I don't know up from down anymore where this woman is concerned. "Viv, I'll come right back. I don't have any clothes here, and I'm full of lake water. I really need a quick shower." I'm drenched. I stink. I have no shoes and abandoned the muddy socks when we got inside.

"Please stay. Abbott has a closet full of clothes in my room. Could you just borrow something of his and shower in my bathroom while I go bathe her?" she pleads. "Please?"

She's so pale and weak. Vivienne is dead on her feet, and I really don't want to be away from them, anyway. "Sure," I answer. "Just let me use your phone to fill Kylie in so she knows where I am, okay?" The last thing I need is her to come over here looking for me.

"Thank you...I-I just don't want to be by myself," she says again with watery eyes as she hands me her phone. Her fingertips brush the palm of my hand, and my pulse speeds up. Staying here cannot be a good idea, but even knowing that it's wrong, I can't ever seem to tell Vivienne no.

Tillie's already falling asleep in her arms. "Go get her ready for bed," I say, rubbing Tillie's back. "I'll stay."

After calling Kylie and letting her know that I'm not sure what time I will be back and why and then listening to her bitch and moan, I head up the stairs to Vivienne's bedroom in search of dry clothes.

BATHED IN UNCLE ABBOTT'S SOAP and dressed in Uncle Abbott's clothes, I step into his bedroom and find his wife perched on the edge of their bed. She's so damned beautiful. I can hear my heart thrumming loudly in my chest as I take a minute to just watch her. The intimacy of the moment has me wishing that I could step into his life as easily as I have the rest of his things.

"Hey," I say softly, crouching down before her. "You all right?" Her body begins to quake with silent sobs like she's been holding it all in and I've just granted her permission to break.

Vivienne shakes her head. "No...No, Reid, I'm not." A lump forms in my throat and tears sting the backs of my eyes.

"Come here, Viv," I offer, opening my arms to her.

She leans forward and allows me to fold her into my arms. I rub her back and kiss the side of her head, shushing her in much the same way that I witnessed her doing with Tillie earlier tonight.

Vivienne cries into my chest, "I'm sorry, Reid. I'm sorry I flipped out on you earlier."

"It's already forgotten," I assure her. "Don't worry about it."

She lifts her head, wiping her nose with a tissue. "Thank you," she says hoarsely. "Thank you for going after her...When I think that I c-could've lost her, too..." She can't even finish as she collapses into me, sobbing.

I hold her tightly, trying to resist the urge to break down, too. I never understood what it meant to be strong for someone else before this summer. I've never had to. These girls have turned me into a man that I don't even recognize. Someone *better* than I ever hoped to be.

"You wanna go downstairs and have a drink?" I ask, needing to get out of this room before I forget myself.

I feel her nod into my chest. "Sure, just let me take my medicine first."

"DID SHE GO TO SLEEP okay?" I ask Vivienne while pouring us each a glass of her favorite wine. I've never really cared for the taste, but I need something to take the edge off.

Nodding, Viv answers, "Yeah. I think she was asleep before her head hit the pillow." Tears trickle down her swollen cheeks. "It's my fault," she whispers, her voice breaking.

"What's your fault?" I ask as I hand her one of the glasses and take a seat beside her on the couch. "What happened tonight with Tillie couldn't have been your fault."

She swirls the ruby liquid around in the glass, staring absently ahead. "I yelled at her, Reid," she says, choking on a sob. "I-I *screamed* at her to leave me alone," she cries, gripping the glass with white-knuckled ferocity. "I've never spoken to her that way. She's just a baby...She's my baby, and I could've lost her tonight."

Reaching out, I take hold of her free hand, attempting to offer comfort. Vivienne relaxes into the couch so I take it a little further and begin rubbing the pad of my thumb over her delicate knuckles. When I pass over her wedding ring, a pang of guilt pierces my chest. I drop her hand, backing away just a little. I wish that I could make my conscience forget that she isn't mine to hold. Vivienne doesn't seem to notice. Her face is blank and her eyes vacant. She seems completely lost in thought. It's almost as if she's sleeping with her eyes open. But then, in a pained voice, barely above a whisper, she says, "If you hadn't seen her...Reid...if you hadn't seen her, I would have nothing left to live for, and this time, it would've been my own fault."

My body shudders at the thought. "You couldn't have known she'd run off like that, Viv. I mean, yeah, you probably shouldn't have screamed at her, but we all make mistakes. We all do things that we end up regretting. Let's just be thankful that she's okay and not dwell on things that didn't happen."

She nods, chewing on her lip, but says nothing. The two of us sit in companionable silence, ruminating over the day's events. We finish the first bottle of wine then pop open another.

At some point during the night, she ends up pressed against my side with her head resting on my chest. I'm not sure how she got there, but I'm too selfish to push her away, and it feels better than it should when I wrap my arms around her and rest my head in her floral scented hair.

I begin to doze in and out of sleep, and when I feel soft lips feathering kisses down my jaw, I'm sure that it must be a dream. But when I open my eyes, there she is...kneeling over me, her wild hair like a curtain framing her beautiful face. My pulse races and that sinking feeling returns in my chest. I swallow the guilt threatening to steal this moment and let my emotions take the lead. Desire, like a wildfire, blazes through my veins, burning through everything in its path until nothing remains but this heat. All-consuming need surmounts any rational thought. I couldn't stop if I wanted to, and I don't want to. Vivienne presses her mouth against mine, and when my lips instinctively part, she slips her warm tongue between them.

I kiss her back, gripping her hair in my hands. Our kiss is long and languid—unhurried. I cherish every second that she allows me to pretend that this is okay. Vivienne whimpers against my lips, and it is the most erotic sound that I have ever heard. Every moan, every touch, I savor, burning it into my memory as if it is the last time I will ever have this chance. More likely than not, it is. Our tongues twirl in sync as if they've done this dance a thousand times before, yet my heart has never felt so heavy.

Vivienne begins to grind her body against mine, and I try to tell myself to stop her, that this needs to end here, but I'm too far gone to be the one to end it, and when she whispers "I need you" into my ear, there is not a chance in hell that I won't give her what we both so desperately crave.

twenty

Vivienne

I WAKE IN THE MIDDLE *of the night with my face in Abbott's lap. It's dark, and I'm disoriented. I try to remember how we ended up here, sleeping in our clothes...but I have nothing.*

His hard bulge presses into my cheek, and my body begins to pulse with desire. I'm overwhelmed with a need to feel close to him. My heart feels so heavy...so sad...and I can't recall why. There's an ache in my chest and the need for him to fix it—to make me feel better—is so strong.

I run my fingers over the mesh fabric of his shorts, tracing his hard erection, and feeling it grow harder still. Crawling over him, I run my hands up his torso, tracing the ridges of his abs and then lean in, trailing kisses along his jaw to his ear. I nibble and suck on his lobe, and when I make my way back up his jaw, brilliant blue irises connect with mine.

He appears a bit startled at first, but it doesn't take long before his eyes blaze with the same hunger that I know he can see reflected in mine. I'm so hot...so hungry, and when I kiss his lips, and he opens to me, I plunge in, swirling my tongue around his.

Abbott groans, fisting his hands into my hair, tugging gently as he takes control, and I am more than happy to relinquish it. He kisses me devoutly, worshiping me slowly, spending long moments exploring my mouth.

My body trembles with need, and I begin to rotate my hips, grinding my wet heat into his hardness...My head falls back, and I whimper as he lowers his mouth to my chest, sucking my breast through the thin material of my cotton dress. His hands ghost up my legs, eliciting a chill as his fingertips skim my sides, lifting my dress over my head and tossing it to the floor.

"Oh God," I moan when he yanks my strapless bra down, taking one of my nipples into his mouth and circling it with his tongue. My head begins to swim... dizzy from the wine and lost in sensation.

"Is this really happening?" he murmurs, lavishing my other breast. "Viv," he rasps out as his lips graze a path up the front of my neck.

He's being so gentle—too gentle—and I just want him to fuck this day out of my mind. To make me forget for a blissful moment how badly I screwed up.

I rock harder, hoping he will take the hint. He usually reads my signals so well, but he places his hands on my waist and slows my movements, whispering into my ear, "Don't...just...just let me enjoy you."

I can't. Not tonight. My eyes well up and a feeling of desperation consumes me. "Please," I cry, blinking away tears. "Just make it go away. Make me forget..."

There's a moment of hesitation, and then as if a switch has been flipped, he delves into my mouth, kissing me with a ferocity I've never experienced from him. It's exactly what I need. He cups the back of my head, and his kisses are hard and bruising. Quick shallow thrusts of his tongue followed by deep almost choking plunges. It's relentless and unforgiving. It's primal. He tugs my bottom lip between his teeth and moans into my mouth. And still I want more. I want him deep enough to cleanse my soul. Hard enough to punish me. Forceful enough to make me forget.

He wraps his arm around my waist, and in one fluid motion flips me onto my back, his mouth never leaving mine. "So beautiful," he growls against my lips before rising to his knees and slipping a finger beneath the black lace band of my thong. Torturously slow, he runs his finger back and forth along my middle while making love to me with his eyes. And just when I think I will explode from desire, he rolls the tiny scraps of fabric down my legs and stands...and I feel his absence everywhere.

I stare with bated breath at the way his muscles contract as he wrenches his t-shirt over his head, and when his impressive erection springs free from his shorts, my entire body clenches with need. "Please," I beg, biting my bottom lip and tasting blood. I slip my tongue out and run it along my lip, savoring the taste of our savage kisses...wanting more...needing more.

He slides his hand up and down his shaft, readying himself for me. I am so wound up, I swear that I will die if I don't get some relief soon. As if he can read my mind, he acquiesces, wrenching my legs apart and kneeling before me.

He grabs onto my thighs, lifting my center, and rubs his cock along my sensitive flesh.

Each stroke of his warm skin against mine is the sweetest torture. It's pleasure and pain...heaven and hell. It's I can't take anymore and please don't stop. His jaw tightens, matching the reaction in my core. It's as if every nerve ending in my body is collecting in my center, manifesting into a tight little ball. A grenade, ready to detonate, and he holds the pin.

I whimper and writhe, clutching the sides of the couch, bucking against him, trying unsuccessfully to force him inside. I am nothing but sensation... nowhere but this moment.

His eyes are fixed on his task...watching with a lustful gaze as if he could do this all day...I can't...The more he teases, the more furious I become. My heartbeat pounds in my ears and my breaths are coming in shallow pants.

When he finally leans over me, and I can feel his head resting against my opening, I begin to shake with silent tears. "Please," I cry.

His face falls at the sight of my tears. "Oh God. Are you okay? Did you change your mind?" he asks, and with a pained expression adds, "We can still... we can still stop."

Stop? Has he lost his mind? "Just. Fuck. Me..." I pant. "Now."

With a renewed vigor and a triumphant smirk, he reaches between us and places his cock at my entrance. "Ready?" he rasps.

I raise my hips, forcing the tip to breach my entrance, and he releases a low chuckle before pushing the rest of the way inside.

This. This is what I've been reaching for. This closeness. This fullness. This connection that only comes from having him buried deep inside me. There is nothing more healing than the feeling of our hearts beating between our chests and our centers pulsing as one.

He pulls back and begins to thrust in and out in long, hard strokes...pounding my head into the arm of the couch. I can feel him everywhere...stretching me... filling me. I'm so close.

"Harder," I moan, needing the pain as much, if not more, than the pleasure.

He circles his thumb over my nub and gives me everything he has. Long punishing strokes. So thick. So deep. So hard.

I dig my nails into his back, holding on for dear life as we pull the pin and explode together.

Gone are the feelings of sadness and guilt as we lie in a tangle of limbs and heartbeats. Breathy sighs and butterfly kisses. We bask in this blissful nothingness that only exists when we come together and purge our souls.

MY EYES FLUTTER OPEN IN the darkness, and I'm feeling a sense of déjà vu when I realize that, just like in my dream, my head is resting on a man's thigh. But unlike in my dream, this man can't be Abbott...The gaping hole in my heart is a constant reminder that can't be possible.

That dream, though...it was so real. I can actually taste the copper on my lips and feel the slickness between my legs. *My first wet dream.* Holy fuck! I had my first wet dream laying in the lap of another man...my nephew at that. *Damn, Viv...how much farther can you fall?*

The night before slowly comes back to me, along with a pounding headache. The lake...Tillie...Reid saving her and the consumption of way too much wine. We must have passed out drinking and my subconscious manipulated reality into my heart's desire.

I need to get up and clean this mess before Matilda wakes up. I should go in and check on her...

Careful not to wake Reid, I lift myself off him very slowly, bracing my aching head with my hand. The room spins. Oh God... the nausea. *Deep breaths. Deep breaths.* I inhale and get a whiff of wine. The smell of sex is evidently burned into my mind because I smell that too and begin to retch.

"You all right?" he asks, placing a comforting hand on my back.

Still reeling from the fact that I just mentally screwed my husband in this man's lap, it startles me and I jump up from the couch. "Yeah...um, too much wine," I offer with a shrug as I begin collecting our wine glasses and the rest of our mess from last night.

"Let me help you with that." Reid grabs the empty wine bottles that are cradled in the crooks of my arms. His hand brushes my arm, leaving goosebumps in its wake. Jesus, my body is still so worked up from that dream. I'm skittish and acting like a bumbling idiot.

Reid follows me into the kitchen and disposes of the bottles while I wash our dishes. Then suddenly, I feel him behind me. *Close behind me*—too close. My body tenses as he leans into my ear and whispers, "That was some dream you had last night, wasn't it?"

I freeze. He knows...He knows about the dream. Oh my God. Of course he knows about the dream. I must have given him quite the show. The wine glass slips out of my hand and shatters in the sink. My entire body heats with embarrassment. I'm going to be sick.

"Shit, Vivienne!" Reid gently pushes me aside to clean up the mess. "I didn't realize you were feeling that bad," he says when my body is wracked with dry heaves. "Go to bed. I'll clean this and lock up on my way out."

I'M SICK.

For hours, I'm in and out of bed, throwing up the entire contents of my stomach and more.

When Tillie finally wakes up, she finds me there, trembling and in a cold sweat. Completely useless. She goes into the bathroom and returns with a wet washcloth which she places over my eyes then cuddles up next to me. "I love you, Momma," she whispers, kissing my arm.

I choke back a sob, still feeling so much guilt over the night before. "I love you more than life, baby," I whisper.

The next time I open my eyes, I find Tillie sitting up in my bed, eating a Pop-Tart. She has the TV on low, watching her cartoons, and I wonder where my baby has gone. When did she turn into a little girl? "When did you start taking care of Mommy and getting your own breakfast, pretty girl?"

"When I gotted free years old," she answers simply, like the answer should be so obvious.

You mean when your Daddy died, and your mommy lost her mind, I think to myself, mentally adding that to the ever growing pile of guilt.

Around noon, Reid peeks his head into the door. "Hey, ladies," he says, looking awfully chipper.

"Hi, Prince Reid," Tillie beams. "Where's Princess Kylie?"

His eyes drift over to me when he answers, "She had to go home, Dimples. I'm sorry." He's giving me a look that I'm not sure how to read. Did he send her home because of me? Because of the scene I pulled yesterday? *More guilt.*

She pouts, hanging her head. "Aw, man...I wanted to show her my princess dresses."

"I'm sorry. You can show me your princess dresses if you want to," he says, giving her a huge, dimpled smile.

Tillie blows out a long breath and rolls her eyes. Those dimples may work on the other ladies, but they do not impress her. "You already sawed them afore."

"That's true," he says, stepping into the room. "But, I would love to see them as many times as you want to show them to me."

"Hmmm...maybe later," she says noncommittally.

"I was actually coming by to see if you wanted to come downstairs and have lunch with me and maybe help me drive the boat the rest of the afternoon since Mommy isn't feeling well." he offers, raising his eyebrows at me in question.

Thank you, I mouth.

The camp. I forgot all about the camp. Thank God for Reid always being here to save me.

Tillie's face lights up with excitement. "Can I, Mommy? Can I go?" Her voice sounds horrible, like her vocal cords have been run through a shredder. Another reminder of how close we came to losing her last night.

My chest tightens as I nod my head. "Of course, baby." Looking over to Reid, I add, "Just make sure she wears her life jacket, okay?"

He looks at Tillie with so much love and genuine affection then over to me. His face says it all. The trauma of almost losing Tillie has connected us on a deeper level. There's a trust that wasn't there before. He saved my baby, and I know that I owe him her life—that I can trust him with her life.

twenty-one

Reid

IN THE FIRST FEW DAYS following the night that Viv and I had sex, I realized that it's not something she is ready to discuss or to repeat. She was really skittish around me for a few days after... embarrassed or worried...maybe even ashamed. It stung at first, and then I had to remind myself that her husband just died and that she must feel like shit. It's too soon. So, I'll bide my time. I'll wait.

The camp has been great. I've learned a lot about myself and life in general. Being able to watch these kids open up, cut loose, and have some fun has been so rewarding. Tonight is karaoke night, and I can't wait to see what they've come up with.

I walk over to the house to see if Vivienne and Cassie are ready to head over to the pavilion. When I step into the kitchen, I find Sierra and Tillie at the table working on a puzzle.

Sierra and Cassie are suddenly a packaged deal. She's a cool enough kid, and it's nice having someone old enough to look after Tillie so she doesn't have to be around the camp kids all of the time.

"Hey, girls," I say, plopping down at the table beside Dimples. "Whatcha making?"

"It's a unicorn, Prince Reid. With a rainbow...see?" Tillie grabs the box and holds it up to my face.

"That's awesome. Leave it on the table when you finish so I can see it when we get back, okay?" Puzzles have become our thing. Every night before bed, she and I put one together before Viv takes her up for her story. As much as I'm looking forward to hanging out tonight, I'm going to miss our new nightly ritual. From the first day, I've felt such a strong connection with Tillie, but since the near drowning incident, it feels as if our souls are somehow connected—bound together through our shared trauma. She's become a part of me. I have no real way of knowing what it feels like to be a parent, but I can imagine that the feeling is something similar to the way my heart seems to grow tighter in my chest when she's not around and how just being in her presence sets it at ease.

I turn toward the doorway when I hear Vivienne and Cassie coming down the stairs. When they walk into the kitchen, I have to do a double take. They look like they've just time warped from the '80s. Their hair is huge—finger in an electrical outlet huge—and I have to stifle a laugh when I see their bright blue eye shadow and Barbie pink lips. The scent of hairspray fills the room. The smell is so strong that I can actually taste it. Viv and Cass are decked out in spandex from head to toe, complete with leg warmers, plastic bracelets, and earrings that look like they should be worn by Tillie... not two twenty-something-year-old women.

Viv looks *happy*. She looks *amazing*.

"The '80s want their hair back, ladies," I say, unable to resist taunting them.

"What's wrong wif your hair?" Tillie asks, grimacing. "You and Auntie need to brush your tangles. It's not fair...I have to."

Viv snorts out a laugh and covers her mouth, turning red in the face. "It's not tangled, Tillie...Well, it kinda is, but it's part of our costumes," she explains, giggling.

"We look hot, baby girl. Like rock stars!" Cassie adds, fluffing up her hair with her hands.

Sierra lowers her head, shaking it from side to side. "So embarrassing," she grumbles, barely loud enough to be heard.

"Hey, Debbie Downer...don't be jealous that you aren't as cool as me. I'll get you an outfit just like this for your first day of school,"

Cassie responds, sticking her tongue out at Sierra.

"Oh God, no." Sierra rolls her eyes, scrunching up her face in disgust, but there's a hidden smile evident in her eyes.

"We should really get going," I suggest, noticing the time on the stove. "We don't want to keep the kids waiting." I ruffle Dimple's hair and lean over to give her a peck on the cheek before scooting my chair back and bidding the girls a good night.

Vivienne and Cassie kiss the girls and instruct Sierra to call one of our cells if they need anything.

On the way out, I overhear them whispering to each other about their upcoming performance, and you could swear that they were going to a club to sing and not on their way to hang out with a bunch of teenagers. It's adorable how excited they are. Their good mood is infectious.

Never in a million years would I have imagined that I'd be looking forward to sober karaoke with a bunch of kids and my *aunt*...but there's no place I'd rather be.

We arrive at the pavilion, and sure enough, find the campers and counselors already there waiting on us. The equipment was set up earlier in the day, and the kids were encouraged to pair off with partners and to come tonight prepared with a song. They've been practicing all afternoon, and I'm surprised at how many of them wanted to participate. It just goes to show how much their time here with each other has benefitted them already. Only four of the twelve don't want to sing, but I hope that when they see how much fun their friends are having, it will make them want to participate next week.

The pavilion is huge with a stage on one end and six picnic tables arranged in two rows of three on the other. It's warm and muggy, but the ceiling fans and the breeze coming off the lake help to make it bearable. I don't know if I will ever get used to this humidity, however. Mosquito zappers hang from the ceiling and some type of spray system set up around the outside along the roof. Both totally necessary. You have never seen mosquitos until you've been on the water in Louisiana on a warm summer night. They will eat you alive.

Not wanting to waste any time, I walk over to the mic, tapping my finger on it a few times to grab everyone's attention. "Good evening, ladies and gentlemen," I say, clearing my throat. "Let's get this party started, shall we? First on stage tonight, we have Mrs. Vivienne Parker and her partner in crime, Cassie Stewart." Following the counselors' lead, the children all begin to cheer and clap while the girls take their positions on stage. "This dynamic duo will be performing "I Wanna Dance with Somebody" by Whitney Houston." More cheers.

"Show 'em how it's done, ladies," I say, handing them each a microphone with a huge smile that I can't seem to help. Then I turn and jump off of the stage, grabbing a front row seat next to the nonperformers.

The music begins, and the two of them sway in time to the beat, exchanging smiles of encouragement. Love and excitement radiates between them. Cassie starts off with a few oohs and ahhs... and then Viv comes in, singing the lyrics, and that voice...God, her voice is unbelievable. It's enchanting. It's alluring. It's...so fucking *sexy*. Cassie continues to sing backup, joining in for the chorus, and she's not bad—not at all—but she's obviously only there for moral support because Vivienne is a star. She shines so brightly that it's almost blinding to look at her. Just when I thought that I'd gotten this attraction under control, she comes out dancing in a pair of skin-tight pants with the voice of an angel and moves that suggest she is anything but...

Her voice caresses me everywhere, leaving gooseflesh in its wake. I feel her pumping through my veins, heating my blood, touching me in all of the places that I dream of someday feeling her again. Her eyes meet mine, and neither of us can look away. There's no way that I'm imagining this connection between us. She has to feel it, too...

twenty-two

Vivienne

THE MUSIC STARTS, AND WITH the first few notes, I'm transported back to the countless other times that Cassie and I have performed this same routine. Visions flash through my mind of college parties and karaoke bars...of drunken nights out by the pool...and of Abbott's smiling face in the crowd. I'd forgotten what a rush it is to be up here on stage...how every cell in my body is electrified—alive and pulsing with excitement. There's a healing that comes from allowing yourself to be completely vulnerable. It's empowering.

I gaze out into the crowd and almost instantly find Abbott's eyes. I know that he is not here—that those eyes belong to Reid... but those are Abbott's eyes. Those eyes are my comfort, and I want to drown in them.

Adrenaline causes my heartbeat to pulse loudly in my ears. I can't believe Cassie convinced me to do this. I've never sung in front of a crowd before, and I never had any intentions of changing that. But Cassie and her big mouth had to mention what a "great" singer I am to Abbott, and he's been begging me to sing for him at our favorite hangout ever since. We've been coming to Joey's Bar as a group on karaoke night for a few months now, and none of us has ever braved the stage. We prefer to sit back and watch others make fools of themselves. At least, we did until tonight.

Abbott promised to perform solo if Cassie and I agreed to a duet. He knew that he would never get me up here alone, and somehow he convinced me that it would be worth it, but now that I'm standing here with sweaty palms on shaky legs, I'm not so sure. I try not to focus on the sea of drunken eyes before me as the music starts and instead hone in on mesmerizing blue in the front row.

Suddenly, I'm less nervous. Abbott has a way of doing that, of making me forget that anyone else exists but the two of us. There's so much pride in his eyes, and that look gives me all of the confidence I need. The rest of the room disappears. There's no band, no Cassie, no crowd. I sing for Abbott, and I perform for Abbott alone. Every sway of my hips, every shimmy, every shake is with the intent to fuel the hunger in his gaze.

Before I know it, the song is over, and Cassie has me wrapped up in her arms as the bar erupts with cheers. "Viv, oh my God, girl. You fucking nailed it! You were amazing! I was so scared that you would back out or freeze up. But, that was so...hot! Who knew you had that in you?"

I squeeze her tight and try to bring myself back into the moment. I feel as though I've just had sex on stage in front of a room full of people and only just realized that they were here watching the whole time. My intimate show is over, and it was anything but private.

Strong arms wrap around my middle, pulling me from Cassie's grip. He smells delicious, and I want nothing more than for him to take me back to his place and make love to me with his body the way he just did with his eyes.

Spinning around in his arms, I lift up onto my toes and whisper, "Take me home," seductively into his ear. I trail my tongue along the edge and feel his grip tighten on my waist.

Abbott chuckles. "Believe me, I want to...but I can't," he says with annoyance. "A bet's a bet."

To hell with the stupid bet. "Babe, nobody cares about that dumb bet. Let's go home." I try pulling his arm toward the exit, but he doesn't budge. Is he serious?

"I care. Don't worry, Hot Pants. I'll take care of you later," he promises, grabbing my ass with both hands and pulling my body flat against his.

I want to go total cave woman and beat him over the head with a club, dragging him out of here to have my way with him. I actually wonder for a moment if his body would still perform while he is knocked out. Would that be considered necrophilia? No. I bet they have another word for it. I'll have to look that up...

"Don't sulk," he says, kissing my pouty lip. "If my singing affects you the way yours just did to me...tonight is going to be one for the record books," he says, waggling his eyebrows with a goofy grin.

"Vivienne!" Cassie shouts, pulling on my arm. She sounds frustrated. I guess she's been trying to get my attention for a while. "We have to get off the stage. We can't just hang out up here. They're ready for Abbott now."

I hang my head like a toddler denied her way and beg Abbott with my eyes to reconsider as I begrudgingly allow Cassie to drag me off to the dance floor. He stares at me, grinning, and shakes his head to himself. Then, pulling at his lips, he turns back to the stage, completely dismissing me.

We walk through the smoky room to the bar and each order a beer. Strangers keep stopping us to tell us what a great job we did, but I don't feel great. I feel horny, and I desperately need a drink.

"You girls were awesome up there tonight," the bartender says as he hands us our drinks. "We don't normally get real singers in here."

Cassie nudges me with her elbow, grinning from ear to ear, and I look up, realizing that he was talking to me. "Oh, I'm not a singer. I just made a bet with my boyfriend. He's up next." I look over to Cassie, who is practically drooling over the guy, and smile. The bartender is covered in tattoos and piercings with well-defined muscles. Such a stereotype, and so Cassie's type. "Come on, we need to get back. I don't want to miss Abbott."

She plants her spandex-clad ass on a bar stool, winking at the bartender. "You go, Viv...I'm gonna watch from here and keep..." she looks at him expectantly.

"Gage," he answers with a sexy smirk.

"I'm gonna keep Gage here company."

Leaving Cassie to do her thing, I squeeze myself through the packed room to the front of the stage. I'm groped and yelled at along the way, but I don't care who I piss off. I'm not missing this for anything. Well, I would've missed it for something...

His music starts, and it needs no introduction. "Water Runs Dry" by Boyz II Men. We are nothing if not ambitious. Whitney Houston and Boyz II Men, I laugh to myself.

Abbott starts to sing, and he's not great...but he's not completely tone deaf, either. He's decent enough for karaoke and shouldn't embarrass himself too badly. We've definitely heard worse. I'm shaking I'm so nervous for him. Maybe even more than I was for myself.

"Let's go into the water and drown, we might watch our whole lives pass us by," he sings, and I question whether I've misheard him because everyone around me is acting normal while I am trying not to fall on the floor laughing. They are either too drunk to care or don't know the song...which is impossible. Everyone knows this song. I must be mistaken.

But then the chorus comes back, and he sings it the same way again, and I feel horrible because I cannot contain myself. I burst into a fit of uncontrollable laughter. Abbott glares at me, not looking my way again for the rest of the song. No one else says a word about his screw up or even cracks a smile. How is that possible?

When he's through, everyone claps and he climbs down the steps to find me on the dance floor. "What the hell, Viv? You almost made me mess up," he says, annoyed.

I snort. "I almost made you mess up?" I ask sarcastically. "'Let's go into the water and drown.'" I tease, making air quotes with my fingers.

"Is it a bad song or something?" he asks, clearly confused.

I chew on my lip, trying not to laugh at him. "Umm...No. "Water Runs Dry" is a great song. This is the first time I have ever heard "Water and Drown"."

He still doesn't have a clue what I'm getting at, so I pull the lyrics up on my phone. "Did you even look at the word monitor once while singing?"

"No, I didn't need to," he answers, puffing up his chest with pride.

Oh, Abbott...

"Well, you should have," I snicker and pass him my phone.

I stand there fidgeting while he reads over the lyrics, and his eyes get big when he realizes his mistake.

"Shit. I've been singing it wrong all this time." Abbott laughs, shaking his head. "But, my lyrics make sense, too," he adds, coming to his own defense.

"Well, yeah. I mean, I guess if you go into the water and drown, you will probably watch your life pass by."

"Right? It works," he says, chuckling. Abbott wraps his arm around my shoulders, pulling me into his vibrating chest. "You ready to get outta here?" he asks, kissing the top of my head affectionately.

He doesn't have to ask me twice. I nod and feel the butterflies return in my tummy as he takes my hand in his, leading us toward the exit. On our way out,

I wave at Cassie, who is still whoring it up at the bar, to let her know that we're heading home.

When we step out into the parking lot and no longer have to shout to be heard, I turn to Abbott. "Oh, and in case you were wondering about the effects of your performance...it was panty wetting."

He stops walking and looks at me with a boyish grin. "Was it?" He darts his tongue out, licking his bottom lip.

"Oh yeah," I say as a smile spreads across my face. "I'm pretty sure I peed myself!"

"VIV!" CASSIE CALLS, PULLING ON my arm. "Where are you, babe? We're done. What are you staring at?"

I shake my head and realize that I'm still staring into Reid's eyes. I force myself to smile at the kids and then follow Cassie down to our seats, feeling dazed and empty. Tears burn the backs of my eyes and the hole in my heart is ripped wide open. *I miss him.*

"Where were you just now?" Cassie whispers as Reid introduces the next performers.

Bouncing my leg nervously, I shake my head and swallow a sob.

Cassie places a hand on my back and kisses the hair at my temple. "You did great," she whispers.

I nod my thanks and reach into my bag, pulling out a pair of sunglasses to hide my tears. I dig around for my pills and tap one into my palm, swallowing it down with one of the bottles of water that we found waiting at our seats after our performance. I just took one before we left to come out here. I've been doing this too often, and I know that I need to stop. But when I feel this bad, all I can think about is numbing the pain as quickly as possible. What's the worst that could happen? I'm already dead inside.

The first pair of kids finish their song, and I'd be lying if I said I even knew what they sang. All of my concentration is focused on not falling apart. It's exhausting. Sometimes the memories make me feel better, make me smile, and others...all they do is make me realize just how much I am not better, and that better may never come. That I may spend the rest of my life treading water—trying desperately not to drown, and praying that I don't take anyone else down with me when I do. Because I undoubtedly will. I can't go on this way forever.

Two more groups have gone, and I play my part. I face the stage, and I clap when everyone else does. But I'm not here, not really. I'm not living in this moment. I'm a body taking up space—a prop. By the time the last performers take the stage, I am blessedly numb and half asleep.

"Hey," Cassie says, shaking my shoulder. "Let's go inside, babe. You fell asleep."

"Huh?" I ask. "Where are the kids?"

"They just left to go back home. They said to tell you that they had a wonderful time."

Shit. I'm ruining Abbott's camp. I'm sad, I'm tired, and I'm completely overwhelmed. I can't seem to do anything right anymore. It's bad enough that I paid absolutely no attention to the performances, but to fall asleep on them. How do I explain my way out of that one?

As if she's reading my thoughts, Cassie says, "Don't worry about it. I told them you weren't feeling well and took some cold medicine that must have kicked in and knocked you out. I gotcha covered, babe...so wipe that frightened look off your face."

"Thanks," I whisper, staring blankly at the stage.

"You wanna tell me where you were tonight? You sounded great, you always do, but you were not with me on that stage, Viv."

Knots form in my stomach. "Joey's Bar...I was at Joey's Bar," I mumble.

"Our first time?" she asks, grinning.

"Mmmhmm."

"That was such a great night. Not only because we totally rocked that performance, but I got to see Abbott naked. That shit should be celebrated!"

At that, I laugh. "You're not right, you know that?"

"Hey, you two freaks were the ones going at it like bunnies on our couch!"

My face warms. We did do that..."Well, we assumed you would be with that bartender all night or at least 'til early morning..."

"Hey. I'm not complaining. I'm totally into a little voyeurism," she teases.

"Voyeurism, eh?" Reid asks, coming up behind us. "Sounds like fun...who are we voyeuring?"

"No one," I answer quickly.

Reid and Cassie both laugh at my expense. I'm getting used to being a source of their entertainment. I think they enjoy embarrassing me a little too much, but I'm okay with it. Embarrassment is better than depression.

I try to avoid looking Reid in the eye as we gather our things and head back to the house. I wonder what he thinks about me staring at him all through my performance, but I'm too embarrassed to ask. Sometimes, I swear I catch him looking at me with the same longing Abbott would and maybe that's why I get lost in his eyes so often. My mind sees what it wants to see.

twenty-three

Vivienne

ANOTHER MONTH HAS COME AND gone. *I can't believe it's July already*, I think as I hang the red, white, and blue streamers from the ceiling of the outdoor kitchen. The Fourth was one of Abbott's favorite holidays. Every year, we had a pool party and barbecue for all of our friends. Abbott was the king of the grill. He said that feeding people made him happy, but I think that he just enjoyed showing off his culinary skills.

This year's celebration will be much quieter than previous years. I still can't bear to be around too many people. The truth is, I wouldn't know how to act. I'm not the same person that I was before meeting Abbott. I haven't been that girl for such a long time. He changed me. We changed each other. There's no going back, but it seems there's no moving forward, either. We danced through life with Abbott always taking the lead. He was my compass...my north star. When he moved, I moved, and now that he's gone, I've forgotten the steps. I'm afraid to make a mistake and land flat on my face.

I don't want to have to see the pitying looks on people's faces or to be forced to lie when they ask how I'm doing. I'm not okay, but that's not what people want to hear. The truth would make them uncomfortable, and I'm not in a place to have to be concerned with other people's feelings.

"Momma," Tillie calls, bursting through the back door.

I glance over at her and smile at her disheveled appearance. Her pigtails are sagging, and she's already lost one of her red bows. Her white skirt is covered in dirt. *She is so Abbott's kid.*

"Yeah, baby?"

"They're here, Mommy," she says excitedly. "I sawed Auntie get out of her car, and she has the guh, Mom!"

The girl is Korie, Sierra's little sister. Cassie arranged it with the Clawsons for the girls to spend the Fourth of July with us. We haven't had the chance to meet Korie yet, but Cassie and Sierra talk about her so often that it already feels like she's a part of the family. Korie is four and close to Tillie's age. To say that she's excited would be an understatement.

I drop the roll of red crepe paper and the tape into the tray on the top of the ladder then climb down so that Tillie and I can go up front to greet our guests.

After slipping my white crochet cover-up on over my bathing suit, we walk around the side of the house, and Tillie takes off running. She has already introduced herself to Korie, and the two have run off together by the time that I reach the car.

I smile when I approach and see that the three of them are dressed festively in red, white, and blue. Even Sierra, which is surprising. She's usually got the whole emo/goth girl thing going on.

"Wow, Sierra, you look beautiful in that dress. You should wear them more often." I walk over and kiss her temple.

An unsure smile moves across her face as she smoothes down her skirt. "Thanks, Mrs. Vivienne. Cassie insisted that dressing up like the flag is a requirement to attend this party, so here we are," she says miserably.

Pressing my hand to my chest, I gasp. "Did you just admit that you wanted to see me so badly that you put on a dress?"

To that, she gives me an impressive eye roll and stalks off, but not before looking back at me with a half grin. *Love her.*

"Hooch!" Cassie comes running around the side of her car, and I shake my head when I get a good look at her outfit. Red and white striped denim shorts with a navy tank covered in tiny white stars and a pair of plastic star sunglasses sitting on top of her head. But the shoes are where it's at. Somehow, this chick got her hands on a pair of star spangled rubber shit-kicking boots.

"Nice shoes, Clotille."

Cassie strikes a pose. "No need to be jealous, Momma. Yours are in the trunk." She winks, smacking her gum.

She'd better be joking. "You're late! You said you'd be here early enough to decorate. Look how sweaty I am from working outside all by myself this morning!" I scrunch my nose in disgust. She knows how much I hate to sweat.

"I know I was supposed to be here earlier, but it wasn't my fault your surprise was late..."

Good grief. Those words shouldn't make me so nervous. "You got me another surprise?"

"Oh, stop looking at me like I'm going to whip out anal beads or something." Cassie laughs. "You are going to looooove this surprise."

I hear a car door open and close, and my heart leaps when I see a familiar face peek around the back of Cassie's car. "Surprise!"

Tears fill my eyes. "Momma?"

"Hey, baby doll. I told ya I'd be back, didn't I?" Her thick country drawl makes me smile.

We meet halfway, and I fall into my mother's waiting arms. The same arms that rocked me to sleep as a baby and held my hair when I was sick. The same arms that saw me through my first heartbreak and lent me their strength as I watched my soul mate being lowered into the cold ground. I didn't realize how badly I needed this. "I can't believe you're really here." I bury my face into her shoulder, breathing in the scent of her perfume, drawing comfort from the familiar cadence of her heartbeat.

"I'm here, baby," she says, rubbing circles on my back. "I'm here."

I peer over Mom's shoulder and mouth the words *thank you* to Cassie. She waves me off like it's no big deal, but this is *such* a big deal, and as I watch her gather the girls and herd them into the house, I'm reminded again how lucky I am to have her in my life.

"How are you, baby? You don't say too much on the phone. I thought that you were doing well...ya know...considering. Now Cassie's tellin' me that's not the case. Talk to me, Viv." Mom pulls back just a little so that she can see my face. With her thumbs, she rubs away my tears while allowing hers to glide freely down her cheeks.

To this day, there's something about Momma's eyes that won't allow me to lie. I can fake it a little on the phone, but standing here in front of her, I feel completely exposed. My lips tremble, and I try to be strong. I shake my head and feel my throat grow thick. "It's... hard, Momma," I cry. "It's just really hard."

Her face contorts with sadness, and I see my pain reflected in her tired brown eyes. "Oh, baby girl...I'm so sorry." Momma pulls me back into her arms, and her body shakes with silent sobs as she runs her fingers lovingly through my hair. And as I fall apart in her familiar embrace, I feel the broken pieces of my heart come together just a little because when Momma whispers that it's going to be all right, I desperately want to believe it.

"I would've come back sooner, but I couldn't afford the flight and the time off of work so soon after the last trip. It kills me that you're going through all of this without me."

I hate my father so much for leaving her to struggle on her own. This shouldn't be her life. "Mom, you know that you only have to ask, and I'll fly you here anytime." Thankfully, money is the thing that I don't have to worry about. Abbott received a ridiculous inheritance from his grandfather on his twenty-fifth birthday, and we also had great life insurance. Even knowing this, Mom is too proud to ever ask for help.

"I know. I just don't like to be a burden. I'm a grown woman and perfectly capable of taking care of myself. But when Cassie called and told me that she wanted to fly me here as a gift to you... well, I couldn't refuse the chance to come and check on my babies. I only have a few days, but let's make 'em count, okay?"

She must really be worried about me to accept such an expensive gift from Cassie. I smile, swallowing hard. "She always knows what I need before I do...I'm so glad you're here, Mom."

"That girl is a blessing. Knowing that she is here to help you through this is the only way I get any sleep at night." Mom laces her fingers with mine and tugs. "Come on, darlin', let's go inside and get ready for your party."

Matilda hadn't noticed Mom when we were outside; she was too focused on her new best friend. So, when we walk into the living room and she sees her Grammy, she lets out an ear-piercing scream and barrels across the room. "Grammy! How did you getted here?" The smile on her face is the very thing Hallmark cards are made of. Seeing her in my mother's arms and the bond that the two of them share makes my heart soar.

I watch their reunion with a smile. After a few minutes of catching up, they walk over to meet Korie at the doll house in the corner of the living room. Momma sits on the floor between the girls, not hesitating to pick up her own doll and join right in. I take this moment to sneak off to the backyard to finish decorating.

When I step through the back door, I find Cassie busily hanging streamers and flags and Reid cleaning the grill. Sierra is setting up the table decorations and snacks. There's nothing left for me to do. It all looks so amazing. He would love this. I half expect to walk back into the house and find Abbott in his white apron and chef's hat. He'd have his patriotic playlist blaring, singing along obnoxiously to every song.

"Hey, Viv, you wanna bring out some meat? I'm ready to fire this bad boy up." Reid's face lights up like a little boy with a shiny new toy.

"You know how to use that thing?"

Reid laughs. "I've grilled before, Viv. Never on anything this fancy, but I'm sure I can figure it out." He winks.

Right. Well, better him than me. I'd probably burn the house down.

I WALK INTO THE KITCHEN and find Abbott seasoning chicken breasts and belting out "God Bless the U.S.A". He's really into it and doesn't

notice when I come in.

I sneak up behind him, wrapping my arms around his waist. "Hey, sexy. You look really hot in that apron."

"You just like watching me rub my meat." He turns his head to the side, giving me a sly smile.

"I do."

"Dirty girl. You kiss your Momma with that mouth?"

"I do lots of things with this mouth." I glide my hand down his waist and palm him, feeling his body instantly tense up.

"Babe, you don't play fair," he says, squirming to adjust himself. "Why do you always do this to me? We have a house full of company. Hands off the goods."

"No one would notice if we disappeared for a few minutes..."

Abbott sighs. "Jake's out back waiting on the chicken titties. Trust me, he would notice."

Giggling, I give him a little squeeze before I let go and walk back toward the door. "Well, by all means, let's not keep Jake waiting."

He pokes out his lip. "But now all I can think about is nibbling on your tender titty meat." He picks up a chicken breast, kneading it. "Chicken titties have nothing on Vivie titties."

"No?" I ask, laughing. "So, you won't be replacing me with poultry, then? That's a relief."

"You two are so fucking weird," Cassie says, slipping in through the dining room entrance.

I burst out laughing, and Abbott turns red in the face. I don't know how he still embarrasses around her. She's caught us so many times...

Cassie walks over to Abbott and grabs the seasoning from his hand. "Go wash up and take care of your wife...I'll handle Jake's meat," Cassie offers suggestively.

"WHAT ARE YOU DOING, VIV?" Cassie asks, walking up behind me in the kitchen. "You came inside almost ten minutes ago to get the meat."

Shaking myself to clear my head, I realize that I have been

standing here staring at the island all this time. "I'm sorry. I was daydreaming, I guess."

"Must've been some dream judging by that smile on your face."

"It was," I say, still grinning from ear to ear.

Cassie walks over to the fridge and starts pulling the trays of food out and setting them on the counter. "Good. Go get the little ones ready to swim, Momma. I'll take this out to Reid."

AFTER SWIMMING WITH THE GIRLS for a bit, I climb out of the pool to relax in my lounger. The biggest downside to taking these pills is how quickly I become exhausted. I begin to doze off almost instantly to the sounds of little girl giggles and the smell of barbecued meat.

I faintly hear the sound of Cassie snickering, but don't open my eyes until...

"Oh my God!" I jump straight up, reaching down into the front of my bathing suit top for the ice cubes that my *former* best friend decided would be funny to pour down there.

"First to fall asleep at a party gets slumbered," Cassie teases. She pokes out her tongue and hides behind Momma for protection.

Momma chuckles, scooting around to get out from in front of my target. "Now, Cassie Lynn, don't go puttin' me in the middle of this."

"Oh, this is war!" I shout, grabbing a handful of ice from the drink cooler and chasing her around the pool. Sierra appears out of nowhere, grabbing Cassie by the arm to slow her down. *Good girl.*

She eyeballs Sierra, trying to look upset. "Traitor!" she shouts, but she's laughing so hard that Sierra isn't frightened at all by her poor attempt at a scolding.

She's got her hands crossed over her chest so that I can't get into her top, so I pull the front of her bottoms open and drop the ice inside there instead. *Hah! Take that!*

Sierra high fives me as Cassie takes off screaming and dives into the pool where she can rid herself of the ice without showing everyone her lady garden.

When she comes up and clears the water from her face, Cassie narrows her eyes at me. "That was a low blow, Vivienne."

"Pun intended?"

She laughs. "Pun intended."

"Hey, uhh, Cassie. You need someone to check out your injury?" Reid calls from the grill, practically pissing himself laughing.

"Keep it up and you'll be next," she threatens, lifting herself from the pool.

"Hey now, Cassie. That boy's too young to be talkin' to like that. Behave yourself," Momma says, looking appalled.

Cassie and I look at each other before bursting into a fit of giggles. Somehow having Mom around has reduced us to a couple of teenaged girls, and it feels incredible because that girl felt happy and protected. That girl hadn't yet had her entire world turned upside down. That girl still believed that Momma could make everything better. Because that's what Mom's do: they share your pain and assume your burden. She's hurting right along with me, and I know this because the only thing that I could imagine to be worse than experiencing this pain myself would be to watch my baby girl go through it instead.

Mom, Cassie, and I sit at the table, watching the girls chase each other around with red Solo cups of ice. We all have a big laugh when Tillie and Korie sneak up on Reid and pour a cup of ice down the back of his shorts. I'm pretty sure he heard them coming and only pretended to be surprised. He's come a long way from the boy we met less than two months ago.

I glance over at Cassie and see the beginnings of tears forming in her eyes as she watches the girls together. I see the way that she smiles without realizing it. How her body involuntarily jerks when Korie, who can't yet swim, gets too close to the edge of the pool. Her body language is telling. It reveals more than any words could.

"Cass?"

"Hmm?" she asks without ever taking her eyes off of Korie.

"What are you waiting for?"

She turns to me with a look of confusion. "Huh? What are you talking about, Viv?"

"You love them," I say simply.

I watch her swallow her tears. "Yeah...so?"

"So...What. Are. You. Waiting. For?"

A lone tear trickles down her cheek, and she quickly swats it away. "I don't know what you mean."

"They love you, too, you know?"

"Mmhmm."

"So, why are you working so hard to find them a family when you know damn well that they belong with you? They belong with us, Cassie."

Cassie shakes her head, choking on a sob. "Why are you doing this? Don't you know how hard this is for me?"

I lean forward, resting my hand on her knee. "But it doesn't have to be. You love them, and they love you. Everything else is just...it's just paperwork, Cass."

"Viv," she whispers brokenly. "I don't know the first thing about being a mother. I didn't even have one...I grew up in foster care. They need a real family. They deserve that. I can't be selfish and take that away from them trying to fulfill some dream of the family I never had."

"Cassie Lynn," Momma calls from across the table. "What exactly do you think a real family looks like? Families come in all shapes and sizes, sweetheart. Love. That's what matters...This," she says, circling her finger between the three of us, "this is a family. This is as real as it gets, baby girl, and if you love those girls the way I think you do...well, they couldn't ask for better."

Cassie wipes her tears before turning her attention back to the kids. "I'll think about it," she says, dismissing me.

I walk over, crouching down before her, and grab hold of her trembling hands. *We aren't finished here just yet.* "I know what's going on here, Cass. You think you aren't worthy...that you don't know how to love..." I look up and meet her eyes through wet lashes. "But, I know what it feels like to be on the receiving end of your love, and it's one of the things I treasure most in this life."

Cassie's green eyes overflow with tears, her body trembling,

172 | HEATHER M. ORGERON

and nods. "I do love you...so much, Viv." I feel her fingers tighten around mine.

"I know, and you do it so well, Cassie. You show me every day in so many ways, and you do the same for them. Those girls will never have to wonder if they're loved because you'll make sure that they know it."

"I'm scared..."

"Do you think I'm not? God, Cassie, we all worry about screwing up with our kids. It comes with the territory. It's time for you to knock down these walls that you keep putting up around your heart once and for all because you can't break through theirs with your own still so firmly intact."

"But what if there's something better out there for them?"

I shake my head. "Can't you see that no one will ever understand them the way you do? You see through all of Sierra's crap because you recognize yourself in her. The two of you have something so special, Cass. Don't let that go. Don't send her to people who won't be able to reach her. You are worthy of their love. Please, believe that."

"Wh-what if this isn't what they want?"

"Well, there's only one way to find out. Talk to them, Cassie Lynn. They aren't too young to know how they feel." Momma walks over, pulling Cassie up from her chair, and wraps her up in her arms. "Give Momma two more grandbabies, sugar."

I move to the side, watching their interaction, my heart nearly bursting. Conflicting emotions wage war in my chest, and I'm finding it hard to draw air into my lungs.

I love that my mom has such a big heart and that Cassie is finally able to experience a mother's love. I'm not jealous of their relationship at all. I want this for her, I do, but the mention of grandchildren has me on the verge of hyperventilating because I still haven't come to terms with the fact that Tillie will be the only one. That was not the life we had planned. This...this is not the life we had planned, and my body's selfish reaction only makes this feeling worse because it's compounded with guilt. I love these girls so much, and I'm happy that Momma wants to take them on as her own, but I'm sad at the same time. I'm sad for what I've lost, and I'm mourning the dreams that Abbott and I shared that will never be.

I turn away, not wanting Momma or Cassie to read my face and feel bad. They've done nothing wrong, and I want them to have their moment. I find the three girls sitting at the little table near the pit having a snack. Then, like a moth drawn to a flame, my eyes connect with Reid's. They always do. I don't intentionally seek him out. In fact, I feel guilty for constantly staring into the eyes of another man, but I can't help myself.

Reid has grown so good at reading my face. He looks at me questioningly, and I shake my head as if to say "not now." I feel trapped...like no matter which way I turn, I'm going to have to explain these feelings that I can't even make sense of to myself.

Quickly, I walk past Momma and Cassie, calling out to them from the doorway that I'll be right back. I grab a pill from my purse on the kitchen counter and hurry into the downstairs bathroom, swallowing it down with a handful of cool water from the sink. Having Mom around has me nervous. Reid never questions my medication but Momma would. She'd want to know what I'm taking and why. She'd pay too close attention. I can't risk losing the one thing that dulls the pain in my chest and makes my life somewhat bearable.

twenty-four

Reid

I'M HAVING A GOOD TIME chatting with Tillie, Korie, and Sierra. These two little ones together are a riot. Glancing up, my eyes meet with Vivienne's. I'm not sure what's happened between now and fifteen minutes ago when she was shoving ice down Cassie's pants but something's wrong. She's been crying. That in itself isn't all that unusual, unfortunately, but there's something in her face that's not sitting right with me.

I look at her questioningly, which causes her to realize that she's been staring, and she quickly turns away. Viv looks around in a panic and rushes off into the house. It's only after she's gone that I notice Ms. Anderson and Cassie crying as well. *What the hell did I miss?*

I pull all of the meat from the pit since it's just about done anyway and ask Sierra to keep an eye on the little ones while I run inside of the house for a moment.

I can't be more than a few minutes behind her, but when I walk in, Vivienne is nowhere to be found. I search the entire first floor, and just when I'm about to go upstairs to check her room, I hear a faint cry coming from the half-bath under the stairs.

I walk over, lightly tapping my knuckles on the door. "Viv...Viv, you in there?" I can hear her moving around and whimpering, but she doesn't answer. "Come on Viv," I beg, letting my forehead fall against the door. "I know you're in there. I just wanted to check on you and make sure that everything's okay."

Viv blows her nose and turns on the faucet. Just when I'm turning to leave and give her the privacy that she's obviously seeking, the door jostles and pops open. She stands before me, a sobbing mess. Her face is red and swollen, her chest shuddering with each intake of breath.

My heart is in my throat. "Are you okay?" I brace my hand on the doorframe above her head, leaning in close enough to feel the warmth of her breath on my bare chest. Every cell of my body aches for her. I want nothing more than to hold her and kiss away her tears. To make whatever has upset her go away. I want another chance to *make her forget*. But, you can't reverse death, and no matter how much I want it to be so, she isn't mine...not yet.

She shakes her head. "No...not really, no."

"Do you, umm...do you wanna talk about it?"

Her lip trembles as she again shakes her head.

I really shouldn't press things. But her eyes...her eyes are desperately begging for comfort. I reach out with my free hand and tuck a long, tear-soaked strand of hair behind her ear, letting my fingers linger for just a moment at her neck. I hear her sharp intake of breath. Knowing that she isn't completely unaffected by my touch strokes my wounded ego. It's not much, but right now, I will take any reassurance that this isn't all in my head.

Vivienne steps into me, wrapping her arms around my waist. Her damp hair feels so good against my skin, and I have to fight the urge to tangle my hands in her long, brown locks. The tropical smell of her sunscreen wafts into the air, drawing my attention to the glistening sun-kissed skin of her shoulder. I want so badly to lean down and press my lips to that very spot, leaving my own mark on her skin, and maybe...maybe even her heart.

We stand there in silence for long minutes. Vivienne's body slowly relaxes as she draws comfort from mine, my own twisting itself into knots. My racing heart pounds against the walls of my chest as I remember the last time that I felt her bare skin against my own. Somehow, I find the restraint to be what she needs at this moment and resist the urge to seek a little comfort for myself.

When the crying has reduced to soft, shuddering breaths, Viv looks up at me with a weary smile. "Thank you. I guess I...I guess I needed a hug." She peels herself off me with an embarrassed laugh.

I'm so wound up that the best I can manage is a tight-lipped smile. "Glad you're feeling better, Viv."

Her smile grows, filling the space that was just occupied by her tears. "I really am. Sometimes it just sneaks up on me..." She looks down, shuffling her feet. "I guess we have a party to get back to, huh?"

"Yeah. You go ahead. I'll be just a few minutes."

"Oh, okay," she says, furrowing her brow in confusion.

"I'm just gonna give my folks a ring," I say, pulling my phone out of my pocket and flipping it in my hand. I'm lying. My parents are probably out in the middle of the ocean on their yacht or something equally as ostentatious, but I can't tell her that what I really need is time to recover from our *hug*.

"Awesome! Tell them I said hello, okay?" Vivienne squeezes the top of my arm in a friendly manner as she walks past me toward the kitchen.

"Will do," I respond with a playful salute, thankful that she's leaving before I do or say something stupid.

Her sudden perk in attitude is a blow to my confidence because while I can tell that she isn't completely unaffected by my touch, it's in no way the same effect that she has over my body. I'm disgusted with myself for being turned on by her at all. In moments of clarity such as this, I feel like a bastard for ever laying hands on her at all. The worst part is that as bad as I feel now, I know that it won't mean shit if I ever get the chance to be with her again. She's like a drug, an addiction I never saw coming. I'm powerless to resist her pull.

I PUSH THE SCREEN DOOR open with my elbow, juggling a tray of sliced watermelon and pineapple for the ladies, and step out into the back yard. The stifling heat is suffocating after almost an hour in the cool air conditioning.

The atmosphere is completely different from the one I abandoned earlier. I find Cassie in the pool with the girls launching those little spongy pool balls at each other. Viv's mom is relaxing on a lounge chair next to Vivienne, who is passed out in hers. I smile at Ms. Anderson as I walk past them to the kitchen area and set the tray of fruit down on the table.

"Reid...you have a minute, son?" Ms. Anderson asks, walking up behind me.

"Sure."

She takes a seat at the table, so I pull out a chair across from her and do the same.

"I just wanted to thank you for giving up your summer to watch out for my baby girls," she says, tearing up. "I worry about them so much."

"It's no problem, ma'am," I assure her.

She smiles at me the way a grandmother would. The way a grandmother should, I should say. Lord knows, my grandmother doesn't quite fit the mold. Her smile is genuine and loving, and she looks at me like I'm something precious, even though she's only just met me. Coming from a family like mine, one founded on social status and reputation, it's not something I've experienced much of in my life.

"How's she been? You spend the most time with her. Do you think she's doing all right?"

I shrug nervously. I don't want to divulge anything that Viv wouldn't want her to know. "I don't really know how to answer that...I mean, she has her ups and downs, but I guess she's doing all right considering."

Ms. Anderson taps her foot nervously and glances over to Viv, who's still asleep in her chair. "Does she do that often?" she asks, tilting her head in Viv's direction. "Fall asleep like that, I mean. This is the second time today that she's passed out cold."

"Sometimes," I answer truthfully. "But she doesn't always sleep well. It's usually in the evening or when she's had a rough day. She's not like passing out all the time or anything." I feel like a narc, and it's making me really uncomfortable.

"Hmm." She purses her lips, deep in thought. "Reid, I have to go home the day after tomorrow, and it would make me a whole lot more comfortable if you had my phone number. I want you to call me if you feel like she needs me. Will you do that?"

"Sure," I answer, and we exchange numbers. Honestly, it makes me feel better, too, knowing how to reach her.

OVERALL, TODAY HAS BEEN GREAT. With the exception of the one meltdown earlier, having Viv's mom here seems to have lifted everyone's spirits.

The sun has begun to set and now it's time for the real fun. I'm probably a little more excited than I should be, but I'm a guy and, well...*fire*. Back home we aren't allowed to set off our own fireworks, and we have to go to watch the public displays. So, in honor of this momentous occasion, I went into town earlier in the week and bought a few hundred dollars' worth of explosives. I've been itching to light them up ever since.

I walk past the girls all stretched out on blankets in the grass on my third and final trip down to the wharf. I deposit the last of my supplies and grab the box of sparklers first. The guy at the firework stand assured me that these would be a hit with the kids. I was a little nervous about it, but Viv just laughed and couldn't believe that I'd never done sparklers before.

I wave them over to join me, and Vivienne pulls out one of those long tipped lighters from her bag, the ones that look like a little gun with a trigger. She hands it to me and grabs a handful of sparklers. Viv holds the first one out, and I light it. When it sparks up, I actually hop back a little in surprise.

"Shit! Are you sure you should be letting the kids handle that?" It doesn't seem very safe to put something shooting actual sparks in the hands of toddlers. I don't know what I expected them to do, but this definitely wasn't it.

"Oh, you poor, deprived child," Ms. Anderson says, chuckling on the side of me. "Can't be you've never seen a sparkler before?"

A nervous lump forms in my throat. "No, ma'am, I sure haven't. That hardly seems safe..." I fight the urge to snatch it away before Vivienne can place the flaming stick in Tillie's waiting hand, but I know that she'd never do anything to hurt her.

When I just stand there, refusing to take my eyes off of Tillie, Vivienne grabs the lighter back and begins lighting more sparklers and handing them off to the other girls. "Here," she says, passing one to me. "No one should go through life without twirling a sparkler."

I shake my head to myself and smile. I can't believe I'm actually doing this. Following Viv's lead, I hold the sparkler away from my body and spin, and the girls all follow suit. It's like were writing on the air, each encircled by a golden band of light. To be honest, I feel like an idiot, but even I can't deny that this is fun.

"Tell me you got Roman candles," Cassie says after the last round of sparklers have burned out.

"Yep, they were on Viv's list." I jog back over to our mountain of loot and grab the two boxes of Roman candles, holding them up to show Cass.

"Bring 'em over here!" she calls, waving me back.

"Oh, oh, oh! Those are my favorite!" Tillie jumps up, trying to snatch one from Cassie's hand. "Can I be first?"

"Hold on, baby. Let's give Reid a turn first, okay? It's his first time."

Cassie hands me a cardboard tube, instructing me to face it out toward the water.

"What does it do?" I had no idea that so many different types of fireworks were made to be set off in your hands.

"You'll see..." She lights the wick and colored balls of fire shoot out from the stick in my hands, and again I am dumbstruck that they are going to allow the girls to handle these things. When it seems that the last of the balls have shot off, I hold the stick toward the water for a little while longer...just to be sure.

Right as I begin to lower the tube to the ground, something explodes at my feet. I jump so high that I damn near fall into the lake.

Cassie, Vivienne, the girls, and even Ms. Anderson are doubled over laughing, and I still have no idea what the hell just happened.

"What the heck was that?"

"These," Cassie says, tossing a little white pouch at the ground. "You should have seen your face."

"I think I may need to go change my underwear," I joke.

Vivienne takes turns lighting Roman candles with each of the kids until we've finished those off, too.

"What's next?" I ask, wondering at which point we start shooting them off from the ground, the way I've always seen it done.

"Whatever you want." Viv collects the trash from the ground and shoves it into a trash bag. "Those were all of the ones that the girls could help with. I'm pretty sure the rest will have to be shot off from the stand that you bought."

They return to their blankets while I fire off dozens of fireworks. It's a completely different experience than watching from a distance the way I've done in the past. It's exciting and makes my blood rush. I guess in some ways, guys never grow up because I think that the thrill of blowing things up will always be there. The big finale is a huge box that will shoot off in rapid succession. After I light the wick, I run over to sit with the little girls on their Dora blanket. They scoot in next to me and squeal each time another one bursts into the air and colors the sky.

I glance over and find Viv cuddled up on her Momma's side, smiling brighter than I've ever seen. She's happy, and for the moment, there's no dark cloud looming over her. It makes me wonder what she was like before. Was she always so carefree and happy? She throws her head back, laughing at something that her mom or Cassie must have said, and my God, she is beautiful. I didn't think it was possible that she could get more beautiful. Her laugh is rich and hearty, completely unaffected. It's the kind of laugh that you can't help but smile when you hear it. The kind that resonates deep down into your bones.

"Hey, Reid," Sierra says, stealing my attention. She sits down beside Korie, placing a motherly kiss to her forehead, and I get a pang in my chest at the realization that in many ways, she *is* her mother. I can't imagine having to grow up the way that they have, with nothing and no one but each other. I don't know why suddenly the reality of her situation is registering with me. I've known all summer that she's in foster care. I guess I just never took the time to think about what that actually meant. I'm not really accustomed to thinking of anyone else if I'm being honest. It's crazy how leaving that bubble that I grew up in has made me realize just how shallow a person I am.

"Hey, Si," I answer, swallowing a lump of guilt. "What's up?"

"I just wanted to say thank you for the fireworks. This was really cool. I've never seen Korie so excited." It doesn't miss my attention the way she thanks me for Korie and not herself.

"You're welcome. I'm glad she enjoyed it...and I hope you did, too."

"Oh, I did..."

"Good."

We sit in silence for a while, watching the fireworks from the neighbors' yards, and after a few minutes, the little ones run off to join the women across the yard.

Sierra looks at me, nervously chewing the insides of her cheeks, the way she has a habit of doing. It's like she wants to say something but can't decide if she should. We've become pretty good friends over the past few weeks, and I'm beginning to think of her like family, so I decide to help her along. "What is it, Si? Just spit it out already."

Her cheeks redden, and she looks over to the other blanket, making sure that no one else is paying attention to our conversation. "Well," she says, her eyes welling up. "Umm, something happened and I just...I wanted to tell someone."

Immediately, my head starts imagining the worst. If anyone hurt her...I can't even go there. "It's okay. You can tell me."

"It's nothing bad," she says as tears roll down her face. I have never seen her cry before, and it makes me feel sick inside.

"Well, what is it?"

"I'm getting adopted. Both of us. We're...we're getting adopted." Her right hand rises to cover her mouth like she can't believe the words that just left her lips.

I can't help the Cheshire cat grin that spreads across my face. "That's great news! Do you know the people? Are you nervous?"

Sierra's head bobs up and down, and it takes her a minute to stop crying long enough to speak. "It's Cassie."

"Cassie," I repeat, stunned.

"Yeah. She pulled us aside earlier and asked how we'd feel about it...It's good, right?"

Wow. I could tell that Cassie really cared about the girls, but I'm honestly shocked. I guess you really shouldn't judge a book by its cover. "Good?" I ask, widening my eyes. "I think it's great. I mean, who wouldn't want this life?"

She smiles with her whole face. "I know, right? I can't believe it...It won't be right away because she has to go through classes and get certified, but in a few months..."

"She has to take classes even though she works at CPS? She's a damn social worker." That just seems really stupid to me. Why make these girls wait any longer than they have already?

Sierra sniffles, drying her tears with the backs of her hands. "I know. It's dumb, but it's okay."

"I'm so excited for you, Sierra. I think you're going to be really happy."

She stares out across the yard. "Yeah..." she whispers, longingly. "Me too."

twenty-five

Vivienne

"WHERE'S PRINCE REID, MOMMA?" TILLIE asks for what feels like the billionth time today.

"I told you already that he had football practice. He'll be home for dinner."

"Ughhh. It's no fun when he's not here." She stomps her plastic heel on the tile and storms out of the room. I don't even bother to correct her because I kind of wish that I could do the same.

It's the beginning of August and the last day of camp. It's also the end of Reid's first week of practice. I can't believe how much I've missed having him around. My stomach begins to churn when I realize that in a few weeks he will no longer be here with us at all.

Blinking back tears, I continue chopping onions to add to the gumbo. The onions are a plausible excuse if anyone were to walk in and find me crying, but I only wish that they were the true cause of my tears. The truth is, the thought of being alone in this house terrifies me.

My phone vibrates against my leg, so I dry my hands on my apron and check to see whose calling. *Hmmm*, the area code's from back home.

"Hello."

"Hi. This is Veronica with Anderson and Associates. Is this Vivienne?"

Anderson and Associates...haven't heard that name in a while. "Hi, Veronica. What bidding does my sperm donor have you doing that requires you to contact me of all people?"

She coughs, clearing her throat. "Umm, well..." she stutters. "Mr. Anderson heard about the death of your husband and wanted me to offer his condolences. He, uh, wants to know if you need any money." *Wow. This is rich.*

"Does he? And he's so concerned about my welfare that he had his secretary call to check on me? How kind," I say, my voice dripping with sarcasm.

"Well...he, uh. I don't..." The poor girl is tripping all over her words, afraid to say the wrong thing and get fired, no doubt. I walk over to the window above the sink and look out toward the lake to calm my nerves before I attack this woman for things that are in no way her fault.

"So, how'd he *find out* about Abbott's death?"

"Oh, he had lunch with a client yesterday who expressed his condolences. Imagine Mr. Anderson's embarrassment when he had no idea what the man was talking about..." Her voice is accusatory, and now she's beginning to really piss me off.

"Imagine that, Veronica. A man so estranged from the daughter that he abandoned as a child that he had no clue that her husband died two and a half months ago! You know...come to think of it, he probably didn't even know she was ever married. It must be the daughter's fault, though, right? Surely, I'm to blame for him leaving and then never hearing shit from him again, right? "

Veronica mutters something beneath her breath that I can't understand.

"I should've called this *stranger* in the midst of my grief to inform him of my husband's passing to avoid the embarrassment that he no doubt felt in front of his colleague."

I hear a click and turn to find Cassie standing in the doorway with a worried look on her face. My lips and hands are trembling but not with sadness. I'm livid. *The fucking nerve of this man.* "Veronica, you can tell your boss that he has never bothered to be concerned for my welfare in the past and that he need not pretend to give a shit now in the name of saving face with his associates. I've been just fine without him for most of my life, and I will be just as fine for the rest of it. I certainly don't want or need his money."

What kind of father has his secretary call his daughter upon learning that her husband died? It should hurt, but I stopped giving him that power long ago. I was only ever a nuisance...a check he was forced to write each month.

Veronica is flustered when she answers, "Thank you for your time, Mrs. Parker, and we are truly sorry for your loss."

I laugh maniacally. "Thanks, Veronica, but please don't attempt to humanize my father by apologizing on his behalf. I'm sure you realize as well as I have that he doesn't give a damn about my feelings."

I can feel Cassie's eyes burning a hole in my back as I end the call. "Hey, Cass, how was work?" I ask, washing my hands off in the sink so that I can get back to cooking.

"Not bad," she says, setting her things down on the counter. "What was that all about?"

"Pfffft." I shake my head and roll my eyes. "It was nothing important. Trust me."

She eyes me skeptically. "Didn't seem like nothing. I know your father had something to do with it."

"Yeah...he found out about Abbott...had his secretary call to see if we needed money," I say, raising my brows. "Can you believe his nerve?"

Her mouth falls open. "Shut up! He didn't?"

"Oh yeah...but only because he found out from a client and he needed to pretend to give a shit," I say, blowing my hair out of my eyes.

"Asshole," she huffs.

"Whoa, what'd I do now?"

Relief. That's what I feel at the sound of his voice. My lips quirk into a smile as I turn my head in his direction. "You're home early."

Reid walks into the room, his hair still wet from a recent shower. The smell of his soap overpowers the food cooking on the stove. "Yeah, coach sent us home. He has some family thing tonight. I'm gonna go spend some time with the camp kids. I'm gonna miss those little shits," he says with a smirk. "Just wanted to let you know that I'm back."

"Well, you better go find Tillie first. She's all kinds of upset that you haven't been around today."

"All right," he says, snatching a piece of smoked sausage from the cutting board in front of Cassie.

Her face screws up in disgust as she watches him pop it into his mouth. "Ew, Reid...that's not cooked yet!"

He chokes. "You're kidding right?"

"You see me standing here cutting it. No, I'm not *kidding.*"

I snort. "Cassie, it's *smoked* sausage."

"So?"

"So..." Reid says, swiping another piece, "it's been *smoked.*"

Cassie shrugs, looking at Reid like he's an idiot. "So?"

"Jesus, Cass, smoked *is* cooked." Sometimes I swear that red hair is artificial.

"If it's cooked then why do you have to *cook* it, hmmm? I don't think you're supposed to eat it raw. That's just gross," she says, cringing.

I release an exasperated sigh, and Reid just smiles, shaking his head to himself.

"I'm going find Dimples. I'll bring the girls out to the lake with me to hang out while you two finish up dinner. It smells delicious, by the way," Reid says, sniffing the air on his way out of the kitchen.

"Thanks, Reid. It'll be done around five. We're going to eat at the pavilion tonight. They're here 'til seven," I call after him.

Reid's head pops back into the doorway. "Sounds good. Call my cell when it's ready and I'll come help you bring everything out."

AFTER WE'RE THROUGH EATING, I give each of the children a memory book filled with pictures from their summer at Camp Aspie, and we spend the evening reminiscing and signing books. A few of the kids even climb on stage and sing.

I can practically feel Abbott's approval, and I know he's smiling down on us tonight. I feel so much relief. We did it. We actually pulled this off. There were times when I felt like I'd made a huge mistake. But now, with the camp ending, I am terrified of what's to come without them here. They gave me a purpose...provided a distraction.

When seven o'clock rolls around and those white vans drive off, I'm actually sad to see them go.

"You did it," my best friend says with tears in her eyes. "I'm so proud of you, babe."

My throat thickens, making it hard for me to swallow. "Thanks," I whisper, waving to the children as the white vans disappear into the night.

"I have to get going, Viv. I need to have Sierra back at the Clawsons' by seven-thirty." Cassie makes a face and rolls her eyes.

It's all so stupid. Those people don't want Sierra there any more than she wants to be there. "It won't be like this for long, Cass. In a few weeks, you'll start classes and then this back and forth will be a distant memory."

"SHE ASLEEP ALREADY?"

"Reid!" I gasp, nearly slipping down the last few steps. "Jesus, you scared me. I didn't know you were here."

He reaches out a hand—an automatic reaction to stop me from falling. "Sorry, Viv." He laughs guiltily. "I finished cleaning up outside and thought I might be able to catch Tillie before bed. Guess I'm a little late."

"Sorry, she was exhausted." I scoot by him to walk into the living room, and Reid follows closely behind. "You wanna watch a movie or something?"

"Yeah...a movie sounds good." I smile, eager to soak up some time with my friend after not seeing him all day. "Grab the remote and find something On-Demand."

He walks over to his usual spot: the recliner. Reid grabs the afghan, kicks off his shoes, and gets comfy. It's going to be so weird not having him here. *Lonely.*

"Viv...hey...you all right?" Reid's voice pulls me from my stupor.

I swallow past the lump in my throat. "Yeah, I'm fine. I'm gonna make us some popcorn. Be right back." I scurry out of the room to the kitchen, and after I've put the popcorn in the microwave, I dig around in my purse. Even though I know that I shouldn't...I take one of my pills.

My mouth starts to water as the buttery popcorn smell fills the room. I dig two bowls out of the bottom cabinet then lean against the counter, tapping my fingers, listening to the steady popping. When the microwave finally dings, I dish it out and grab a few sodas from the fridge. I return to the living room and hand Reid his bowl, getting mine situated on the coffee table in front of the couch. I'm already feeling better. I know a lot of it's psychological. Just knowing that relief is on the way has my body returning to normal.

"Thanks," Reid says, still browsing through the movies. "Are you sure you're okay? I sort of heard what happened with your dad earlier. I didn't want to bring it up in front of anyone else...but you just seem sort of down. If you want to talk about it..."

My eyes roll back in my head. "No. Really, Reid, that's not what's bothering me at all. I'm completely serious when I say that his disinterest in my life no longer affects me whatsoever. It's almost comical," I laugh unconvincingly.

Reid presses his lips into a flat line, nodding his head. "All right, but there *is* something bothering you, then?"

"Just a rough day. I'm fine...You'll be a great dad someday, Reid. I can tell by the way you were with the camp kids and by how much you love Tillie. That's so important. If you take nothing else away from this summer, please don't ever forget how important it is to make your children feel special. Tillie got more in three years from Abbott than I've gotten from that asshole in my entire life. I'm so sad that she won't have more memories with him."

"I won't forget," he whispers back. "You'll be enough, Viv."

"Huh? Enough for what?"

"I just wanted to tell you that you're a great mom...and Tillie's gonna be okay."

How'd he know that I needed to hear those words so badly?

"Thank you for saying that."

"No problem," he answers, smiling nervously.

The room grows uncomfortably silent, neither of us knowing what to follow that conversation up with. After a long and awkward pause, I break the silence. "Woo, you better pick something with some action so I don't fall asleep on you," I say, yawning and stretching my arms and legs.

"You sure you don't wanna just call it a night? If you're tired..."

"No," I say too quickly. "I want to watch a movie." I sit up to help keep myself awake and cradle my bowl of popcorn in the middle of my legs.

Reid seems relieved not to have to cut our night short and smiles back at me warmly. "Action it is."

He rents some guy movie, and I hardly pay any attention at all. I keep glancing over to watch him. He's so into it, mumbling and jerking with surprise. It's true that boys really never grow up. Abbott was the same. Anything with guns or fighting and he was like an eight-year-old kid.

I try so hard to keep my eyes open, but I keep feeling my head fall back and then jerk myself awake. Finally, I give in and rest my head on the couch. I end up dozing off, and when I peek through my barely opened lids at the television, it's no longer the same kind of action we were watching before. The room is filled with breathy moans and grunts of passion. On the screen is a tangle of naked, sweaty limbs. I turn my head to the side to avoid watching and find that Reid is no longer watching the screen either. He's watching *me*.

Reid stares at me with hooded eyes. He must think that I'm still asleep, and I don't tell him any different. I watch his hungry eyes rove up and down my body, and it causes my pulse to race. It's a look my body recognizes and responds to. One that makes me tingle in places it shouldn't. It makes me feel alive and desired, and it makes me feel guilty as well. If I didn't know better...if I didn't realize that this was all in my head...I'd swear that Reid just made love to me with Abbott's eyes

twenty-six

Reid

A TAP, TAP, TAPPING SOUND rouses me from a dead sleep. I grab the ends of my pillow and pull them up over my ears, squeezing them tightly to my head in an attempt to drown out the annoying sound. The goddamn wind must be blowing something up against the pool house, and I have no desire to go outside and check it out in this weather. The room flickers bright yellow with a flash of lightning, which is almost instantly followed by a loud, resounding boom. The rumbling of the thunder causes the metal frame of my bed to rattle, so I squeeze the pillow even tighter, letting out a frustrated sigh when it seems to do no good. Finally, there's a moment of silence. I toss and turn, trying to find a comfortable position. Just when I think that I might finally get a little sleep, I hear a faint cry coming through the window. There's a very good chance that it's only a stray cat, but I don't want to take any chances with Tillie next door. With that thought, I jump right out of bed, taking only a moment to slip into the basketball shorts from the floor, and rush over to the front door. Through the peephole, I can barely make out the top of Tillie's little, blonde head.

What's she doing out of the house at this time of night? Instantly, I begin to panic because I can think of no good reason for Tillie to be standing outside of my door in the pouring rain, especially in the middle of the night. My hands shake as I fumble with the locks and yank the door open.

I'm greeted by a frantic little girl. The rain and thunder are so loud that I can barely make out what she's saying, but I hear the words "blood" and "mommy", and I begin moving on autopilot. Lifting Tillie into my arms, I run over to the main house and up to Vivienne's room.

I find her curled into a ball in the middle of her bed, whimpering in pain. There's blood covering the sheets and her shorts. I blanch at the sight as I set Tillie down on the chair next to the door. I tell her not to worry, and that Mommy will be okay, but what the hell do I know? I feel like I'm borrowing someone else's body, walking through someone else's life, because this cannot be happening to me.

"Vivienne?" I walk over to the bed, unsure of what it is that I'm supposed to do. *How the hell do I keep finding myself in these situations?* I reach out a trembling hand and place it gently on her back. Vivienne flinches, cowering away from my touch. "What happened? Are you okay, Viv? Do you...do you need a doctor?"

"Reid?" Her voice is pained but laced in relief.

"Yeah, Viv. It's me. I'm here." I reach out a tentative hand, running the backs of my knuckles gently down the side of her tear-soaked face.

"Ow! Oh my God...Oh God, it hurts..." Vivienne cries out in pure agony. She clutches at her stomach, releasing a deep, guttural moan. Even in the darkness, I can see the red stain on the bed growing larger.

"Talk to me, Viv. What happened? Is it your period?"

"No, this is different...I don't know. I don't know. I just woke up and...oh God." She twists her hands up in the sheets, moaning and rocking through the pain. "Reid...it hurts so bad," she sobs.

Reaching over to the nightstand for her cell phone, I rub her back and try to sooth her with my words. "It's going to be okay. I-I'm going to get you to a hospital, Viv. Everything's going to be okay." I don't know which one of us I'm trying to convince more, and I hope that she doesn't recognize the panic in my voice. I call for an ambulance, and while waiting send Tillie to put on some dry clothes...anything to get her out of this room. Cradling Vivienne in my arms, I wipe sweat-soaked hair from her face and try to keep her calm with whispered words of assurance. The coppery smell is nauseating. There is just so much blood.

Everything from there happens in a blur. The EMTs arrive and place Vivienne on a stretcher. Tillie starts screaming for her mother—blood-curdling screams. I'm sure after witnessing her father leave in an ambulance and then never come home this is really traumatic for her. Seeing Tillie so upset only causes Viv to cry harder, and with all of the chaos, I barely understand anything the medics are saying.

They're taking her to Memorial, so I grab Matilda, Viv's cell, and keys on my way out of the door. I put her in her car seat and try to calm her down. This is so out of my comfort zone. I don't know how to ease Tillie's fears or how to handle the gamut of emotions I am feeling.

On the way to the hospital, I call Cassie from Vivienne's phone and pray that she leaves her ringer on at night. It's close to 3 A.M., and I know Viv would want her there. Also, she'll know how to handle Tillie.

On the third ring, Cassie answers. "Hello?"

Thank you, Jesus!

"Cassie, hey, it's Reid. I'm on my way to Memorial with Tillie. The ambulance just took Vivienne. She was in a lot of pain, and there was so much blood...Tillie is freaking out. Can you come to the hospital?" The words pour out of my mouth, and I hope that I'm making sense because my thoughts are all over the place.

I hear Cassie moving around in her house and the absolute fear in her voice. "Oh my God, not Viv...Reid, what happened? What do you mean she's bleeding? Oh my God, of course I'm coming... Tell Tillie I'm coming."

"I honestly have no fucking clue what happened. Tillie came to the pool house to get me, and I found Viv keeled over in her bed, full of blood. I called the ambulance, but everything was so hectic. It all happened so fast. All I know is that they're on their way to Memorial, and we're right behind them. Tillie is so upset. I don't know what to do, Cassie."

I pull the phone away from my ear and look over my shoulder at Tillie. "It's okay, baby girl. Aunt Cassie's on her way, too, okay? Everything's going to be okay." She nods her little head at me, but the tears keep coming. I can't get the image of Viv covered in blood out of my head...I hate seeing Tillie so upset. I just want to fucking punch something. I don't know where I find the strength to keep myself together, but in order to spare Tillie this pain, I would do anything.

She has to be okay.

I hear Cassie begin talking again and press the phone back to my ear. "I'm getting in my car now. I'll be there in a few minutes. Thanks for calling me, Reid," she says as she ends the call. White knuckled and consumed with fear, I try to focus on the sound of the rain pelting down on the windshield to distract myself from Dimples crying in the back seat.

I'M PACING IN FRONT OF the information desk of the emergency room when Cassie comes bursting through the glass doors. Thank God for small miracles. She rushes over to me and pulls Tillie from my arms. Immediately, I feel immense relief. I don't want to mess that kid up more.

Swaying back and forth with Tillie wrapped around her neck, Cassie asks about Vivienne, and I have nothing. I tell her that they rushed her back and said they would come and let us know when they knew something, but no one has come back out yet.

It's at this exact moment that I realize just how much this woman has come to mean to me. I'm in love with her. I didn't mean for it to happen, and I know it's not right. It's fucking sick, but I need her like I need air. She's beautiful, so beautiful, and it's so much more than a physical attraction. Vivienne's beauty exists in the way she loves that little girl. It's in the spattering of freckles that dot her cheeks. The delicate heart that lies broken in her chest. It's in the way she aches for Abbott and how she loves with her entire being. She makes me better—makes me want more. I didn't realize how much was missing from my life before I met Vivienne, but now that I have, I can't let her go. I know she's just lost her husband, and that now is not the right time, but she'll make it through this, and someday...when the timing is right, I'm going to make this girl mine.

After almost an hour of pacing, a doctor comes through the double doors and asks for the family. Cassie and I walk over. "She's stable," Dr. Monroe says, "but she's lost a lot of blood and will need to remain here for a few days. I'll let her explain to you what's going on herself. Only one of you may see her at a time."

Cassie starts to pass Tillie back to me when the doctor interrupts. "She's asking for Reid."

The look of hurt and betrayal that crosses Cassie's face is brief, but I see it. At this moment, all I care about is getting to Vivienne and finding out what's going on with her.

I lightly rap my knuckles on her hospital room door, and she calls out for me to come in. Her voice is weak...she sounds so small. When I step through the doors and see her looking so frail and helpless in that hospital bed, I want to run to her, to hold her and protect her, but she is not mine, and I don't have that right.

Vivienne looks up at me with watery eyes, and she says my name like a prayer. "Reid..." There is so much emotion, so much pain in those eyes...in her voice.

I walk over on shaky legs and stand at her bedside. "They said you were asking for me?" I ask while she fidgets with the hospital bracelet on her wrist.

She responds with a slow nod of her head and tears streaming down her beautiful face. To see her like this...in so much pain makes me feel sick to my stomach.

"Reid, I have to...ummm....to ask you something...and I don't really know how to ask it." Her shoulders begin to shake as she chews on her bottom lip nervously.

I move closer. "Don't be afraid of me, Viv. You can ask me anything."

Another nod.

I hand her a wad of tissue, and she dries her tears, but it's pointless. They just keep falling.

"What is it, Viv?" I ask, rubbing my sweaty palms on my jeans.

I watch her suck in a long breath and blow it out slowly. My heart begins to race. "Okay...Did we.... umm," she says, wringing her hands. "Well, did you and I...?" Viv motions between the two of us. "You know? Did we sleep together?" She whispers the end of that question like she's deathly afraid that someone might overhear, and it pisses me the fuck off.

I can feel the temperature of my blood rising as the heat begins to radiate from my face. My pulse hammers in my ears and my entire body tenses...veins pulsing with rage. I don't care how irrational it is, how wrong what we did was...to be her dirty little secret after just realizing how much I care for her *hurts*. I drop her hands like they're on fire and step back, scrutinizing her with a murderous glare.

"Are you fucking serious right now?" I roar, my jaw plummeting in disbelief. "Did we sleep together?" I sneer as I shake my head in disgust. "Like I'm supposed to believe you don't remember?" My hand rises to my chest, and a snide smirk moves across my face. I lean in close, digging my fists into the mattress on either side of her body. "Is this really how you're going to play this, Viv? Like you weren't fucking there...*begging* me to fuck you?" I grit out through clenched teeth, our noses nearly touching.

Vivienne's breath hitches...her bottom lip trembling wildly. But her pitiful state does nothing to slow my anger. "To make it all go away," I continue. "To make you feel *good*...Are you seriously playing this game? Huh?" I shout, causing her to jump back. I can feel my heart breaking into a million fucking pieces. Who knew heartbreak was a tangible thing? "Why? Why are you doing this, Vivienne?" I ask with a lump lodged in my throat.

Viv's eyes widen...her head rapidly whipping from side to side. "No...Reid, we didn't...How could I not remember? I-I...No! I wouldn't do that. I-I wouldn't do that to Abbott." She lets out a wail, and her body convulses with the force of the sobs that follow. "Oh God. Oh God, what have I done?" She raises her fingertips to her quivering lips. "I'm so sorry, Abbott. God, I'm so...sorry."

She slinks back into the bed, covering her face and crying into her pillow. It's as if I'm no longer in the room. Like she didn't just rip my heart from my fucking chest and stomp on it repeatedly.

Abbott...? I'm fucking fuming. "What the hell's going on, Vivienne? What does the two of us having sex have to do with why we're here?" I ask, ripping the pillow away so that she has no choice but to look at me. "And we did have sex. *Consensual* sex," I add, glaring at her.

Viv's cries are agonizing to hear and even more so to watch. They are gut-wrenching. She sounds like a wounded animal, but where she is wounded, I am *rabid*. I need to hear her say it...to confirm what I already know to be true.

She can't...or won't look me in the eyes. Staring down into her lap she whispers, "I had a...a miscarriage. I thought it was Abbott... You. I thought that you were Abbott. The dream, it was so real." Realization dawns on her. "Oh God, it wasn't a dream. It was you." She lets out a wail, and I don't even have it in me to fucking care about her feelings right now.

I reach out, lifting her tear drenched chin, forcing her eyes to meet mine. "You..." I spit out with disgust. "I don't know what you're playing at right now. You make me sick. While I was falling in love with you, you were fucking a ghost. You used me, Vivienne. You fucking used me to feel close to him, and you broke me. Do you hear me? Don't say his fucking name. Don't you dare call out for another man while *my* baby spills from your body. This," I say, pointing to her stomach, "this moment doesn't belong to *him*. This is mine. That baby was mine!" I shout furiously, feeling warm tears run down my cheeks. In a fit of pure rage, I swing my arm, flinging the little table and all of its contents into the wall. I have never experienced pain like this in all of my life. Her complete disregard for my feelings is a fucking bullet to the chest. How can I both love and hate her with the same breath? Two opposite feelings felt with such intensity that it literally feels like my heart is being ripped in two.

Vivienne cowers and at least has the decency to look remorseful. "Oh, Reid. What have I done? What have I done to you? I'm so sorry. I...I didn't know."

At that moment, Cassie comes rushing in with Tillie still asleep, cradled in her arms. She must have been waiting near the door and heard the commotion. So much the better because I do not need to be alone with her right now. "What the hell are you doing?" she whisper-hisses. "Viv is in the hospital, and you're in here *yelling* at her? What's wrong with you?"

I clench my jaw, looking between the two of them, and I know that I need to leave. I can't trust myself not to go crazy. I won't hurt Tillie by carrying on in front of her. Viv may deserve my wrath, but that baby doesn't. "Your friend," I say glancing over to Vivienne, who is curled into the fetal position, crying pitifully, "is what's wrong with me. I can't be here right now."

Cassie could not be more confused or angry. She looks ready to murder me for hurting her friend. *If she only knew...* "Why is she crying like that? What did you do, Reid?"

I shake my head with a cynical laugh. "Ask your friend. I'm gone." I pull Vivienne's keys and phone out of my pockets, set them down on the counter, and then storm out without giving either of them a backward glance.

twenty-seven

Vivienne

THEY SAY THAT GUILT WILL eat you alive if you let it, and I never knew how very true those words were. Like an incurable cancer, it grows and festers inside of you. It has destroyed my self-worth and tainted my life with misery. All of the good memories that I once shared with Abbott are no longer. When you've betrayed your dead spouse, there is no way to atone for it. There's no way to beg and plead for their forgiveness. I'm drowning in this guilt, and the only person with the ability to absolve me of it is buried in the ground, two miles down the road.

My once perfect life has spiraled so far out of control so quickly. I just want to know how to dull the ache. How to make the most of this hand I've been dealt. I need to find a way to forgive myself for what I've done. I can't be whole carrying this weight. I can't be the mother that my daughter deserves. It pains me more than anything to admit that I've failed my baby.

I haven't seen Reid since he stormed out of my hospital room three days ago. I don't blame him. I can only hope that what he said wasn't true. That he hasn't wasted his love on someone as fucked up as I am. Reid is a great guy, and I know that he has a lot to offer the special girl in his life, whoever she may be. Unfortunately for him, that girl can't be me. That piece of my heart was buried along with my husband, and I have nothing left to give.

There are moments in life that you can't ever forget. They are the ones that define us. Moments that we don't only experience but change who we are as a person. From that moment forward, who you were five minutes ago no longer exists. And this person I've become, this mess he left behind, she's an empty shell of the woman I used to be, and I know in my heart that I will never get that girl back. I don't know how to navigate this new life, and I don't think I like the new me.

My heart grows heavier with every piece of clothing that I add to my suitcase. I've agreed to enter a treatment facility at Cassie's and Dr. Benson's request. After the hell I've put Cassie through and all that she's done for me, I owe her this much. I owe Tillie this much. They've promised to visit me every day, but I've never spent the night away from Tillie, and the anxiety is almost too much to bear. As much as it hurts, I know that I need to do this. I need help finding a way to deal with Abbott's death and to forgive myself for the mistakes that I've made in the aftermath. I have to find a way to live with these life-altering moments that have left me drowning. I'm in desperate need of a lifeline, and I pray the damage I've done isn't beyond repair.

I wish that I could go back in time to when my heart was merely empty; I'd take the emptiness any day over this heart of guilt.

twenty-eight

Reid

FOR TWO WEEKS, I HAVE been living in my own personal hell. As pissed as I am at Vivienne, and believe me I have never been so fucking mad in my life, I can't stop my heart from loving her. No matter how much I don't want to, I still care. I need to know that she is okay...that Tillie is okay, but my stubborn pride won't allow me to do anything but wallow in my misery. I'm a prisoner of my own mind...bound by hurt and anger.

After leaving Vivienne at the hospital, I went straight to her house to pack my things and then checked into a hotel near the university. My dorm was ready after only a few days, so I wasn't displaced for very long.

Since then, I've kept myself busy with football practices during the day and partying with my teammates on Bourbon St. every night. I've been drinking myself stupid and not enjoying any of it. I just need to do something to pass the time. This past summer spent with Vivienne and Tillie changed me. Before, I couldn't wait to get out here, to live it up. Now, what I want more than anything is to cuddle on the couch with the girls—*my girls*—watching stupid Disney movies and eating popcorn.

I haven't been able to bring myself to call or go to the lake house to check on Vivienne. I'm still reeling from the shock of everything that went down. Most of all, I can't believe that she had the nerve to put everything that happened between us on my shoulders. She "didn't know". What a fucking cop out.

I've never had my heart broken before, and honestly, I wasn't sure that it was even possible. But, now I see...I see how women can get men to act like fucking pussies because I miss her, and I miss Tillie. I miss them so much that it's crippling, and it makes no fucking sense to me. How can I miss something that was never really mine?

I WALK INTO THE COFFEE house on campus, and when the doorbell chimes, I get a tight feeling in my chest. I glance around the almost empty café until I find Cassie waiting in a secluded corner booth. She waves me over, pointing at the two cups on the table in front of her, and then watches me with a nervous smile as I weave my way between the tables and chairs.

After weeks of avoiding her calls and messages, I finally agreed to see her. I can't go on not knowing any longer. It's tearing me up inside.

When I reach the table, Cassie stands and instantly wraps me in a welcoming hug. I'm a little shocked. It's no secret that I'm not exactly her favorite person. "Hey," I say, returning her embrace. It's incredible how good it feels to be comforted by this woman, who as far as I could tell barely tolerated me all summer. "Everything okay?"

She looks up at me and her eyes glaze over when she answers, "No...No, Reid. Nothing's okay...but it will be." Even run down and broken, she has this fierce look of determination, and I don't doubt her for even a moment.

Right away, I notice how exhausted she is. She appears to have aged ten years in the two weeks since I've seen her last, and it begins to eat away at my resolve. "Is Tillie okay? How's Viv? Do you girls need anything?"

"Reid, Vivienne is in the hospital..." she says, sliding into her seat.

"What...still?" I jerk back in surprise. "It's been two weeks. Did she have complications from the miscarriage?" My stomach knots up with guilt. "Is she okay?" I'm such an asshole for not making sure she was all right before pulling my shit.

She flattens her lips into a straight line as she shakes her head. "Not that kind of hospital, Reid," she says, pulling me down into my seat. "Sit down, please. You're causing a scene." Cassie looks around as I reluctantly lower myself into the booth across from her. "She's in a psychiatric hospital," Cassie whispers, and I don't know who she thinks might overhear her. No one knows us here. "Viv is having a lot of trouble accepting...well" —she eyes me nervously— "everything that happened."

By everything, she means me. All the blood rushes to my head, making me dizzy, and I feel the tips of my ears begin to throb. Just the mention of what happened between Viv and I brings back all the hurt and anger I've felt over the past two weeks.

"Reid...just let me finish before you get upset, please. Just...just let me explain." There is desperation in her voice, a pleading in her haggard eyes. A look of absolute defeat moves across her face, and I know that I need to hear her out. No matter how much this hurts or how much it pisses me off, Cassie needs to say whatever it is that she came here to say.

I glance down, realizing that my hands are balled into tight fists, so I unclench them then open and close my fingers a few times to help release some of the tension. Then, I shove them under the table and nod. "Go on. I'm sorry."

She smiles at me sympathetically before breathing out a sigh of relief. "Well, uh...after you left and she filled me in, I just couldn't understand how she could get pregnant without ever realizing it. I could tell that she truly believed what she was saying. Reid, I know her. She would have never slept with another man so soon after Abbott's death. Honestly, I'm not sure that she ever will. I know it's hard for you to hear, but you didn't know them together...as a couple. You didn't see the way they lit up in each other's presence. It was magic. It made you feel good just to breathe their air."

I flinch and gnaw on the inside of my cheek. It's not easy listening to her go on about the two of them and their epic love.

It hurts, and for a moment, I start to hate him. When did I get so possessive of Vivienne? When did I begin to think of her as mine and not his? How have I managed to turn my dead uncle into the bad guy?

"Hey," Cassie says, reaching across the table and cupping her hand on my cheek tenderly. "It's okay. I'm sorry. I got a little carried away."

I clear my throat. "No, it's okay. I, ugh...I kind of got lost in my own head there for a minute. Go ahead."

"Okay. Well, when she finished explaining about the miscarriage and how she knew that it could not be Abbott's baby...that only left you. You're the only man she's really been around since his death... Viv told me about the dream, of what she thought was a dream, and it still wasn't adding up. I couldn't understand how she could've actually mistaken you for Abbott and dismissed it as a dream."

I scoff, "Yeah, I'm a little confused about that myself."

"I know you are. That's why I needed to see you...to explain. Vivienne finally broke down and told me that she's been taking pills. They're prescription pills for her anxiety, but she wasn't supposed to be drinking while taking them. She also confessed to taking a lot more than she should have."

"I knew she took some medication, but I had no idea that she had a problem," I interrupt. Vomit rises in my throat. I'm nauseous because I was with her every single day. I should have noticed. I could've helped her. "Is Tillie okay? Is she with you?" I look around. "Where is she now? I can move back to the house and stay with her until Vivienne's home. We can get a babysitter while I'm at classes or something..."

Cassie reaches out her hand and covers mine. "No, Reid. That's not why I asked you here. We're fine. I'm staying at the house with Tillie and put her in a preschool near my job during the day. We're making it."

I should feel relieved, but I just feel lost and alone. I want to be needed. I want my family back.

"Reid, I need you to do something for me."

Finally. "Okay, sure. Whatever you need, Cassie."

She swallows. "Reid, I need you to stay away from Vivienne...."

I shake my head. She came here to ask me to leave them alone...I can't. I can't lose them.

"Let me explain, Reid," she rushes out. "Vivienne really does not remember sleeping with you. The medication she was taking when mixed with alcohol...it causes memory loss. All of those nights that we had a few drinks and Viv seemed way too drunk...she wasn't drinking before we started...She was on those pills. When she added the alcohol, it screwed with her head. You look so much like him, Reid. She convinced herself that you were Abbott. She wasn't using you. Vivienne never meant to hurt you. She honestly believed that you were him."

Finally, the reality of what she's saying hits me. How could this all be completely one sided? How could I love her so fucking much...and she feel nothing?

"She's so messed up right now, Reid," Cassie says while tears pour from her eyes. "Viv feels like she cheated on Abbott. I don't know if she will ever come back from this, but I know that seeing you would not be good for her. She needs to find a way to forgive herself. She hurt you, Reid, and I am so sorry. Vivienne is sorrier than you will ever know. She's making herself sick with guilt. I'm begging you to let this go. Let her go. Let her heal and try to move past this."

"I love them, Cassie. I know that you think I'm just some stupid kid with a crush, but I love them."

She nods. "I know, Reid. I believe that you really do love her because she's impossible not to love."

I feel what's left of my heart crumble to dust because I know that this is it. "You'll let me know if y'all need anything?" It's a reach, and I know it.

Cassie shakes her head. "We won't. Reid, go to school. Play football. Fall in love. Fall in love with someone who's capable of loving you in return. You deserve that, and nothing would make Viv happier than to know that you've moved on and found happiness—that she hasn't completely destroyed your life."

"You're asking too much...How do you two think this is going to work out? We're family, or have you forgotten that part?"

"I've already spoken to your parents."

She what? I feel the color drain from my face.

Cassie rolls her eyes and smirks. "I didn't tell them about the two of you or the baby. God, I'm not crazy, Reid."

I breathe out a sigh. "What exactly did you tell them?" I've been avoiding Dad's calls, not in the mood to hear whatever it was he was calling to nag me about. Now I know, and I'm glad that I chose not to answer.

"I told them that she's in the hospital, and I explained that while she loves you all very much, it's just too difficult to be around you."

I flatten my lips and nod. "And what did Dad say?"

"First, he made sure that you hadn't done anything to upset her, and I assured him that it was nothing any of you did. That the resemblance you all bear is unreal and just having the face of her dead husband around was too much. He understood...I think. Told me to be sure to call if we ever needed anything."

I can't believe that I won't ever see them again. It doesn't seem like a long time...only a summer, but in the space of that summer, everything has changed. Somehow these girls have infiltrated my heart, and I know it won't be easy to eradicate them. Slowly, I begin to nod my head because that's all I can manage without breaking.

"Thank you, Reid," she says, reaching across to squeeze my hand. "I'm sorry," she adds, chewing on her lip. "I'm sorry about the baby and that you got hurt." Cassie dabs at her tears and continues. "I'm sorry for how I've treated you, too. I was...I was jealous. Viv is all I have, and I couldn't stand to see her leaning on you instead of me. I was wrong, and I'm...I'm just sorry."

My eyes burn, and I fight back tears, refusing to let her see me cry. "Thank you," I rasp out. I give her hand a squeeze as I slide myself from the booth, clearing my throat. "Cassie, I have to go," I murmur.

She stands, blocking my exit, and wraps her skinny arms around my neck. When I enfold her in my arms, Cassie completely falls apart, so I stay for a while longer and give her the only thing I can: understanding. I hold her and allow her to release all of her pain and frustration.

When she's through, I pull back and look her in the eyes. "Take care of them, Cassie." I feel a warm tear sneak down my cheek and swat it away.

She nods, sniffling, "Always, Reid."

"And take care of *you*, too," I stress. "You can't do it all."

She shakes her head as the tears start up again. "I'm...I'm fine. I'll be fine."

"You are not fine, Cassie. You need a break. Call Viv's mom...a friend...call *me*," I beg, but I know that I'm the last person she would call. "You need to eat, and you need time for yourself. You're no good to Viv and Tillie if you're gone."

I leave Cassie at her car with a tear-filled goodbye. I know that this is the last I will see of her and that Vivienne and Tillie will soon be just a memory.

twenty-nine

Vivienne

I PULL UP TO THE wrought iron gates of Magnolia Cemetery and place the car in park, taking a moment to look around. I notice how much everything has changed already. I haven't been here since the day that we put Abbott into the ground almost four months ago, and the place is nearly unrecognizable.

Death is all around me; the leaves are rotting and withering away. The once green vines now brown twigs entangled around the fence posts. They mock me. I feel as if those posts are my life, and the breath is being squeezed right out of my lungs.

How fitting.

I know that I need to get out of this car, but I can't seem to pry my body from the seat. I don't want this. I don't want to have to visit my husband in a graveyard. I don't want to only be able to see him in photographs...to have cement and dirt between us. I don't want to do this because then it becomes real. Then this becomes normal and I. Don't. Want. This.

Panic rises in my throat and I swallow it down with deep calming breaths. Just like the doctors taught me.

I step out of the car and place my feet on the muddy ground. The gate squeaks loudly as I pull it open, and I jump up in fright when it slams shut behind me. My heart races in my chest and the leaves crunch beneath my shoes as I make my way through the seemingly endless rows of headstones. All of these sounds echo in the eerie quiet. The sound of my own heartbeat loudest of all.

It's like a death march ringing in my ears, getting louder and louder the closer I get to my destination. Blinded by tears, I fall to my knees, fighting for each and every breath. "Oh, Abbott," I cry out as I drag myself through the dank sludge to his grave.

I drape my body across his tomb, resting my cheek on the cold cement. I'm as close as I will ever be to touching him again, and I have never felt more alone in my entire life.

The wind begins to pick up speed, whipping my hair into a wild, tangled mess as the dark clouds continue to roll in. My body begins to shake uncontrollably.

I lie there for minutes? Hours? Time simply stands still. I just need to feel close to him. God, I would give anything to spend one more minute in his arms

Thunder rumbles in the distance and still I can't move.

"Abbott," I whisper hoarsely, my face pressed into the hard surface. "Abbott, I'm so sorry. I'm so sorry, baby...Forgive me...Oh, God, please forgive me, Abbott." I can barely breathe with the force of my sobs. The grief, the guilt, the sadness all culminate into a gaping wound. I'm cut open, raw and bleeding out.

Closing my eyes, I rub my fingers lightly over the course surface beneath my face, and I hope that he can sense my presence. That he can feel my love. "I miss you," I cry. "I miss you so much. I don't know what to do.... I'm so lonely, baby."

Gripping the edge of the stone and squeezing my eyes shut tight, I try to regain some semblance of control. I cry. I cry until my eyes burn so hot that I'm sure there will be permanent damage to my retinas. I cry until I can no longer find air to fill my aching lungs. I cry until it is physically impossible to cry anymore.

"Abbott," I croak. "Please forgive me...There's only you. It's only ever been you. Forever."

That's when the rain finally begins to fall, and the sky takes over, bathing us in her tears. It's a violent storm reminiscent of the one brewing in my heart. Still, I don't move. I'm not afraid. I live with this devastation inside of me every single day. As strange as it may seem, I feel comforted. Like Mother Nature herself is showing her displeasure over a loss so great. She rages on, expressing her devastation. Lightning strikes and leaves and branches are tossed around in the wind. I stay through it all, soaking in every last drop. When the clouds are all cried out and begin to move away, they leave behind the most magnificent rainbow I've ever seen.

Even the most violent of storms can leave something beautiful in their wake. *A sign.* A smile spreads across my face. This is Abbott's way of telling me that it's okay to enjoy the rainbow.

It's his forgiveness.

It's my salvation.

five years later

thirty

Vivienne

I RUN THROUGH A MENTAL list of what I will need to prepare Cassie's surprise birthday dinner. Shivering through a chill from the coolers, I add eggs and butter to my basket. I can't wait to see her face when she walks in tonight and sees what we've done. She's going to flip!

As I round the corner into the next aisle, I slam right into another basket. Mortified, I look up to apologize, and all of the air leaves my body. I can't find words. I can barely hold myself upright. I brace myself on the basket and just stare.

"Vivienne?" His voice is so much older now. So much more mature. So much like *his*. He's filled out...grown up, and he still looks so much like my dead husband that it knocks the sense right out of me. "Wow, Aunt Viv. It's been so long," he says with a genuine smile.

I'm relieved that he's able to smile when he sees me, but then I remember that he doesn't know the whole story...and that if he did, he would most definitely not be smiling at me this way.

My heart races as I force a smile. "Reid. Wow. Look at you all grown up."

He walks right up to me and wraps me in his arms. "You look great," he whispers, rubbing my back.

My body trembles as I hug him back, breathing in his manly scent. His arms feel like home, and for the first time in a very long time, I allow myself to miss this man. This man who at one time meant so much to me...who helped me through one of the darkest times in my life. I forget how badly I've hurt him and all of the reasons that I should wrap up this reunion as quickly as possible.

A delicate cough catches my attention, and I see a beautiful brunette standing to the side of Reid's basket with a baby cradled in her arms. She smiles at me warmly.

I smile back, realizing that this must be Reid's family. "Reid, would you like to introduce us?"

"Of course." He moves away and reaches out to the woman. "Vivienne, this is my wife, Julia. Julia," he says, waving his hand at me, "this is my Aunt Vivienne. She was married to my Uncle Abbott," he explains.

I reach out to shake her hand, and with her free arm, she embraces me around the neck. "Sorry, I'm a hugger," she offers with a shrug. "It's so nice to meet you."

My eyes fill with tears when I look down at the beautiful baby in her arms. "A girl...Reid, what's her name?"

The pride in his face when he introduces me to his daughter is *everything*. It's affirmation that I did the right thing. This is what I prayed for. He deserves this happiness. "This is Amelia," he says, smiling down at her with such tenderness that my heart skips a beat. "Amelia Rose Parker."

"She's perfect. Congratulations to you both."

"Thank you," they both reply in unison. They are a striking couple. The love between them is palpable. Reid has found his person, and I could not be happier.

"How are you, Viv? I've thought about you a lot over the years. How's Tillie? " Reid asks, and before I have a chance to respond, Tillie rounds the corner with AJ following closely behind.

"Reid?" Tillie asks, narrowing her eyes in uncertainty.

"Hey, Princess." He stares at her in awe, no doubt trying to absorb all of the ways that she's changed over the years.

"Oh my God!" she screams, lunging at him.

"Dimples, I can't believe how much you've grown," he says, enveloping her in his arms. Tears of joy are shared amid whispered words of affection, and then I see it. The moment the color drains from Reid's face.

"Who's that, Mommy?" AJ asks, tugging on the hem of my shirt. "Who's that man?"

It's one of those moments where time stops. Where no one moves nor dares to breathe...Reid looks at me quizzically, taking in the little boy with brown hair and freckles and piercing blue eyes, and I know that he knows. I can see him mentally calculating.

"Mommy?" More tugging.

"Yeah, baby?" I ask, forgetting the question.

"Who is that man wif Sissy?" AJ asks again.

My heart begins to pound in my head. This is it. The moment I have dreaded. The moment I wished would never come.

With vomit rising in my throat, I answer my son. "This is your cousin...Reid."

"I have a man cousin?"

"Yes," I answer simply. I look over to Reid and mouth the words *I'm so sorry*. And yet again, they do nothing to reveal the true depth of what I feel.

Hurt, betrayal, confusion, and contempt flash across Reid's face. No one else notices, but I see it all. I feel it all because I am the cause of it all.

Reid sets Tillie back on her feet and forces a smile for *our* son. "AJ, huh? That's a cool name," he says, shooting me a look.

We communicate in discreet looks and glances, and I can feel the heat coming from Reid. I wish that he could yell at me. That he could get it all out. That I could apologize and explain, but surrounded by our families, by our children, is not the time. This was not the way he should have found out. *He never should have found out.*

Reid lowers himself to his knees and reaches out a hand to AJ. "Come here, buddy, and shake your *cousin's* hand."

AJ walks over timidly and takes Reid's hand. Reid pulls him in for a hug, and I know it must have taken all of the strength he possesses not to show the deep emotion he feels. "How old are you, AJ?"

"I'm this many," he says, holding up four fingers excitedly.

"Yeah, I thought so, buddy," Reid answers, clearing his throat. "I'm so glad to meet you. Maybe we can hang out sometime, huh?"

My son's face lights up. "Do you like to go fishing? We have a lake and a boat!" AJ volunteers.

"I do. I love to fish." Reid forces another smile. "I've been to the lake house. I actually worked at the camp the summer before I started college. I'll come by really soon to take you and your sister fishing, okay?" he offers to our son, ruffling his hair as he looks pointedly at me.

I do the only thing that I can. I nod, and I smile. "We would love to have you guys over anytime." What I really wish I could say is: *Take your hands off of my son.* I wish that I could erase this entire meeting. Because as wonderful as it was to see Reid settled and happy...as much as it warmed my heart to see he and Tillie reunited, none of that is worth the fear of not knowing what Reid is going to do. Will he respect my decision or is my entire world about to fall apart again?

Reid nods. "Great."

"Reid, we really have to be going. We're having company tonight. Julia, it was a pleasure to meet you. You have a beautiful baby," I say, trying to get out of this awkward situation as quickly as possible.

"Likewise," she answers, completely oblivious to the havoc unfolding around her. "It's exciting to have cousins nearby for Amelia to grow up with."

Reid walks over and leans in for a hug. "How could you?" he whispers, and I can't stop the tears that spill over.

"I'm really sorry, Reid." I murmur, squeezing him extra tight for support, hoping for some sign of forgiveness.

Reid pulls away. "I'm so glad we bumped into each other today. I'll be seeing you soon."

I gather my children and head to the check out without even finishing my grocery shopping. We will just have to make do with what we have.

AFTER GETTING TILLIE AND AJ situated in their seatbelts, I round the car to the trunk and begin loading my groceries inside. I feel him before I see him. If hatred had a form, it would look exactly like the beast of a man standing beside me. I look up from the trunk to face my consequences. "Reid."

He stares at me for a moment, unable to speak. He asks a million questions with that look alone, and I'm not going to make him drag it out of me. He's going through enough.

"He's yours..." I whisper while staring into blazing blue eyes.

"How?" he asks. "Why, Vivienne? Goddamn it! Why would you keep him from me?"

"Reid..."

"I know my name, Vivienne. Start fucking talking," he fumes. All happy pretenses are now gone.

"Please lower your voice...the kids..." I say, motioning to the back seat.

He purses his lips, clearly done with my stalling. "Just tell me," he says quietly.

"There were two," I whisper, staring down at my feet.

"Two what? You aren't making any sense."

"There were two...babies. I...*we* lost one at the hospital, and I didn't find out about the other baby until after you were already gone. I didn't know what to do. I'm sorry, Reid. I'm so sorry, more than you will ever know. I don't expect you to forgive me, but I hope you can at least try to understand what a difficult decision I was faced with. I'm sorry for hurting you, and I'm sorry for not telling you about AJ, but I don't regret my decision," I say with finality. As hard as it is, he has to know that hasn't changed.

"You don't regret your..." Reid shakes his head. "You are a piece of work, you know that?"

"Just hear me out, Reid. You were just a child, and I was sick and so confused. I didn't even see what was happening in my own home...what I was doing to you. I hurt you. I unknowingly led you on, my husband's nephew, and for that I will forever be ashamed. But you have to know that I made this decision as much for you as I did for myself and my children."

Reid scoffs, "You named my kid after your dead husband, Vivienne. Who were you trying to fool?"

"Everyone!" I shout, finally breaking. "I was trying to fool *everyone*. What other choice did I have, Reid? Can you imagine what the truth would have done to Tillie, to AJ, to you, to all of us? Have you thought about that for even a second? Because I did! My God, that's all I thought about for months and months. Not only would it have humiliated us and our families but our children. How would I explain to my daughter that her baby brother's daddy is her cousin? It would have completely derailed your life, too. You had already convinced yourself that you were in love with me. This would have made it that much harder for you to ever move on, and look..." I say, glancing across the parking lot, "you have a beautiful family...a wife...a child..."

He shakes his head. "I have *children*, Vivienne. A *son*. A son I don't even know! A son who I never held as a baby. Who I never was able to feed or change or rock to sleep. A son who is *mine*! And it was *my* decision too."

"Maybe I was wrong, maybe I..."

"*Maybe* you were wrong?" he interjects.

"Yes, Reid, *maybe* because maybe I was *right* and maybe if you had known about AJ, you never would have gone to college and met Julia, and you never would have had that beautiful baby. Maybe you would have kept trying to create something with me, and that would have never happened. Don't you see, Reid? I could never have been what you needed. My heart is dead and gone. It was buried with Abbott, and I'm finally okay with that. It took me years of therapy to feel confident in the choices I've made, and I know that you need time, too. I hope that with that time you will see that I did what was best for all of us. That I had all of our best interests at heart...including yours."

"You have no idea how much I loathe you right now, Vivienne," he hisses.

As if he slapped me in the face, I recoil, trembling with barely contained emotion.

"Don't worry," he says spitefully. "I'll keep your secret because now it's too late for me to change anything. But you listen to me and listen to me good. I *will* be a part of my son's life, so if seeing my face is too hard for you, well, that's just too damn bad...Get over it."

"Okay, Reid. I'll deal with it. Whatever you need."

"We're going to be one big *happy* family. You will have us over for dinner regularly. I'm going to be the best damn cousin those kids could ever dream of."

"Okay..." I nod, ready to agree to just about anything if it means that our secret stays hidden.

"Starting this weekend. Saturday. I'm going to tell Julia that you've invited us over for a barbecue. We'll be there at six o'clock."

"Okay," I whisper through tears.

"I wish that you'd had just a little more faith in me, Vivienne. It hurts. I'll get over it...eventually, but it fucking hurts."

"I'm so sorry, Reid."

"I know you are," he says calmly—almost too calmly.

He slams his fist down on the trunk of my car. Gasping, I jerk back in surprise, but I don't utter a word as he hangs his head in defeat. There is nothing that I could ever say to make this easier for him. So, I stand there in the crowded parking lot, crying like a fool. I just...stand there...watching this man's heart break for the second time. All these years later, it's still just as brutal.

thirty-one

Reid

"REID, DOES THIS LOOK OKAY?" Julia asks while adjusting her top in the bathroom mirror. "I feel fat," she huffs, frowning at her reflection. Julia was never self-conscious before having Amelia, and I wish there were some way to erase this negative self-image she's developed over her post-baby body.

Walking up behind her, I brush her hair aside and snake my arms around her waist. I nibble down the curve of her neck, and just like I knew she would, Julia melts into me. "You look beautiful, babe."

"Thank you," she says, whimpering. "I just...I just wish everything would go back to the way it was before."

"Jules, you just had a baby...not even two months ago. Cut yourself some slack. You were beautiful before, and you're beautiful now. These are quite nice," I tease, cupping her swollen breasts in my hands.

She squirms in my arms, giggling. "You like those, do ya?"

"Mmmm," I say, rubbing my thumbs over her pert nipples. "I like these very, very much."

She moans, grinding her ass into my crotch. "That didn't take long...Little Reid seems to like them as well."

"Hey, we're just coming off of a six-week dry spell, and you are sportin' some major ta-tas. Give *Ginormous* Reid a break," I retort, laughing.

"How much time do we have?"

I glance over at the clock. "About ten minutes, fifteen if we're fashionably late."

Julia turns in my arms, wrapping her own around my neck. She presses kisses across my bare chest. "That's plenty of time, right?"

"Damn, Jules..."

She trails her fingers down to my waist, playing with the band of my boxer briefs. "I didn't mean it like that...I just meant that maybe we could be quick or...fashionably late."

"Hmmm." I pretend to mull it over while pulling her shirt over her head. "I think you've just challenged my manhood." I slip my hands into the waist of her skirt, pulling it down past her butt and letting it fall to the floor. "Challenge accepted."

WE'RE MAKING THE FORTY MINUTE drive to the lake house—fashionably-fashionably late—and Jules is out cold. *Guess we showed her, didn't we, Gargantuweenie.*

I feel bad about the fact that we're running late to our first visit, but it's only a few minutes in the grand scheme of things. And, Julia needed me. If I'm being honest, I needed her just as badly. There is nothing more healing or more invigorating than being inside of that woman. A connection so deep, no words are needed. It's the only place that I can apologize, and the only way to seek forgiveness for this guilt that is eating away at me.

It's been so damned hard keeping this secret from Julia. I swore I'd never lie to her, but I also swore that I'd never intentionally hurt her, and this...this would destroy my wife. So, I'm going to do it. I'm going to keep this secret until I draw my last breath because I would rather live with this pain than to inflict it upon the lives of everyone that I love. I will live each day with the shame of knowing that every time I look into my wife's trusting eyes, I'm lying through omission. I will bear the guilt that comes with allowing my son to go through life believing that his father is dead when I am very much alive.

My gut reaction was to blame Vivienne. If she hadn't taken

those pills and led me on...if she hadn't lied to me...if she hadn't hidden my child away for all of these years...I walked around for days pissed off at this woman all over again, and then something clicked, and I realized that none of this is her fault, either.

Vivienne and I are victims of circumstance. Shitty fucking circumstance. The product of two people thrown into each other's paths when we were most vulnerable. Viv didn't ask for her husband to die. She didn't choose to fall so deeply into a depression that she felt the only way to survive was by taking those damn pills. She didn't ask to become pregnant or to miscarry. Vivienne didn't intentionally hurt me, and that's the biggest revelation of all. Because it's easier to have someone else to blame.

I was young and impressionable. A horny kid, who'd never been exposed to anyone genuine in his entire life. I was raised in a place where love is superficial, and marriage is of convenience. And then I met Vivienne. A woman who loved with every fiber of her being. Her unwavering devotion to Abbott made me long for something more. I wanted it so badly that I wore blinders, only seeing the things that I wanted to see. I misread Vivienne's signals and saw something that wasn't ever really there.

The love I felt for her was real. I fell fast, and I fell hard. I went off to college with a broken heart, fucking anything in a skirt. I cursed her name for years. God, I hated Vivienne for showing me what was possible and then crushing any chance I had at finding it. No one made me feel even a fraction of what I felt for her that summer.

And then, halfway through my junior year, I met Julia and everything changed. From our very first meeting, I knew that something was different. She had a confident air that not many girls possessed at our age, and I found her maturity refreshing and so fucking sexy. For the first time since Vivienne, I wanted more. I wasted no time in making my intentions known, and for reasons I still can't comprehend, that feisty Italian girl saw something in me as well. Every moment we spent together only made us yearn for more. We fell in love quickly and effortlessly. Loving this woman was as easy as breathing. She filled my heart so completely that there was no room for resentment. Loving Julia made me realize that what I felt for Vivienne was only scratching the surface. I stopped thinking of her as the woman who broke my heart and instead became thankful to her for saving me from the path that I was headed down.

I've thought of her and Tillie often, and when we literally bumped into each other at the supermarket, I can't even explain the level of happiness I felt. It was like returning home after being away for five years. I didn't realize how much I still missed them.

But when I looked up and saw him...my son, all of that hatred for her came rushing back tenfold. It's never easy to learn that someone you love has been lying to you, but this was more than just a lie. This was an outright betrayal. Vivienne robbed me of a relationship with my child. She stole years that I can never get back. I felt cheated.

Nearly a week has gone by and the choice that I'm making to keep this secret from my wife, the woman I would lay down my life for, has forced me to consider the situation from Vivienne's perspective. On some level...I get it. Whatever pain I felt that night in the hospital, Vivienne felt it so much worse. I understand all of her reasons, and I know that the truth would have been messy and painful. Selfishly, I still wish that she had chosen differently.

I flick on my blinker and turn down Vivienne's long driveway, and while passing beneath the canopy of oaks, a feeling of nostalgia hits me. This is my family...my home. I glance over at my Jules sleeping so peacefully, and I know in my heart that I would do anything to protect her. I would shelter that woman from pain at all costs.

As I pull up next to the house and shift the car into park, I realize that Vivienne was only trying to protect me. She shouldered all of the responsibility so that I wouldn't get hurt. While on the surface it seems wrong and selfish, she did the most selfless thing that she could. She tried to shelter me from the pain of having to make the most difficult decision of my life. Because there was only ever one way that this could end.

I have to let him go.

epilogue

12 years later

Vivienne

THIS ISN'T HAPPENING. IT'S TOO soon. *I'm not ready...*

I pace the hall, listening to the clicking of my heels echo throughout the wide open space. Taking slow, measured breaths, I try desperately to ward off the panic that's growing rampant in my chest.

The bitch with anxiety is that the harder you work to get it under control, the worse it seems to get. Stressing over the anxiety just leads to...yep, more anxiety. Heat floods my cheeks, and I don't even need to see my reflection to know that my face is beet red. I walk over to stand beneath the air vent, hoping that it will cool my skin enough to bring it back to its natural shade of tan. The ceremony is going to be starting any minute now, and I'm a complete fucking mess. *Lovely.*

I lay my head against the wall and shut my eyes, trying to calm my nerves and clear my head. I breathe in and out slowly, and after a couple of minutes, my frantic heart slows to match the rhythm I've set. Feeling slightly more in control and realizing that I don't have much time left, I lift my head and open my eyes. "Holy shit!" *Where the hell did he come from?*

Reid chuckles, standing only a foot or so away. "Hey, beautiful...

been looking for you everywhere. It's just about showtime." He takes my hand into his own, squeezing it gently. "It's okay, Viv. Breathe." Then, he lifts his other hand and begins righting my flyaway hairs without even giving it a second thought. *After all these years, he's still taking care of me.*

I swat his arm playfully. "Don't sneak up on me like that. Jesus, Reid...you made me curse in church!"

"Whoa, I didn't make you do shit." He laughs, shaking his head. "I walked right up to you and even called your name a few times..."

"Liar," I say, rolling my eyes. "And you can't curse in here."

"Shit, my bad."

"Ugh." I look around, making sure that no one was listening, and narrow my eyes at him. "Stop it...I mean it." That Catholic guilt is in full effect.

Reid throws his hands up in surrender. "All right, all right. I quit. You know I just like fuckin' with ya."

"Oh my God!" I suck in my cheeks, trying not to laugh. "I cannot believe you just said that."

He smirks. "You can't believe I said what? Fuck? I say fuck all the time, Viv. It's like you don't know me at all."

This time, I can't hold it in. I bust out laughing. "You are terrible!"

"Sometimes," he admits with a shrug. "Seriously, though, are you all right? We got worried when we couldn't find you."

"Yeah, I'll be fine. Just needed a minute to regroup."

Reid pulls out his phone and starts typing. "Gimme a sec," he says, holding up his finger. "I need to call off the search party."

Whoops! "Search party? Who's all looking for me?"

"Just Julia and your mother," he says, shoving his phone back into his pocket.

Reid looks up and smiles, and I finally pause to take a good look at him...Dear God, he looks amazing in his tux with a fresh haircut and clean shave.

"Reid, you look so handsome," I say, trying not to cry. It's still hard sometimes to look at him and not picture Abbott, especially today.

Over the past twelve years, Reid has become a constant in our lives. The first few months were a little rough. There was a lot of resentment. Time lost that could never be reclaimed. But, he forgave me, and true to his word became a beacon in our lives. He has taken our son to all of his sports practices and has never missed a single game. He's also been at every one of Tillie's dance recitals, and today...today, he will give her away.

"Blake's a good guy," he says, trying to offer me some reassurance. "She's going to be just fine. You know I wouldn't support this if I didn't truly believe that, Viv."

I bite my bottom lip and nod, feeling my chest tighten. Then, shaking my head, I whisper, "But, Reid, she's my *baby.*" I try so hard to fight back the tears, but there is just no stopping them. "He should be here. Today is hard. It's so hard," I sob. "Abbott should be here."

"Shh, come here," he says, pulling me into his chest. "I know, Viv. I know it's hard." I snuggle into his familiar embrace and allow him to comfort me. It's a position I've found myself in many times over the years, and I don't know where I would be without my family today. They can never replace Abbott, but for me, there is no greater therapy than love.

"Thank you, Reid," I utter between sobs. "Thank you for doing this. For...for being here for my kids. Thank you for just...just everything. Your friendship. God, Reid, you and Julia. I don't know where I would be without you."

"You'd be just fine, Viv." With his thumbs, Reid wipes away smeared mascara from beneath my eyes. "You're stronger than you think, and you are one hell of a mother. You would've been just fine. But thank you for sharing them with us. Thank you for allowing me to love them."

Our secret is one we will take to the grave. Some truths are better left uncovered. Instead of tearing us apart, it has created an unwavering bond. We are family, in every sense of the word. Reid is one of the strongest people I have ever known. It couldn't have been easy letting AJ go, but since the day he learned the truth, Reid has never again referred to him as his own. It's better this way. One slip up would blow all of our lives apart, but I know that it must still lie heavily on his heart.

Reid laces his arm through mine. "Ready?" he asks with a tearful smile.

I close my eyes and inhale deeply. "As I'll ever be," I say, opening my eyes and meeting his with a smile. "Lead the way."

When we reach the entrance, I feel Reid's body vibrate with silent laughter. "Did she have to go there with the pink runner?" he whispers out of the corner of his mouth.

I look down at the hot pink runner in place of the traditional white and grin. "Is that a serious question?"

"Nah," he answers, shaking his head, "I guess not."

He walks me down the aisle to my seat in the front pew where AJ, Momma, and Julia are already seated. Before he walks away, Reid whispers with a slight catch in his voice, "We've got this."

And in this moment, I realize that I'm not the only one feeling emotional today. Of course he's a little choked up. He is the closest living thing that girl has to a father. "I love you, Reid," I whisper back. "It's hard not having him here today, but we are so lucky to have you."

"Thank you," Reid says, his eyes glistening with unshed tears. Then, he turns around and leaves the way we came. The next time that I see him, he will be handing my daughter over to another man.

My eyes wander, admiring the beauty that surrounds us. It's a fairytale brought to life, my little girl's every dream come true. Pink and white roses fill every surface of the room. They drip from the ceiling and line every doorway and pew. The air is floral scented and the ambiance so serene.

The organ music begins, and every head turns toward the back of the church. The double doors swing open, and little Amelia steps through. She's pretty in pink and looks so much older than her twelve years. *It seems like Tillie was this age only yesterday.* She's met by her groomsman midway down the aisle where they lace arms and continue down to the altar together. Korie is next, followed by Sierra. Then comes Cassie, her matron of honor, and my girl is crying before she even makes it through the doorway. She's the most beautiful disaster of a bridesmaid I've ever seen.

It's not like I didn't know it before today, but it touches my heart to see how loved my baby girl is.

Sierra's daughter, Riley, is the flower girl, and just like her momma, she's a little pistol. She flat out refuses to hold the little boy's hand. Riley takes off, walking without him, tossing her pink petals and smiling like she's in a Miss America pageant while poor little Owen crosses his arms on his chest and follows behind her, pouting the entire way, giving us all a good laugh. When they've finally reached the front of the room, the doors at the back of the church shut. The music stops, and the room goes completely silent in anticipation.

Here she comes.

When the first note of the wedding march is played, I reach out for AJ's hand. Together, we rise, and holding onto my son, who is now taller than me, I watch my beautiful princess escorted by Prince Reid, as they make their way down the aisle. And, my God, she is the most beautiful bride there ever was. Her long, blonde hair lays in ringlets down her back, topped with an exquisite tiara. The skirt of her dress is compiled of layers upon layers of tulle, and I can't even breathe because of how beautiful she is right now. She is a real life Cinderella, and my little girl is finally getting her ball.

Her eyes meet mine from across the church. Words aren't needed to convey what we both feel in our hearts. I nod, just barely, and she does the same.

Tillie pauses when she reaches the front pew where I sit, handing her bouquet off to Reid. Then she melts every piece of my heart with the emotion in those baby blue eyes. "Momma," she cries, falling into my arms. "Momma, I love you so much." I feel her body tremble with tears and my heart nearly bursts.

"Oh, sweet girl," I cry out, breathing in the sweet scent of her perfume. "I love you...more than life."

We stand there holding onto one another and crying. I kiss her beautiful face and wipe away her tears. "It's not too late," I whisper, trying to lighten the mood.

Matilda Grace rolls her eyes and laughs. "Stop..."

"I mean it. We can run out of here right now."

"I'm with Ma...let's go," AJ teases. He's a boy, so he doesn't show it, but Tillie leaving is weighing on his heart as much as mine. It's been the three of us for so long. For all of his life.

Tillie just shakes her head at the two of us.

"Go get your prince, Bossyrella," I say finally, and Reid links his arm with hers and leads her right into the arms of her soon to be husband.

I watch Blake's face as Tillie approaches, and I remember a time when I saw that same look on the face of her father. Tears unabashedly fall from his eyes as he looks at my daughter like she is the answer to every question. Like she holds the stars in her eyes. If love had a face...it would be his. My baby girl is going to be just fine.

I wiggle my bare feet nervously in the hot sand. This is it. Today, I will marry Abbott Parker.

"Stop doing that, Vivienne. You're going to mess up your pedicure. You can't get married with fucked up toes."

Oh, Cassie. I laugh. "Says who?"

"Says your best friend and wedding planner extraordinaire!" she huffs.

I still my toes while she fusses over my hair and makeup one last time. "You know, it's not too late," she offers. "We can hightail our pretty little asses out of here right now."

"Really, Cassie?" I thought she was on board with this.

"Hey...I'm just checking off all of the boxes. I'm supposed to say that." Cassie shrugs, nonchalant.

I shake my head and roll my eyes.

"For real, you can look it up," she insists.

"I'm not changing my mind, Cassie," I say seriously.

"I know, babe. I would kick your ass if you tried. You've got a good one. Now, let's go make it official."

I can't believe how lucky I am, and I don't know if I will ever accept that this is actually my life. "Let's do this." I lace my arm into the arm of my best friend and together we make our way down the sandy path. I've chosen Cassie to give me away. I know it's not very traditional, but next to Abbott, she owns the biggest piece of my heart. There is no one else on earth that I would want to share this moment with.

As we draw nearer to my groom, my heart rate speeds up. By the time that Cassie places my hand into his, I feel like it may very well beat right out of my chest.

I look up into the eyes of my soul mate, and I know without a shadow of a doubt that I am making the right decision. I have never felt more certain of anything in my life. Abbott looks at me like I am the very air he breathes, and my heart comes alive whenever he is near.

I stand there in awe...in a love-induced fog. Vows are exchanged, and it all goes by in a blur, but I will never forget the moment when he takes my face in both his hands and places his lips to mine as husband and wife for the very first time. In that kiss, we communicate emotions so deep we could never find the words to describe it, and it feels like coming home.

He is mine.
I am his.
This is forever.

acknowledgements

There's so much that goes into the process of writing a book. It's scary and exciting. There are days when the words seem to fly right out of your fingertips and others when you can't seem to string two words together. It's such an emotional journey, and I could not have done it without the help of so many people.

First, thank you to my husband, Adam, for believing in me and for supporting my dream. Thank you for all of the times you've kept our six children for entire weekends so that I could work on this book, and for listening to me go on endlessly about the voices in my head.

A huge thank you to Shanora, Kate, and Edee for not only believing in me but for your constant support. You've been my biggest cheerleaders, amazing friends, and many times my therapists, as well.

Shanora, without your insistence, Vivienne would not exist. You saw something in me that I didn't even see myself, and you've awakened a passion for writing that I otherwise may never have discovered. I can never tell you what that means to me.

Kate, my eggplant! The way you've embraced me throughout this journey and held my hand throughout the entire process is everything. You are so generous and supportive. From the bottom of my heart, thank you for everything, especially your friendship. Soul sisters.

Edee, I feel like I hit the jackpot on my first spin. You are so much more than an editor. You are a beautiful person inside and out. Thank you for going above and beyond the call of duty and for teaching me all the things!

Nicole...you are the other half of my brain, and I will never be able to thank you enough for the help you've given me. Thank you for your excitement, your encouragement, and your love for my characters. If there is one person who knows them as well as me, it's you.

Thank you, Juliana for designing my beautiful cover. You captured my vision perfectly! You are a jack of all trades and have made this entire publishing ordeal so much easier for me.

To my beta readers: Shanora, Kate, Edee, Pam, Nicole, Selene, Karla, Megan, Ashley, Jessica, Sara, and The "Dude" Reviewer, thank you! Thank you for assisting me in making this book the best that it could be. It's not easy to separate yourself personally and to provide unbiased feedback, but it's so necessary, and I can't thank you enough.

My book besties, Selene and Brandi, thank you for sharing this journey with me. From books and blogging to best friends. Your support is invaluable. I love you BBs!

Thank you to my author friends over at The Indie Squad; Shanora, Kate, Tina, Ava, Nicole, Rose, Mo, Emily, Leia, and Nevaeh . . . I am incredibly lucky to have you in my corner.

Thank you to the girls in my reader group, "Heather's Hunnies." I appreciate your excitement and that you've given me a place to share my thoughts throughout this process.

To all of my book friends I've come to know while blogging at The Real Housewives of Romance Book Blog, who have followed me and supported me in my writing career, thank you so much.

Thank you to my family and my closest friends for listening to my ideas and for never telling me to shut up when I've gone on and on about different stages of this process: Mom, Tasha, Sandie, Ashley, Krista, Liz, Karla, Candy, Jo, Julie, Leslie, Abby, Lindsey, and if I've left anyone else off, it wasn't intentional and thank you as well.

To the readers and bloggers who I hope will read this book... thank you for taking a chance on my book baby, and I hope you've enjoyed the time you spent with these characters as much as I have

about the author

Heather M. Orgeron is a Cajun girl with a big heart and a passion for romance. She married her high school sweetheart two months after graduation and her life has been a fairytale ever since. She's the queen of her castle, reigning over five sons and one bossy little princess who has made it her mission in life to steal her Momma's throne. When she's not writing, you will find her hidden beneath mounds of laundry and piles of dirty dishes or locked in her tower (aka the bathroom) soaking in the tub with a good book. She's always been an avid reader and has recently discovered a love for cultivating romantic stories of her own.

If you would like to connect with Heather M. Orgeron, you can find her here:

www.heathermorgeron.com

www.facebook.com/AuthorHeatherMOrgeron

www.twitter.com/hmorgeronauthor

www.instagram.com/heather_m_orgeron_author

HMOrgeronAuthor@gmail.com